May the Best Man Win

May the Best Man Win

M.T. Pope

www.urbanbooks.net

Urban Books, LLC
97 N18th Street
Wyandanch, NY 11798

ISBN 13: 978-1-60162-387-4
ISBN 10: 1-60162-387-9

First Trade Paperback Printing September 2013
Printed in the United States of America

10 9 8 7 6 5 4 3 2 1

Distributed by Kensington Publishing Corp.
Submit Wholesale Orders to:
Kensington Publishing Corp.
C/O Penguin Group (USA) Inc.
Attention: Order Processing
405 Murray Hill Parkway
East Rutherford, NJ 07073-2316
Phone: 1-800-526-0275
Fax: 1-800-227-9604

More from M.T. Pope

Novels:

Both Sides of the Fence 1
Both Sides of the Fence 2: Gate Wide Open
Both Sides of the Fence 3: Loose Ends
A Clean Up Man

Novellas:

Lost Pages of Both Sides of the Fence Vol. 1
Stick Up Boys

Anthologies:

Anna J. Presents: Erotic Snap Shots Vol.1
M.T. Pope Presents: Boys Will Be Boys
Don't Ask, Don't Tell

Short Stories:

"Don't Drop the Soap"
"I Saw Daddy Doing Santa"

Acknowledgments

I started "writing" in February of 2008 and never thought I would be here and finished another title, but, yeah, it's done. Yippie! I can still say that I'm surprised at the success of them all. I am humbled by the people who support with money, time, words of encouragement and the hard work that goes into completing a story.

My family, especially my mommy, is very supportive of me. My two very good friends that keep me in line. I am grateful for all the people that come into my life and for the love and happiness they deposit. Especially when I need it and they don't know that they are helping. I am told that God uses us best when we don't know it. So thank you to all for the deposits and withdrawals. Peace!

This is my fifth full-length novel. I owe it all to God for blessing me with a wonderful gift that He chose to spring forth at the appointed time.

To my Mom, Lawanda Pope, a little woman with big strength. You make me smile every time I see you. You are the best mom in the world. I love you. My brothers and sisters: Shirley, William, Darnell, Darlene, Gaynell, Latricia, Nathon, and Yvette. I love you guys.

To my Pastor, Melvin T. Lee and First Lady Tanya Lee, for coming out and showing love at my first book signing and everything else I do in this life. I promise Dad that the Christian Fiction is coming . . . lol. To all

my Because He Lives church family members. I lov
you with only the love that God shines through me. W]
ARE! . . . BECAUSE HE LIVES!

To Tracey Bowden and Arnisha Hooper, my two best
friends in the world. I can't even begin to say how much
you mean to me. I don't say it enough and I don't show
it enough, but I can't pay for friends like you two. You
put up with my mess and my mouth and I am grateful.
For all the book signings you drove me to, all the books
you sold for me and all the bookmarkers you passed out.
I appreciate it so much. There are just some things in
life that you just know. I know that only God could have
put together and you two were chosen just for me. I am
honored to have you as my friends.

Carl Weber once again, thank you for this opportu-
nity, and all that you do.

To all the Urban Knowledge Bookstore workers that
pushed my book, it is appreciated. May God bless you
in all of your endeavors.

To the Urban Books home office family: Carl, Karen,
Natalie, George (Gee).

To Nichelle Washington-Davis, Darlene Washing-
ton, Karen Williams, Aaron Brown, Deterrius Woods:
Thank you for reading the first draft of this book.

A special shout out to Anna J. for the encouragement
and the GEM.

To all the book clubs that hosted me, thank you for
the love and support as well.

Thank you for another slamming cover. Davida
Baldwin, Oddball Designs (www.oddballdsgns.com)

I want to give a special thanks to couple of people
who really supported me from a distance:

Martina Doss, thank you for giving me my first official review and selling my books down there in Atlanta.
Also, thank you for calling me and letting me know

how my books moved you. Thank you for hanging in there with me support wise since book one. You have to finish your book now . . . lol.

My literary friends, J'son M. Lee (Just Tryin' to be Loved). Man you are the best. We clicked from day one and we have so much in common. Thank you for answering the phone every time I call. Dell Banks, for the encouraging phone calls. Anna J for being one of the hardest working renaissance women in Philly. Leave something for somebody else to do . . . lol. Oh, Thanks for the pointers and lifelines. *wink*

To the people that encouraged me along the way. Kenneth Goffney, your words are so inspiring. I am glad to call you friend.

Deterrius Woods, an extraordinary Facebook buddy. Don't be afraid to finish your book. You have some great stories to tell, so get to work.

Kyeon, you have so much talent that it is ridiculous. So get started and get yourself out there.

My E-supporters: I have never met you in person but you always are encouraging and honest about my work: Patrick Irené Plante, Aaron Brown, Shawna Brim, and to the MANY that e-mail me and hit me up and spread the word. It is too many of you all to name. Just know I appreciate all of you.

My Walmart family: Shernae, Tamara, Renee, Gary, Ms. Val, Danuiella, Keisha, Wayne, Sharon. Thank you guys for your love and support. I still miss you guys . . . lol. But, not the work . . . lol.

If I left you out, put your name here:_____, because you are important to me too. *Smile*

I can be reached at www.facebook.com/authormt-pope, www.twitter.com/mtpope, www.instagram.com/mtpope or e-mail me at chosen_97@yahoo.com. Thank you for the love.

P.S. Please please leave book reviews on Web sites like Amazon, Barnes & Noble, and Books-A-Million. It means a great deal to authors no matter how you feel about the book.

A Letter to the Reader

Hey Everyone,

Thank you for picking up this book. It is appreciated. I hope you have read my other books, especially the *Both Sides of the Fence* trilogy. I think you'll love it. Also, check out my anthologies and novellas.

Didn't know that I would be a "writer" or "storyteller" and a lot of the time I don't think that I am very good at it. I quit writing every other day . . . lol. It takes everything in me to write sometimes because I'm a procrastinator.

I started this novel in 2010 right before I was surged with requests for *Both Sides of the Fence 3*. The storyline evolved over time and the characters did as well. This is a different type of story for me altogether. It is still adventurous in theme, but with a little more heart. I wanted to get away from the "revenge" novels, per se, and focus on something a little different for me. I hope you enjoy it as much as I like writing it.

M.T. Pope

Prologue

"What the hell is going on here?" I walked up to the table where my man and my new enemy sat across from each other, talking, one hand covering the other's hands. It was a sign of affection to them but a sign of betrayal to me. There was a few people staring at me and the scene going on, but I didn't care at the moment. I had completely forgotten my reputation as an upstanding, law-abiding citizen and my senses. I was seeing red. I wanted to flip the table over in a tirade. My man looked at me calmly and the "enemy" had an evil smirk on his face. I wanted to smash his head into the glass window and watch the blood run down the side of his face and then do it again. This was my man he had his hand on. He had his filthy, hoeish hands on my man.

"Hello, Kardell. How are you?"

No, this bitch didn't just ask me how I am doing while he is sitting across from my man. I didn't answer him at first because I wanted to retain my dignity and some of my reputation as an upstanding citizen; but, as they say, shit was about to get real.

"Have you lost your fucking mind?" I couldn't believe I was speaking in such language in front of my man, but I was seething hot and didn't care at the moment.

"My mind is great right now. It couldn't be better. I'm out with my man and we were having an almost quiet meal together before you showed up and showed us your ghetto side." He looked at me and then at my man and then smiled slyly, like he was winning.

"Your man?" I asked, looking at my man, waiting for him to answer.

"Did I stutter? You have a degree or two and you mean to tell me that you haven't grasped all of the English language?" Lewis said sarcastically. "How could he be your man if you didn't want him?"

"You're in my business and I'm about to be in yours," I threatened.

"Like I said, my man and I are enjoying ourselves and we don't want the interruptions, so we would appreciate it if you found you a man, if you can, and leave us two lovers alone."

"Are you forgetting the fact that you work for me and not the opposite?" I stated matter-of-factly.

"Is that a threat? . . . Are you threatening me?" He turned toward me in his seat as if he was about to get up.

I took a step back just in case he was about to swing or something. I can say I wasn't planning on this shit happening today. I guessed there was something that could change my mood today. I never thought in a million years that it would be this.

"It is what it is," I replied.

"Excuse me is everything okay over here?" A male and female member of the museum's security walked up to us. The male asked the question.

"No, everything is fine . . . Just a little miscommunication." Mateo finally decided to talk by answering the officers. "Kardell, have a seat so we can discuss this rationally." His smile, his calming voice was all I needed to hear, so I hesitantly pulled out a chair and sat down at the table. I was breathing hard, and looking at Lewis's ass was not making it any better.

"Okay, any more profanity or arguing and we will have to ask you to leave the grounds. This is a family-friendly environment and we like to keep it that way. Have a great day at the Walters Art Museum, fellas." They walked off and left us to hash out the mess that we were in.

"Gentlemen, this is entirely my fault. I wasn't being honest with either of you. I like both of you and couldn't decide on which one of you to see exclusively. You two are very good-looking guys and it is hard to decide when two guys meet my standards. I like you both." He looked at both of us, one to the other, intensely.

I was shocked at what I was hearing. *Here I am thinking I am the only one and he is dating Lewis and me.* I wanted to get up and walk out and leave them both here looking stupid, but that would only make Lewis the winner and I wasn't going out like that. I found him first. The truth is I probably fucked myself by seeming uninterested in Mateo when I first met him and denying that attraction to Lewis. His fast ass swooped right in and made his move. I had to give it to him: he was a go-getter. I guess he was looking for love too. It just happened to be the same guy I was interested in.

"Mateo, it's okay," I spoke up first. "It can happen to anyone."

"Yes, I forgive you," Lewis stated, and then reached his hand across the table and placed it on Mateo's hand that was resting on the table. I reached over, knocked it off, and placed my hand on his. I knew it was petty and downright childish, but I wasn't giving up that easily. Pretty soon we were pushing each other's hands off of Mateo's before he finally pulled his hand back.

"No need to fight, fellas. I have a great way to solve this dilemma." He looked at both of us and smiled. "Since I can't possibly choose between the both of you

I propose a contest of sorts to see who the best man for me is. I love games, and why shouldn't life be interesting?"

"A game?" I spoke hesitantly.

"Yes. I know it is totally unconventional, but I think it would be fun to have a little friendly contest. Think of it as *American Idol* for dating." He laughed lightly.

"I'm game if he's game." Lewis looked at me sharply. I eyed him back in the same manner.

"But you can't take it out on each other at work."

We both nodded our heads yes even though I knew that it was going to be hard to keep this from spilling over into the work atmosphere.

"Great. It will take me a few days to think about what I want to do, but expect a text with the first challenge," he said, getting up from the table. "I'm looking forward to this. Have a great day, gentlemen."

We both watched him walk off and then we looked at each other in silence for a few seconds.

"May the best man win." I stuck my hand out to shake Lewis's hand.

He hesitantly did the same before he said the same: "May the best man win."

Chapter 1

Kardell

A Piece or Some Peace?

I jumped up out of a good sleep to the sound of some fool banging on my door. I lived in a pretty decent neighborhood in the suburbs of Baltimore County, Maryland. My neighbors were quite uppity and this sound just wasn't tolerated. I scrambled to get myself together and focused my eyes on the clock on my nightstand. It read 7:15 A.M. Now I was pissed. I liked to sleep in on Saturdays, especially when I had no man in my bed. I moaned and groaned as I slipped on my housecoat and slippers, making my way downstairs to the door. My house was immaculate and I glanced around to make sure that everything was in place. I glanced into my full-length mirror on my living room wall to make sure my hair wasn't all over my head before I opened the door.

The banging sound echoed throughout my quiet home causing me to hurry my pace.

"Okay, this is ridiculous. This better be Publishers Clearing House and Ed McMahon rose from the dead with a huge-ass check, because all this noise whoever this is is making is uncalled for," I mumbled to myself as I unlatched the locks to my door.

I opened the door and—guess what—no Ed McMahon. No check. Nothing. Just a fool. Just like I thought,

Ronald was standing in my doorway with all the fineness he could muster up. About six feet tall with deep brown eyes, tight curly black hair, and he had a creamy chocolate complexion that was my weakness. I loved brothas! I mean real, sexy brothas who knew how to use what they had. And Ronald had everything going for him but a damn job. He stood in the doorway looking at me like I owed him something when, in actuality, he owed me. The last time I saw him, he had borrowed some money and that was right after he got a good nut off on me an hour before. That was about two weeks ago. Sorry-ass mother-ump-ump-ump.

"Hey, Kardell, baby." He flashed his pearly whites.

He got no response.

The first time I met him was at the supermarket. He was standing outside the market doing only God knows what. He offered to help me with my bags. I looked him up and down. *Pretty hot and tempting,* I thought. I said yes and headed toward my car with him in tow. I got to the car, pressed the button on my key ring that popped the trunk, and started loading the bags that I had in my hand. He in turn did the same. But, as he did it he rubbed up against my butt with his crotch as he hovered over me. I instantly jumped and turned to see if it was an accident. I was pinned between him and the car. The look on my face said it all. I was appalled and turned on at the same time. How dare he assume I was gay, and easy, too?

"Oh . . . my bad." He looked at me and smiled. "That's not you?"

"Look, brother," I said as I eased from under him and closed my trunk. "It's not that kind of party." I had to admit he was sexy, but I couldn't let on that easy. We were in a parking lot full of cars and people. I looked around to see if anybody had noticed us. I sighed in relief, because everybody was doing their own thing and not paying us any attention.

"Again, my bad," he said as he licked his lips, stepping back and simultaneously looked me up and down. I had to admit I had that effect on people. I was hot and I knew it. Not arrogant, but confident. I garnered the stares of many men and women. I was a nice-looking brother with a toasted-almond complexion and I had shoulder-length dreads that I loved to death. They were one of my best features, I thought. I was about five feet seven and a little muscular. I wasn't a geek, but I was quite intelligent. I was 150 pounds easy and I wore that well. One would say I had it going on.

I wasn't shocked at his stares. It's was his boldness that sent me over. It's was like he just didn't care.

"I just couldn't help myself," he said with a smile. He was cocky and confident.

"Really?" I said as I made my way around to the driver's side of my car. I pulled out ten dollars and handed it to him. He looked at me with confusion.

"What's that for?" he asked.

"It's for helping me with my bags."

"Nah, shorty," he said, waving his hand. I noticed his pants hung off his butt a little. That turned me on, too. "I'm not a panhandler."

I laughed. He sure could've fooled me, because he was sure trying to handle me.

"You know what I want," he said as he moved in closer. My door to my car was open. I backed up and I put my hand up to signal him to stop. He proceeded anyway. I was now touching his chest—a firm, well-built chest. My stomach rumbled and I shifted my eyes away from his. I was uncomfortable and horny. Things were about to get ugly.

"I'm going to need you to back up off of me," I said with little force. He did as instructed.

"What's wrong?" he said with a smile. "You're not feeling me?"

Feeling you, touching you, groping you, slobbing you down. That's not all I want to do to you.

"Look . . ." I paused, looking around again. "You are good-looking and all, but how did you know I wasn't straight?" He laughed. I didn't.

"Look, baby boy. I scoped you out when you first went into the market. I knew without a doubt that you were about that life."

"Umhmm," I said as I now leaned back on my car and I put my hands in my pockets. "So you're psychic, too?"

"Nah, shorty, but I knew." He looked me up and down and then he pulled up his pants a little.

"How?" I posed the question. I couldn't wait for his answer.

"Because of the way you walk." He was smiling hard now. "You're not a sissy; you carry yours like a man should. Not like you on a runway and shit."

"Oh, really," I said, trying not to blush. He had me. "What if my walked fooled you?"

"Nah, man, my dick never lies to me." He grabbed his crotch.

I laughed. He just smiled. I took a quick glance at his bulge. It was adequate from what I could tell. My mind was like, Damnnnnnnnnnn! But I held it together, trying not to let on to being into him. I was easy by nature—something that I hated about myself.

"Is this how you always pick guys up?"

"Usually, I don't. They usually come to me. But you, you had me going the moment I laid eyes on you."

This guy looked like trouble. His lines were weak. I'd heard them before. So why was I falling for it?

"You really are sure of yourself," I said and then smiled.

"This ain't no game, shorty. I gets mine."

"Can you lay off the 'shorty' talk?" I said with attitude. I really wasn't an around-the-way type of guy. I
wasn't better than, just not 'round-the-way.

"You're feisty, too. I can work with that," he said,
rubbing his hands together.

"Work with what?"

"You!" he said boldly. "You look like the next chapter
in the book of my life."

"Well, let's skip to the end of the chapter because I
have to go home."

He laughed, showing his pearly whites again. My
knees got weak and I knew I had to make a run for it.
I turned to get in my car.

"So it's like that?" he said. "You're just going to pass
up a good thing like me and walk away? I think you
will regret not taking this chance with me."

I chuckled at that one. "I think I'm going to have to
go ahead and take that chance," I said as I closed the
door to my car and then stuck my head out of the window. "Got to go."

"Damn, you straight cold," he said with a smile.

"Yep, so put on a coat because I'm out."

Just as I started the car, this fool jumps in front of
my car. Then he started yelling like a maniac.

"Baby, don't leave me," he yelled. "I love you, baby!
Just . . . don't . . . leave me!" He banged on the hood of
my car. "Please, baby, pleaseeeee!"

I was mortified. People started looking and staring.
I couldn't believe that dude was acting like this only a
couple minutes after meeting me. I switched my car
into drive, intending to scare him into going about his
business. It didn't happen. This fool decided to jump
on my car hood. I was done. I stopped, turned my car
off, and then signaled him to go to the passenger door.

I didn't like being embarrassed, ever. He jumped off the car, straightened his clothes, and walked around the car. He opened the door and hoped in. He buckled up and then looked at me.

"We're going to your place right?" Ronald said as his smiling face gleamed at me. I just shook my head and pulled off toward my house.

I should have known then he was going to be a pain in my ass.

I was brought back to the present by Ronald kissing me on the lips.

"What do you want?" I asked tired, pissed, and leaning up against my front doorpost. And his juicy lips just made me even more pissed that he was such a loser. I was mad at me for accepting it, too.

"Kardell, baby, you know what I want," he said, pushing past me and making his way into my house.

"No, tell me," I said, closing the door, trailing behind him like it was his house and not mine. His confidence was ridiculous and hypnotizing. And his muscular shoulders reminded me of his strength in bed. He also had an ass to die for. All of these things were my weakness.

"I missed you, babe." He was now in my kitchen and in my refrigerator, pulling out something to eat. He had nerve.

"I guess two weeks will do that to you," I said sarcastically as I sat down at my kitchen table and watched him.

"Baby, you know I was out taking care of business."

He was jobless. It was the only kind I attracted. Funny, I say. So what he was doing for the two weeks that he was gone, I didn't know. In the four weeks that I had known him, I found out he was jobless and he lived with a relative. He had no kids, no girl on the side, and no diseases. *Why is he still here?* I asked myself. *Four words: I must be desperate.*

I sat at my kitchen table and watched Ronald fix breakfast for one: himself. He looked like Chef G. Garvin when he moved around the kitchen. I shook my head at all the wasted talent and sexiness. Why did I allow this behavior? I must have been crazy. Certifiably so.

He was excellent in bed and that was his only plus. Everything else he took: my money, my time, and now my patience. He finished his food, threw the plate in the dishwasher, and headed toward my bathroom. I stayed at the table, contemplating dating women. They had to be easier.

I heard the shower running, so I made my way toward my bedroom. There was a trail of clothes up the stairs and down the hallway that led to the bathroom. Like a neat freak, I picked them up and threw them in my hamper.

After about fifteen minutes, he sauntered out of the bathroom in the nude. I was lying in the bed, watching television, trying hard to ignore him. But I couldn't help it. I watched him go toward my linen closet and grab a towel. He toweled himself off, threw the towel in the corner, and climbed into bed with me. Okay, I know what you are saying. This Negro had balls. Well, yes, he did and big ones, literally, and that was why I put up with him. I pretended to be engrossed in a television show, fighting hard to not give in to his banging body, which was now pressed up against mine. He smelled good, too. I loved a clean-smelling man. It woke up every part of me that should have stayed asleep.

He started with my ear. Small circles with his tongue at first until my entire ear made its way into his mouth. His dick was pressed up against the back of my thigh and I felt it throbbing. Then it started. My dick began to rise. I was a goner; he took his hand and turned my body toward his. He kissed me softly, and then he pulled me in tightly. Fighting was futile and I knew it. His hands massaged my back and moved down to my butt. He squeezed hard and long. I was at his mercy. My legs had a mind of their own as I wrapped myself around him. He rolled over on his back and I straddled him. I reached over, fumbled through the nightstand, and pulled out a condom. He quickly eased the condom on and I eased down on his dick like a hot knife cutting through butter. He was well endowed and each time we had sex I had to get used to his size all over again. It was that good pain, too. I started slow, up and down.

"Mmmmmmmmmm," he moaned. "This is what I was looking forward to all day." he slapped my butt and palmed it like a basketball. That sent me into overdrive and before I knew it I was rodeo riding and holding on for dear life. *Buck 'em. Ride 'em.* After about twenty minutes he came and I pulled off and lay next to him, sweaty and drained.

After a couple of minutes, I heard my house phone ringing. I rolled over, picked it up, and answered.

"Hello," I answered, annoyed that whoever it was calling was ruining my sexual high.

"Is Ronald home?" I heard a man's voice.

"Is Ronald home?" I wondered the same thing out loud. "Who is this?" I said with an attitude. Ronald followed up behind me with the same question.

"Who is that?"

"Tell him it's Tony," the stranger said as if Ronald was paying bills here.

"Tony?" I repeated, confused. "You have the wrong number," I spoke before I knew it.

"Hold up, baby." Ronald reached around me and grabbed the phone from out of my hand, just before I could hang it up. "This is an important call."

He got up out of the bed, stark-naked, dick swinging, and walked into the other room like I was not even there.

He was back in the room within two minutes.

"Who said you could give out my number?" I asked angrily.

"Babe, Tony is an associate of mine. He called to tell me about a job he was trying to hook me up with."

"Why couldn't he call your cell phone?" I said, getting under the covers and rolling over.

"It's off," he mumbled.

"I thought you paid that with the one hundred dollars you borrowed two weeks ago," I said matter-of-factly.

"I had to pay my aunt rent money I owed her."

"Yeah, okay." He must have thought I was a dummy. *He doesn't know he just got cut off financially.* I was not an ATM. I could tell now that he was on his way out of my life. *I don't get it. These guys don't have anything. They're not willing to work.* And they thought paying back owed money by fucking me good was breaking even. *Hell naw!* I wasn't a call girl and I wasn't going to be treated like one.

"Baby, you mad at me?" Ronald said as he snuggled up against me, trying to smooth me over with sex. It wasn't working. *I swear, Negros must be learning this shit in a secret club or something. Because every one of these bastards I have dated thinks that their dick is good enough to give me amnesia.* This was the last one. But what I was going to do was get me one good fuck in before I kicked his ass to the curb.

"Nah, baby," I said, pushing my ass toward his dick, giving him a hint. "I'm not mad at all."

That night was the last night I saw Ronald. I told him to keep the money he owed me and the dick I had ridden in on.

Chapter 2

Lewis

Knock Knock

I woke up feeling around in my bed with my hands like a fat man trying to find his dick. My eyes were still trying to focus in the darkness of my room. There was a small bit of light that was coming through the curtains I had in my window. I was expecting someone to be in my bed with me. At least there was someone there last night. I had spent another night with a strange guy who I thought was "the one." Again. Don't worry, we practiced safe sex and all of that. I was a latex ho for sure. His ass must have slipped out the door when I rolled over last night. *I guess he wasn't the cuddling type.* He busted and broke out like a bad rash. But it was all good. I knew *he* was coming. You know . . . the one.

"Shit, I'm going to be late for work." I jumped up out of the bed and briskly walked down the short hall to my bathroom. It was almost seven o'clock and I had to be in the office at eight. "I'm so dead."

I took my job seriously and my boss did too. He was such an uptight, by-the-rules boss. He was gay and he acted like he didn't get the memo. He didn't have to be me and my fabulous self, but damn get the dildo out of your butt and live. I never said that to him, thank God, even though it almost slipped a couple of times.

I didn't hate him. I just thought that he should loosen up a little.

I walked into work and breathed a sigh of relief because I narrowly made it to work on time. I looked at Janice as I walked by and smiled. She smiled back. Before I got to my cubicle, I peeked back at her to see if she was writing down anything. She was so by-the-book as well. She said she minds her business, but I don't trust her as far as I can throw her. I wasn't good at any sport, so throwing her would be a feat. I laughed to myself and kept it moving toward my desk.

As soon as I sat down I got a text on my phone: Can I come over tonight?

Who is this? I texted back.

Damn, how many people you doing? ... lol

I still had no clue as to who I was talking to. My nose was wrinkled up in disgust and wonder.

Apparently, you weren't good because your number is not registered in my phone. Chew on that! Limp Biscuit! I was now smiling from ear to ear. *That will teach whoever his ass is to text me with some foolishness.* No text followed after that one.

I threw my phone in my top drawer of my desk and logged on to my computer. I had work to do.

My boss was unusually late coming in. I heard him greet Janice and a few others as he made his way in.

I peeked out of my cubicle briefly to see a slight smirk on his face. He was so uptight most of the time I didn't know if he was upset or his normal self. I just ignored him for the day and went on about my job tasks.

I loved my job and my life and, with the exception of no love life, I was a happy guy. I was raised in a two-parent home in Philadelphia along with one older brother and one older sister. Yes, I was the baby of the family and I loved it. I got everything I wanted or even asked for as a child; my parents conceived me ten years after my brother and sister, who were a year apart in birth. They were practically out of the house when I was in my teen years. I came out of the closet at about fifteen years old and both my parents took it well, although they were a little hesitant in the beginning. I migrated to Maryland when I decided to go to school out of state. I decided to get my schooling done at University of Maryland Eastern Shore. Being away from home was so liberating and scary at the same time. I had flare and an opulent taste that many weren't ready for. Don't get it twisted, I wasn't a complete fem queen or anything, but I dressed in any color I felt like and I wore whatever I put on well. I was on every committee they had when it came to design and fashion, hence my major in design technology. Colors were my best friend and I worked UMES overtime when I attended the school. That's what I did here at the advertising agency. I worked my magic with design and I was getting paid well to do it. I lived here on my own and I was happy. Again, with the exception of my love life.

My workday went by pretty smoothly and I exited the building promptly at 5:00 P.M. I had my shades on and my haircut was edged up to the T. I hopped into my little Honda Civic and pressed on my way. And, yes, I said Honda Civic. I was fabulous in everything, even my car, but I was not going to let a car drain my pockets. My clothes had to be top notch at all times and "fresh" cost money.

I pulled up to my house in the Avalon, a gated housing community, and exited my car, but before I could walk toward my door an Asian-looking woman popped out of a car that was parked right behind me, blocking me in.

She was yelling at me in her language, which I assumed was Chinese or something. She was one of them Rice-A-Roni, no-chairs-at-the-table-having bitches. She had a deranged look on her face. I eased my hand in my pocket for the Mace that was on my keychain.

"What? Who are you?" I said as I consciously backed up onto the cemented sidewalk. She kept on rambling in her language.

"Lady, what are you talking about? English . . . speak English." I looked around, hoping no one was lurking or looking. It was a quiet community and I liked it that way.

"You fuck husband?" she asked, but already knew the answer. She was going to have to prove it or get the hell out of my face.

"Who *is* your husband?" She looked like no man would go near her with a ten-foot dick but I didn't say that. She looked like she wanted a fight. I was a lover and a fighter, meaning I loved a good fight, verbally and physically, as a teenager. I had grown out of that at my age, but she looked like she wanted me to dip back into my past and have me pull out a good ol' ass whipping for her ass.

"You know husband , because he not come home. I watch he come out you house. Us live across from you home. How could you ruin happy home?"

"Miss, he said you all were sister and brother." I'd seen them before in the exercise room and they showed no type of affection toward each other. I just took him for his word that they were brother and sister. He was a very attractive Asian man and I couldn't see him with her so I believed him when he said that they were brother and sister. I guessed this was entirely my fault for not investigating and only going by what it looked like. He was in a hurry to get down with it, too, which should have been my first clue. He was also too familiar with my asshole. He knew how to tease it and then please it. No hesitation. A newbie would have fumbled around a little but he didn't. He went straight for it the first time we fucked.

His ass wasn't lacking in the dick department, either. That little dick Asian myth must have skipped him. He banged it out for a good hour. He loved me long time. I snickered out loud at my last thought.

"You think me laugh?" She lunged toward me and the pepper spray materialized out of my pocket and right in front of her face. She froze instantly.

"Make my day, bitch, and your ass will be scrambling on the ground and crawling around like Ray Charles reincarnated trying to find the ass you didn't have to begin with." She backed up as I knew she would. "Confront your husband. He lied. Plus, I can't turn off all of this goodness. Shit, but I can take you in my house and make you over so he can give you what he gave me last night."

Her mouth dropped in shock. I was serious. She just turned and walked away from me. A sloppy-haired ponytail, Juicy Couture jogging suit, and a flat ass is not a good combination.

"And let something happen to my car and I will do what I did with him last night again, but on purpose!" I spoke loud enough for her to hear me. She kept on walking and I turned and went to the door of my humble abode.

I couldn't believe that she caused a scene like that in front of my home. "I guess everybody got a little ghetto in them, especially when it comes to some good wood." I spoke and then laughed to myself as I entered my apartment.

I had showered and shaved, and was getting ready to doze on off to sleep when my front doorbell chimed.

"I know this ugly Asian bitch isn't knocking on my door about her well-endowed husband." I was still naked and loved to be that way. I huffed as I threw on some boxers, lavender silk lounging pants, and slippers and walked to my door. I peeped through the peephole to see who it was. I was angry with whoever it was because I was watching *The Color Purple* and Celie had just got to my favorite part when she fell out on the dirt road when Shug left her hanging.

When I saw who it was I perked up a little and opened the door. He didn't even say hi; he just pushed the door open, and walked past me and into my living room.

"Your wife confronted me today!" I stood with my arms folded against my chest, waiting for an explanation.

"Me give her two Benadryl in wine. Her pass out and me come over here. I fuck you hard and fast and then me home." He stepped out of his pants and underwear and started to stroke his dick. I knew I was wrong, but I had to get it at least one more time so on my knees I went.

After the blow job we made it into my bedroom; here he bent me over the foot end of my wooden sleigh bed.

"Him like this?" he asked. He was punishing me some kind of good. His wood was good.

"Yes." I grunted out a moan because he bent me over so quickly that I didn't have time to put a pillow or towel in between me and the hard wood of my bed, which was pressing against my pelvic bone. I was a petite guy and right now I was wishing that I ate more like my mother had told me the last time I saw her about two weeks ago. "Give it to me . . . Give it to me hard." I didn't know the next time I would be getting any so I might as well take what I can and suffer with the bruises later.

He pulled out. "Get on bed . . . on all four."

I did as I was told as he climbed right behind me and entered me from behind. He immediately began to go back to work. My joyful whimpering encouraged him to thrust harder. He went from doggie style to froggie style and fucked me ferociously. He finished about fifteen minutes later and got up as quickly as he entered me.

I lay there while he walked into the bathroom. I heard the condom snap as he pulled it off of his penis and then he flushed it down the toilet. The shower ran for the next ten minutes while I continued to lie in the same spot he left me in. He dried off, dressed, waved, and then left. I didn't get up. I didn't move. I stayed in the position of a used fool for the rest of the night.

Love needed to find me and fast.

Chapter 3

Kardell

Fooled Again

I sat on my chocolate suede chaise in front of my bay window with a bottle of wine and a broken heart. I cried as I stared out the window at the people passing. I was home alone, again. I had "Through the Rain" by Mariah Carey playing on the stereo. I was completely bummed. It had been weeks since I showed Ronald the door. On some nights, I was so lonely that I contemplated calling him up just to have someone to hold me at night. But I knew that it wouldn't be long before he was in my bank account again, so I ditched that thought.

I looked at the clock. It was only 8:30. I was a thirty-year-old young man sitting in the house on a Saturday.

"What in the hell happened to me?" I wondered. A year ago I was up in the club, sweating so hard that my shirt would cling to me like I had showered in my clothes. I had no friends, well, real ones anyway. Those days a gay man couldn't have gay friends and a man, because somehow my man and one of my friends would always end up sleeping together behind my back. Gay men are so promiscuous that it's a shame. So now I had neither.

I picked up my cell phone and scrolled through the possible candidates I could invite over for company—

someone from my past. I knew I was acting desperate. Chalk it up as me being human and horny. Yes, I had my moments of promiscuity but for the most part I pretty much kept to myself. As I scrolled down my phone it began to ring. The caller ID showed it was my mother.

"Hello," I answered with a sigh.

"Boy, what's wrong with you?" my mother asked. "You sound like you lost your best friend."

"Nothing, ma, I'm just a little down."

"My baby needs his mama to come over there and fix you some of my lasagna. That always makes you feel better."

"No, ma, I'll be fine. I just need to get out of this house before I jump out the window."

"Kardell, baby, you know I can always call one of the Carter girls over to cheer you up." Mom loved me just as I was, but she still tried every chance she could to get me to go out on a date with a girl.

"Now, ma, you know that will only happen when pigs fly."

"Don't make Mama throw some bacon out the window."

She laughed. So did I, but harder.

"You never said how the pig was going to get in the air." She laughed again.

"I knew that would get a laugh out of you."

"You know ya sister baby daddy is acting up again," she huffed into the phone. My sister, Angela, was a single mom, well sort of. She had a man, but he was in and out of her life like a three-minute man during sex. It was like choosing losers ran in my family. Truth was I wasn't surprised to hear this, because he did it all the time. She refused to let him go because she said "he has potential." And she didn't want my nephew to grow up in a single household. She was blind because most of the time he was doing what he wanted to do anyway. When the street called, he answered, and she waited around for him to make it back home. When he made it back home.

"I don't know what to do with that girl." She huffed again like I was going to try to offer a solution to the problem. She didn't know I was in the same type of predicament myself: denial. My sister didn't know that her baby daddy swung both ways either. It was news to me, too. About three months ago, I was downtown and I bumped into him in the Sportsman bar in Mount Vernon. I remembered it like it was yesterday.

I was in the club doing what I did worst: trying to find a man. I was on the dance floor, giving the boys a show, and a good show, too. I was hot and sweaty, but I kept it going. A classic song came on that had everybody scramble to the dance floor and dance. At the club, you know, sometimes you let a few guys grind on you and get their feels so you saw how much they were packing and if they were packing at all.

The guy who was rubbing on me was grinding like he was ready to fuck, and, truth be told, I was down for it. I wanted to get laid that night too. He was packing, too, and that made me turn around to see the face that came with the dick.

"Wassup, shorty, you tryin'a go somewhere?" His eyes were glassy and his breath was laced with the smell of hard liquor. He was just as sweaty as I was.

"Alex?" I looked at him, shocked. Neither one of us was dancing anymore. The thrill was gone for me.

"You know me, shorty?" he asked as he reached to squeeze my ass.

I knocked his hand away and walked back toward the tables that were near the walls of the club. He followed me.

"And you know me," I countered angrily. How someone could be this drunk, where they didn't recognize their baby mother's brother? I mean it was a little dark in the place, but not that dark.

"I do?" His ass was toasted. He was almost pissy drunk.

"My sister is your baby's mother. You remember her right? Your son's name is Anthony," I reminded him.

"Ohhhhh, shit." He covered his mouth in shock and shook his head from side to side. I was pretty sure his high was gone. He was quiet for a few seconds. I would be speechless too if my girl's brother caught me in a gay club grinding up on him.

"So are you going to tell her or am I?" I asked him. He was still silent.

"Yo, this not what it looks like. I was just in here getting a drink and just getting my party on." He actually looked like he believed he was telling the truth.

"You expect me to believe that this is the first time you were grinding up on another man?" I was looking at him with doubt all over my face.

"It's the truth. I got no reason to lie. I just wanted to see what it was like. You know . . . try it out." He looked pathetic. I almost felt sorry for him.

"Okay, let's say this is the first time. What are you going to do after this? Leave and never do it again?"

"Yeah, man, this is it. I won't do this again. I promise." He actually put his hand over his heart like he was sincere.

"No, I can't do that. I can't do that to my sister or my nephew. I am going to give you some time to tell the truth and if you don't then I will. I promise."

"Okay. I will."

"Also, I need you to get tested for everything and have it to me ASAP. And you don't have sex with my sister until I get this."

"Okay," he agreed. I watched him leave and shook my head in astonishment.

Alex was your typical sports-watching, booty-chasing brother. I had seen him on several occasions and we never really paid each other any mind. Come to think of it, on every function we had as a family, he never said anything to me and he always stayed clear of me. It all came together as I drove home that night. He must have been scared that I was going to notice his secret or something. The truth was most people thought gay men could tell who was gay and who wasn't, but that was so far from the truth. I couldn't have cared less about his or anybody else's choice of dating.

That was about three months ago and I never told anyone, yet, and each time we saw each other now he tried to have conversations with me to ease the tension between us. He was an attractive man and I could see why my sister kept him around as long as she did. He was quite easy on the eyes.

"Ma, I don't know what to tell you. She loves him and he is her son's father. We just need to mind our business and let her be." I know what you're thinking. She was my sister and I should have been spilling the beans. But she was one of them people you had to show and not tell. She's a "kill the messenger" type of person. I wasn't even going to touch that with a ten-inch stick. We already didn't see eye to eye most of the time as it was. *All I need is for me to go and tell her that her man is a bisexual and she is liable to curse me out and try and tell me that I pursued him.* She believed that all gay men were on a course to take men from women for spite and sport. So not true, we only pursued the pursuer. If your man was gay, then it would come out eventually. Gay guys didn't have to take what was already taken. She didn't believe that at all though. My sister, Angela, was a very pretty girl, but she had a nasty attitude and I wasn't going to add wood to an already-burning fire.

"Well . . . you're right, baby." She sighed. "Your sister is just as stubborn as her father." She laughed at that one. I did too. "So what are you doing tonight, just sitting in the house and moping?"

"I guess so, Ma."

"Baby, why don't you come over here and keep me company since your father is gone again?" Oh, Lord, I loved my mom, but I could not get through a night with her. *She will have me shifting furniture or playing Scrabble or gin rummy all night long.* That wasn't my kind of night.

"No, thanks, Ma. I think I'm going to get dressed and go out."

"Sure, baby, be careful. Love you, baby." She blew a kiss into the phone.

"Love you too, Ma." I hung up the phone and headed toward my closet in my bedroom. I pulled on some black linen slacks and a cream-colored short-sleeved button up. I hopped in the shower, washed off, and then got dressed. I practically ran to my Volvo and pulled off. I didn't even know where I was headed. I just needed to get out of the house.

I ended up heading out to the Sportsman bar/club. It was a familiar place to me. There was nothing like the familiar. I had some good times here and I met some good prospects. *Maybe, just maybe, I might find me a good guy out of the bunch who is in the club tonight. It isn't likely, but it's worth a try,* I figured.

I walked in the club at about 10:30; it was not jumping with young hoppers yet, so I was good. All I needed was a couple of twirling prissies to come in and ruin my night. I went to the bar and ordered me a rum and Coke, just to add to the buzz that I got from the wine I was drinking at home. I wasn't a heavy drinker, but tonight was different; I wanted to be. I was alone and I was disgusted with my choice in men. Maybe the drunken me could pick out a winner, because the sober me sucked.

I found a table in the corner in the back with an eagle-eye view of the bar and dance floor. I could see everybody who came and went. I sat in the corner for about forty-five minutes and three drinks later I was swaying to the beats of some of my favorite singers: Mariah Carey, Janet Jackson, Ciara, and, my ultimate favorite, Jennifer Hudson. Homegirl was a vocal force to be reckoned with.

The crowd was getting heavier as the night wore on. I noticed nothing but losers walking through the door. A couple of them had been bed buddies of my past. They glanced my way and scurried away like mice toward a hole. I didn't care, because I was over them.

But one dude caught my eye. He was a well-dressed older-looking guy. I'd say around forty years old. Low cut curly hair and goatee. He had toasted hazelnut–colored skin. My eyes danced with excitement. He looked sophisticated and classy, with a hint of a rough edge. *My type of guy.* This was the drunk me talking now. In my mind we had already done the deed and were nestled, sleeping in each other's arms.

"Excuse me, can I set my drink here?" I was brought back to reality with the brother I just sexed up in my quickie fantasy.

I screamed, *hell yeah!* in my mind. My mouth said, "Sure."

"Thanks," he said with a smile. His lips looked soft with a hint of wetness. "This place is packed," he said as he took his jacket off and set it on the open chair next to me. He was well dressed with denim jeans and a cream-colored sweater vest alone. His arms were muscular but not overly so. I liked what I saw, but I didn't let on.

"Yeah, it is," I said back nonchalantly. Before I knew it he was out on the dance floor, getting his groove on. All the young bucks flocked toward him as he jammed to song after song. He was out on the dance floor for about twenty minutes before he came back to the table to get his drink. I wanted to go out there and dance with him but I wanted to see what he could do first. I liked to observe my prospects for a while. I usually just sat here and let them come to me. Dancing was optional for me.

He looked good out there. I couldn't help but wonder how this brother worked in the bedroom. He had to be good. When I was a kid Mama always joked around with my aunt in the kitchen about their one-night stands from time to time. One time I heard her say, "He was good on the dance floor, girl, so I had to try him out in the bedroom." They would both break out in a fit of laughter, carrying on wildly.

"Whew!" He came back to the table, grabbed a napkin, and wiped his sweaty brow. "Those young boys know how to work it out there on that floor. They keep an old boy like me blood flowing to all the right places if you know what I mean," he said with a huge smile.

"Yeah, I bet," I said with a little contempt in my voice. I wasn't a hater, but these young boys knew nothing about how to get and keep a man. All they wanted was a quick fuck and moved on. I knew how to romance a brother. Keep him coming back for more, and not just sexually either. I was smart, funny, and I knew how to hold a conversation. In retrospect I guessed none of that mattered to men and I was in the same vicious cycle as them.

"I'm pretty sure you know all about that though," he said, sitting down and facing me. He was even more attractive up close. He had a few gray hairs in his goatee; to me that meant he was experienced. At least I hoped so. "What are you, about twenty-one, twenty-two?" he asked me.

Okay, was this a line or was he serious? I had to be smart about this and not get played like I had in the past.

"No, actually I'm thirty," I said proudly, as I picked up my drink and sipped it.

"Really? . . . Nah, man . . . you are lying," he said, grinning. "You're going to have to prove this to me. Show me some ID."

I quickly whipped out my driver's license and he looked at it and handed it back to me.

"Umph . . . umph . . . umph, time has sure been good to you. You look *good,*" he said, shaking his head.

"Well, attribute that to no smoking, very little drinking, and plenty of good sex," I said, shamelessly flirting. This guy looked like he was relationship material. I had to go in for the kill. "Then again you probably can say the same thing. What are you thirty, thirty-two?"

"Yeah, about ten years ago." He chuckled.

"Well, I guess time has been good to you too." I showed my pearly whites.

"My name is Darius." He reached out to shake my hand.

"I'm Kardell."

"Now that we got the age and name thing cleared up, I think we've checked each other out long enough. Unless you want to see a brother's social security card, so you can run a criminal and credit check on me." I laughed very hard. He was on to me. *I take it he's been in my shoes before.*

"So, how can a brother get a dance out of you?" he said, looking out at the dance floor and back at me. "I know you aren't going to let them young bucks outdo you out there on the floor."

"Young bucks?" I said as I faked being offended. "You're on," I said, stepping out of my chair and onto the dance floor. I wasn't about to be shown up. I had a couple of good moves in me still.

We danced until about two in the morning. I walked off the floor tired and drenched. The liquor had completely worn off. When I got back to my table, I figured it was time for me to go and make a night of it.

Darius, the older guy, met me back at the table just as I was getting my coat on.

"You're not leaving yet? The night just got started."

"I don't stay out this late. I like to get at least eight hours of sleep before I have to get up for the next day."

"Well, can I at least walk you to your car?" He looked at me with a disappointed look on his face.

"Um . . . sure," I said, a little uneasy. I'd just met this dude, and he could be trying to set me up or even rape me or something.

I walked out the door with Darius in tow. I had my hand on my keys in my coat pocket. They had an emergency-size pepper spray on them that I could easily unlatch if somebody broke bad on me.

My car was about three blocks away, so we chitchatted a little as we walked. Out of the corner of my eye I thought I saw somebody following us. It was late and I didn't take any chances. I eased the top off of the pepper spray just in case.

"So this young tender you leaving me for, Darius?" I heard someone yell. I turned around to see an older guy, probably about sixty-five years or older, standing with a bat in his hand. My mouth flung open.

"What in the he—" That was all I could get out before the old dude started swinging. I ducked just in time, but Darius wasn't so lucky. When I looked over I saw him on the ground balled up. I looked at the old dude, who still had rage in his eyes. He looked as if he was going to swing again. I quickly pulled out the pepper spray, sprayed his ass like I was using a can of Raid on some roaches, and then hauled my ass out of there. I sprinted all the way to my car. As I got there I was shaking, fumbling my keys, and looking behind me to see if I was in the clear like a white girl in a horror flick. I jumped in my car and sped off like a bat out of hell. I wasn't going to that club ever again.

As I was driving down the block, which happened to be the one I had just sprinted up to get to my car, I noticed that the old dude was still whipping Darius's ass. I just shook my head and kept it moving. I dodged a bullet there. *Just think, I could have taken that chump home and old dude probably would have followed me home and bust out my car windows or something.* I did not need that shit in my neighborhood. I was still apologizing to my neighbors who were awakened by Ronald beating on my door weeks ago.

As I pulled up to my door, guess who was sitting on my stoop? Yep, it was Ronald. I must have talked his ass up.

"Hey, baby," he said as I got out the car and made my way up to the steps.

"What do you want? Didn't I put you out weeks ago? Why are you back here?" I asked as I walked past him and up to my door. This guy was a thorn in my side. Really!

He walked up behind me and pressed up against me with his hard dick against my ass. He reached around and grabbed my dick with his hand and massaged it. I fumbled my keys, missing a lock for the second time in an hour.

I turned around, angry and horny. "Look, I'm tired and—"

He cut me off with a kiss that made my arms go limp. I dropped my keys and let him take advantage of me. After about a minute he pulled away and looked at me with his eyes piercing me. He was intoxicating, sexy, and irritating as hell.

"Now what were you saying?" he said as I just stared into his eyes.

"Um . . . Um . . . What was I saying?" I stood there on my stoop with my hand on my forehead. His kiss had left me absentminded and dazed.

Chapter 4

Lewis

Love . . . Is That You?

"Hey, boo." I kissed my best friend Dennis on his forehead as we sat down for lunch. Dennis was a white boy with just as much flare and charisma as me. Though he wasn't overly feminine like I sometimes could be. I'm not hating I just know who I like to hang out with. We complemented each other well. The only difference between me and him was he had a man. A deep, dark chocolate man. A working man. A construction worker who was all man. He was built strong, just like a Ford truck. Dennis and I met while waiting tables when we worked at Applebee's during my college years. We had clicked from the start and we had been friends ever since. Dennis was a clothing designer for a reputable fashion line out of DC and he was very good at his job. I even wore some of his designs.

"Hey, sir," he spoke before he took a sip of his tea. We were in Mount Vernon in a quaint little restaurant with a table or two outside. We would meet up here for lunch about twice a week to chitchat and gossip a little. "So what's going on in your world?"

"Not a thing." I smirked.

"Good day, sir. Can I get you something to drink?" A petite black woman politely interrupted me before I could go into detail with Dennis about the last couple of days in my life.

"Yes, I'll have a chocolate Frappuccino with whipped cream and a vanilla scone," I ordered.

"Sure, I'll be right back."

"All that sugar goes to the hips, you know that, right?" Dennis scolded me.

He always chastised me when it came down to my weight. I was a regular-looking guy, not fat or thin, but I was fit. Dennis was always fit. He looked good. But he wasn't always like that. Getting and keeping a man would do that to you. He was a gym freak. He lived inside Bally Total Fitness.

"I don't have anybody to worry about that for anyway. I don't have a man like you do." I threw a little shade his way. It was innocent though.

"And you won't get one with a gut and thick thighs, unless you meet one who's a chubby chaser." He smiled.

"Bitch, please. Chubby is not for me. Now don't get me wrong, I will fuck a thick guy, because I like me a thick man working me over, but I don't want to be one." We both laughed.

"Anyway," I pushed to change the subject from me to him. "How is Charles doing? Mr. Work Hard For The Money?"

"Chile, he is doing it and doing it well. I just can't keep him off of me. I'm surprised that I could sit down in my office chair this morning." He was smiling extremely too hard. I was envious on the inside. Extremely envious.

"Damn, he got it like that." I scooted up my chair a little closer to the table. The waiter came and brought me my order. She asked if I needed anything else, but I waved her away in an effort to get back to the conversation with Dennis.

"Well, baby, let's just say he brings his own jackhammer home and into the bedroom. He breaks ground every time he enters me."

"Ump . . . ump . . . ump." I shook my head and marveled.

"And get this. He talks to me afterward. Not that I be listening, because I be so spent afterward. He holds me and kisses the nap of my neck. I wake up to breakfast in bed sometimes, and when he leaves for work before I get up there are love notes plastered all over the house to see when I get ready to leave out for the day."

I could have flipped the table over and walked off. I was so jealous. Not at Dennis, just that I didn't have a man like that. I got stuck with losers, leeches, or ones already on leashes.

"Damn, what the hell am I doing wrong?" I asked out loud after a few seconds.

"The right one will come along. You just have to be patient. Don't rush it. I had to go through the whole United Nations just to find mines." We both burst into laughter.

"Now, that is true. You was a ho back in the day." I laughed.

"Boy, please. They gave you an honorary star up on the Meat Rack for all the men you were serving up," he said and then we both laughed again.

We ragged on each other for about another half hour before we both made our way back toward our perspective jobs. When I got back to the office I was a little peppier than I was when I had left for lunch.

Back at my desk, I was going through my "to do" list for the rest of the day. But my mind kept wandering back to the conversation that I had with Dennis today. We had fun and I loved every minute I spent with him, but he had someone to go home to. Colors and schemes weren't making me happy at home or comforting me at night. I needed a living, breathing body to do that job. I wanted someone to talk to about my dreams and aspirations. I needed someone to sit across a table from and just to stare at for as long as I wanted to without saying a word. Why couldn't I have that? Was I asking for too much or were my standards too high?

I reached in one of my desk drawers and pulled out a Dove Dark Chocolate with Almonds bar and started to devour it. Dennis was right; I was going to eat myself heavy. And I knew all too well that color on a fat man was a no-no, but I was an emotional eater. And right now I was an emotional wreck. I threw the wrapper in the trash and continued to do my work for the rest of the day.

On my way home from work I hoped and prayed that the unhappy Asian across the complex was up for some "unhappy" sex. Since we were both unhappy with our present situations, why not have some "unhappy" sex?

But I pulled into my parking spot in front of my house and sat there for a minute, hoping that he would come out of his door "coincidentally." I hoped that he waited by the window for me to come home like a mate would do. I looked in the rearview mirror a few times before giving up and getting out of my car.

"Excuse me, can you do me a favor?" I turned to see a fine—and I mean fine—light-skinned guy standing before me.

"What can I do to you?" I blurted out my innermost thoughts inadvertently.

"Huh?" He looked at me, confused.

"Wow, I'm so sorry." I was completely embarrassed. I looked away for a second before I spoke again. "That wasn't supposed to come out."

"It's all good, and we've all had those moments," he said, trying to make me feel at ease.

"I guess." I shrugged my shoulders. I was still embarrassed.

"Anyway, I am new to the complex and I locked my keys in my car. Could you call a locksmith? Because I left my phone in my house, too."

"Sure." I pulled out my phone and Googled locksmiths in my area and within minutes he was on the phone arranging for a locksmith to pop his lock.

"Thank you so much." He handed me back my phone. He had a well-manicured afro-type haircut and exquisitely tapered up goatee and mustache. He was gorgeous. Then he smiled and his teeth were subpar, a little dingy. It wasn't a total mood killer but I wouldn't kiss him right off either. "How can I pay you back for this?"

"Pay me back?" My mind wandered off to all types of places and I was in heaven just thinking about the possibilities of him and me getting it in sexually. "Don't worry about it. It's just a phone call. It was no problem at all, quite a pleasure actually."

"Nah, tell you what. I'm a cook and I'll invite you to the restaurant I cook at and cook you whatever you want on me."

"Oh, you got it like that huh?" I looked him up and down lasciviously. I didn't have a pure thought in my head right now.

"Maybe, you'll just have to come and check me out."

Too late for that, I thought as he handed me his card and smiled. I didn't know what that smile meant but I wanted it to mean some fabulous, mind-blowing sex. I could see me going off into the sunset with him.

"Well, let me go stand by the entrance gate so I can let the locksmith in when he comes." He then turned and walked in the direction of the front gate. He had a fabulous walk and a nice butt, too.

"Daniel Asher, master chef." I looked at his card and smiled. "I wonder what else you're a master at doing," I said as I smiled and grinned as I walked to my front door and entered my apartment.

I was definitely going to find out about Daniel and *all* of his skills. I could only hope he was at least on both sides of the fence or hopefully just my side. The shower I took before I went to bed was all that. I couldn't help but masturbate in the shower just from the thought of maybe having a man who could cook in and out of the bedroom. Both were still to be determined. I was going to do my best to bring him on home.

Chapter 5

Kardell

A Day in the Life

I woke up in bed with a snoring Ronald next to me. I put my hand on my forehead, because I could not believe I ended up here once again. Maybe I was fooling myself by going out and looking for Mr. Right last night. Maybe Ronald is Mr. Fuck-it-he'll-have-to-do. Is every man a liar and a cheat? Or was I just a magnet for losers? The hell if I knew, but I was surely getting tired of the runaround with these men I'd been stumbling on to.

I got up and stretched as Ronald shifted in the bed, but he did not get up. Of course he didn't; what did he have to get up for? He had no job with prospects, that was clear. I sluggishly headed to the shower. After about fifteen minutes in the shower, I was out and drying myself off. While I was in the shower I did have a conversation with myself about being optimistic and sticking it out with Ronald and his flaws.

As I was in my walk-in closet, trying to get myself a suit to wear to work, Ronald snuck up and grabbed me from behind.

"Where do you think you are going?" he said as his muscular arms wrapped around me, threatening to break my smaller ones.

"To work," I said, while he licked the back of my neck. He eased his hands under my V-neck undershirt and caressed my pecks. He was turning me on. He was very good at getting me hot and bothered within seconds of his touch. I had a floor-to-ceiling mirror at the end of my closet and I looked at the two gorgeous guys who stood in front of it. I wasn't sure of how long this was going to last, but I liked what I saw in that mirror. I saw a glimmer of hope. "Ummmmm . . . Not now, baby," I said, struggling to ease my way out of his grasp.

"You sure?" He started to take of his shirt. His body was almost flawless. His pecks were huge and his abs could wash a couple loads of clothes easily, they were that tight. He stood there in his boxers and a fresh pair of my socks.

"Um. Umm. I have to get to work," I said, trying to keep the snake in my pants from growing. It was a losing battle. As I looked into his soft eyes and a smirk on his face that made me melt, I knew if I didn't go now I would be late, if I went at all. It had happened before.

He eased his boxers down and his manhood, which was curved and hard, beckoned my lips like a mouse to cheese.

"Are you sure?" he asked again. This time he made it jump and slap his thigh. He smiled as if he knew he had me. I shook my head and pushed past him with my suit in hand. It took everything in me not to go back and finish him off in the closet.

"Yep." Somebody had to bring home the bacon. And I surely couldn't rely on him to get the job done.

I stood at my dresser as I fixed my tie and made sure my hair was in place. Ronald sat on the corner of the bed and watched me as I finished my ritual. I watched him from the large mirror that was on the same dresser as he made his pecks dance. He knew I was watching him and he also knew that I loved his chest. He was really trying to entice me.

"So what are you going to do today?" I asked as I walked away from my dresser, out of my room, and down the steps toward my kitchen while he was in pursuit. He came in the kitchen right after me and sat down at the table.

"I'ma go holler at a couple of my boys and then I'm going to check out a couple of spots to see if I can get me some work." He was drawing circles in the table as he talked, which made me think he was just talking to be talking. I wondered if he was one of those pretty boy airheads. Was I just keeping him here as a placeholder for the man of my dreams or maybe so my bed wouldn't be cold at night? He was getting on my nerves.

"All right, whatever," I said nonchalantly. I made a cup of coffee, made my way toward my office, and got my laptop and some papers for work. I was trying my best to get out of the house before he wanted to try to get a piece before I left, again.

He went into the living room and cut the television on. As I made my way toward the door, I turned toward him as he sat in my chocolate and cream leather and suede sectional with his feet propped up on my matching ottoman.

"Are you going to be here when I get back or is this the last time I am going to see you for a while?"

"Sure, baby boy. Because that fat ass you got right there belongs to me tonight." He was smiling ear to ear and laughing. I just shook my head and exited my home.

"I guess this is my life," I mumbled to myself as I walked out of my door. I'd have to say that I wasn't too comfortable with this situation. Here I was portraying one thing at work and being another thing in my personal life. I just wanted to be happy and in a relationship with someone I could depend on. Was that too much to ask?

I walked into work with a frown on my face and a frown in my heart. I just wasn't sure how I was going to put up with Ronald and his shenanigans for a long time. I walked into my office and shut my door. My secretary waved a couple of messages or something in the air, but I was too preoccupied with my defunct love life. I was a successful marketing executive of a marketing company (Bankable Advertising, Inc.) that I launched right after I graduated from college. I was on the right track with a heavy client base that rivaled any other marketing firm in the area. I had several junior execs and one intern who were in my staff of professionals. All I needed to complete the puzzle of my life was a life partner I could lean on for love and support forever. It just didn't seem like it was ever going to happen. Ever.

Knock. Knock. Knock.

"Come in," I said, logging on to my computer system and checking my e-mails.

"Mr. Spencer, is everything okay?" My secretary, Janice, walked up to my desk with a notepad in hand. She was a petite woman. Her skin was as chocolate as a Hershey Kiss and she was as sweet as one, too. She was a bit older than I wanted to hire, but she was efficient and meticulous, which was why I hired her. I had just launched my company and my office was in disarray. In the middle of her interview I had to use the bathroom and within ten minutes of my absence she had completely organized my entire desk and half my office. I knew I should have been annoyed by her touching my things but she showed that she was orderly and professional. She also reminded me a little of my deceased grandmother. Needless to say, I hired her on the spot.

I continued to type away, partially ignoring her. "No, Janice, everything is fine. Sorry for ignoring you earlier. I was thinking about something and I wanted to write it down before I forgot. How are you doing this morning?" I said all in one breath.

"Wonderful, Mr. Spencer. Just marvelous. God is good." She was now smiling and that alone caused me to smile. She was infectious and lighthearted all the time. I'd never heard her raise her voice once.

"That's great to hear, Janice," I said with a bit of envy in my voice.

"Here are your messages," she said, placing them on my desk. "Do you need anything to drink, Mr. Spencer?"

"Sure, I'll have a mint tea and a bagel with cream cheese, please."

She shuffled out of the door making her exit.

As I looked at my messages I had noticed one from my father. He was estranged, or strange if I had to tell it. He and my mom were together, but they were separated. He came and went as he pleased and she let him. Maybe that was where I got my ways from. Letting men do and act the way they wanted to.

My dad was a good provider from a distance even though he wasn't always around when I needed him. And he asked me if that was the reason I was the way I was. You know, gay and all. Blaming him for me being gay was not even an option. I was gay because I liked men, plain and simple. He was not to blame and I never made him feel that way. Anyway, he wanted me to call him. He said he was worried about me. This had my mom written all over it. *She is such a blabbermouth. She just couldn't keep it to herself, could she?* Now he was going to be all in my business.

Like the procrastinator I was, I pushed that message to the end of the day, maybe even the end of the week. I was not comfortable with my dad asking me about how the men in my life were treating me. It was just too freaking weird, SMH (shake my head) kind of weird.

I continue to sift through the rest of the messages, none striking me as urgent: a few prospective clients and one from my sister, another busybody. I wish they would just leave me alone.

Janice came back in with tea and bagel and my itinerary for the day: a couple business meetings and project projections, nothing too heavy.

"Thank you so much, Janice."

"No problem, boss." She was just so refreshing, a needle in a haystack of people, very reliable and dependable.

"Oh and, Janice, I appreciate all that you do around here for me and the company." I had to make a mental note to put a little extra money in her paycheck this week.

"My pleasure," she said, making her exit.

I turned back around toward my computer and proceeded to start my day.

About an hour into my day Janice buzzed my office to tell me I had a call. I was a little miffed but I kept it to myself. I hated being sidetracked when I was working. When I had a set pace I got a lot done. Any interruptions were costly. Janice knew this and she only let in calls that the caller deemed necessary.

"Okay, I got it," I slightly yelled to her. When I saw the light flashing on my phone line I picked up. "Kardell Spencer speaking."

"What are you doing, baby?" Ronald asked.

It's called work. You should try it. That was what I wanted to say to him but I kept my cool.

"Nothing, I was just thinking about you," I lied.

"Yeah, 'cause daddy can't wait to get with that tonight," he cooed into the phone with seduction. I was not as enthusiastic. I mean I loved having sex with him and all of that, but there wasn't any other incentives for me to come home to. He was eye candy and a warm body. I kept conversation to a minimum with him.

"I'm sorry, baby, I have a little shift in plans. I have to be here a little later than expected."

"How late? 'Cause it is getting lonely up in here."

If you had a muthafuckin' job you wouldn't have to worry about that shit now would you? Again, I kept that one to myself. I was such a coward when I came to confrontation and men. No backbone at all. Just lying the fuck down and letting them walk all over. It was getting so bad, I was about to get WELCOME tattooed on my back, because I felt like a doormat most of the time.

"I don't know," I said, blowing out some air, hoping he would get the point and hang up.

"You mean to tell me you're the boss and you don't know what time you getting off?" he said with an attitude. "Let one of them muthafuckin' flunkies do that shit. I need you home on time tonight."

I looked at the phone in disbelief. *I know this dude is not trying to call shots up in my shit.* He was but a trip and a fall down my steps from being on the street and he was telling me what I should and shouldn't do.

"Well, what am I supposed to do until you get here?" he questioned me again.

Try looking in the classifieds, bastard. You just might find a job. "Well, baby," I said with some sweetness in my voice. I wanted to blast his ass and he didn't even know it. "Could you clean up for me a little? I have some laundry that needs to be washed and I would love to have one of those delicious meals you cooked for me the other day."

"Man, what do I look like, Uncle Ben or Benson?" he said like he was offended. "And I ain't about to be getting on my hands and knees and cleaning anything. That shit is women's work."

"Okay, then, baby, you going to have to find something to do then, because I can't help you," I said, sounding defeated. I was stuck with a loser and I couldn't get rid of him all because he could sex the hell out of me.

"Okay, I'll find something to do," he said, hanging up the phone.

I leaned back in my chair and looked out the window down at the people passing by once again. A couple of people with bright, cheery smiles were holding hands. I looked over into the park across from my building and I saw various couples having picnics on blankets while children played feverishly. I was jealous to say the least. A single tear slid down my face as I knew I was sacrificing my happiness for sex. Great sex, but sex nonetheless. Out of all the people in the world, I could not find one man who would love me and treat me with respect. I felt robbed and rejected. I wanted happiness and love. And I didn't want to pay for it. I felt like it was my fault these men used and abused me. Mainly because I let them. The ones I picked were almost always good-looking. It was a weakness. A physically strong man was a weakness to me. I didn't want a man who couldn't protect me in an altercation. *Maybe that is where I'm going wrong. Maybe I could find a man if I just let go of my standards. Maybe I will try a regular guy.*

I was not in a mood to be in my office, so I decided to take a walk to clear my head before I got back to focusing on my work.

"I'll be out of the office for a little while, Janice. Can you reschedule my appointments for the day?" I said, walking toward the elevator. I needed to get away fast before I broke down right then and there. I didn't need her or anyone else in my business.

Chapter 6

Lewis

The Runner-up

Fast forward a few days and, yes, I was at the restaurant that Daniel invited me to eat at on him. I was dressed in light blue ultra-thin pants and a simple white H&M short-sleeved slim-cut shirt. No wild colors for me today. I didn't want to scare the brother off before I got my hands on him. I had on some really cute white Gucci sandals that showed off my magnificently manicured feet. They looked so good I wanted to suck my own toes.

The restaurant was located in historic Catonsville, Maryland, and the ambiance was fabulous. The place was filled with couples and there was some soft angelic music playing from the speakers.

I was seated for a few minutes before Daniel came out to the table and greeted me. "Thanks for coming out." He reached over and shook my hand and smiled. It was a firm handshake, too. It gave me hope that he was a firm lover in the bedroom. He probably could hold his own and then some. "I hope you will enjoy the food and the evening."

"Just being here is a pleasure." I gave him a light smile. I didn't want to seem overanxious with a full-fledged smile. He looked really nice in his chef's outfit. It was clean and crisp.

"There will be a live harpist and soloist coming out in a few minutes to give the customers a treat, so enjoy." He smiled and turned back to go into the kitchen.

The restaurant wasn't a large restaurant. It had about thirteen tables and a small stage located in the back. There wasn't an empty table so I knew that the place was doing well.

I'd put my phone on vibrate a few minutes ago and the buzzing against my thigh let me know that I had a message. I pulled it out of my pants pocket, read the message briefly, and then put it back in my pocket.

"I will have to deal with that later." I spoke to myself as I took a sip of the complimentary champagne that was placed on my table a minute after I arrived. I grabbed a piece of the complimentary Gouda cheese and a cracker from the dish in the middle of the table.

There were a couple of fine guys in the restaurant and I eyed some of them to see if they gave off anything, but none of them were giving off any signals. I even smiled at a few and nothing come of any of it. I guess I was fishing hard for affection today. It's not like I didn't get enough as a child or even as an adult. I just wanted some personal attention and not just sex, even though that was a plus for me.

Just like Daniel said, the female performer and harpist came on to the small platform and began to entertain the small crowd of people present. Soon Daniel had presented me with my meal personally.

"Lamb, squash, and my special sautéed mushrooms." Daniel set my extremely well-decorated plate in front of me.

"Oh, wow. This is just wonderful." Daniel ate up my praise as I put my hand over his hand that was still on the table. I noticed no ring on his finger. *Yes!* But I didn't get too happy just yet because he didn't show me any clear signs that he was interested, or even gay for that matter. "I can't wait to dig in and tell you how good it is and I know it is." I winked at him at the end of the comment. He smiled then walked away.

I enjoyed my food and the music as the evening went on. I savored every bite of my food. G. Garvin had nothing on Daniel's cooking skills and his looks were much more appealing as well, but maybe that was me being biased. I was hoping I could get good food and some good loving from the cook for a long time to come. I already saw him serving me breakfast in bed with nothing on but an apron and the fine body I knew he had underneath his clothes. We would have to work on his teeth though, because, again, that was a no-no.

Chapter 7

Kardell

Boiling Point

I ended up sitting in the park until about ten o'clock that night. I had a lot of thinking to do. I left my phone in the car because I did not want to be disturbed. It was my time to myself and I felt like I deserved it. I couldn't keep going this route with the wrong choices in men. It's like I was a bum magnet. If there was a no-job-having, down-low, lowdown brother in the world chances were I dated him and his cousin.

When I finally decided to get my butt home, I walked to my car and got in. I checked my phone to see who called me. I had ten missed calls: eight from Ronald, one from my mom, and the other from my dad. And I even had a text from my sister as well. *Do these people love me or are they just too damn nosy?* I had already come to the conclusion of nosiness, but they would overall say it was love. *Liars!*

I called no one back as I made my way home. I had no energy or explanation for Ronald, so I decided to sex him down to keep him quiet. Maybe even give him a couple of dollars. I pulled up to my door and put my car in park. I sat back in my car seat and exhaled and mentally prepared myself for Ronald. Before I exited my car, I prayed that he would be asleep from clean-

ing the house. Yes, I knew it was a stretch, but, hey, a
brother could dream, couldn't he?

I opened the door to soft music playing; it was Lu-
ther. Was Ronald one step ahead of me or what? I
smelled incense and candles burning. They were all
over the place. I softly put my stuff down and walked
toward my bedroom. The music was loud enough that
he couldn't hear me. I passed my kitchen and I noticed
that he had indeed cooked us a meal. I immediately
felt bad for not calling him back. I had even noticed he
had mopped the floors. *I'm going to have to make it
up to him big time.* Maybe there was hope for him yet.
Maybe I was not giving him a fair shake.

I softly made my way up my stairs toward the bedroom. He was probably tired from all the cooking and
cleaning he did and I didn't want to wake him; at least,
not with a lot of noise, that was. As I got to the bedroom
I heard what sounded like a porn tape on.

"He must have been bored," I thought out loud.

I peeked in the door and almost lost my lunch. My
eyes were watching Ronald having sex in my bed with
another dude. And guess who the other dude was? Darius, the old-man lover from the club. I couldn't believe
this shit. *My luck can't be that bad.* My nose flared up
instantly. My first impression was to burst in the room
and start throwing punches. But, I decided against it.
I had a trick up my sleeve that was going to be a long-
lasting memory in both their lives.

I crept back down in to my kitchen and quietly put a
large pot of water on the stove. The hotter the pot got
the hotter I got, so I threw some hot sauce in the pot
to make it an even more painful experience for them.
I heard somewhere that that was a lethal combination
on the skin at those temperatures. I grabbed the pot off
the stove with some potholders and made my way up to

my bedroom. They surely would remember my name. I set the pot down briefly as I made a quick detour to my office to grab my gun I had stashed in the closet. No one but me knew that I had bought a gun. I was a new homeowner and I lived alone. I felt that it was a necessity.

I stashed the gun in the back of my pants so they wouldn't see it. It was unloaded, but they didn't have to know it. I brought it thinking that I would never actually have to use it.

I picked up the pot of boiled water and hot sauce and crept to the door of my room in hopes that I could still catch them in the act. And sure enough I had made it just in time. Ronald was fucking Darius from behind and as they both climaxed I burst in and threw the boiling water on them. Screams and yelling filled the room as they both jumped out the bed with looks of surprise and shock on their faces as they patted their skin, trying to make the burning feeling go away. I was truly hurting. They were patting their skin as if it were on fire. They looked pitiful.

"Baby, I—" Ronald said after a few seconds of just standing there with fear on his face.

"Save it!" I yelled, cutting him off and pulling the gun from behind my back. "There is no way you can explain this one." They both stood in the middle of the floor stark naked, dripping dicks and all. I shook my head in disgust.

"How could you?" I said with a broken-down mug. I was on the verge of tears, but I was tired of crying for these sorry-ass fools I encountered.

"It was an accident," Ronald spoke. I must have been playing the part of the fool so good that he thought that that was going to float with me.

"So you are telling me you accidentally started fucking him?" I said, pointing the gun at Darius. He was quiet as a mouse and could have been mistaken for a mute if I didn't hear him moaning in pleasure minutes ago.

"That's not what I mean," he said, coming toward me. "Baby, let me explain it."

"Muthafucka, I'm good with this gun. You take another step and you going to be looking for one of your balls underneath my bed. And you!" I said, now looking at Darius. "How in the hell did you end up here?"

"I memorized your address when you showed me your identification the other night. I was trying to come by and apologize for the other night."

"So you said, 'What the hell, let me get a nut since I came all this way,' huh," I almost yelled.

Ronald chuckled. I couldn't believe this Negro thought this situation was funny. I got even madder.

"This is not a standup show, bastard." I looked at him with disdain.

He quickly quieted himself.

I shook my head again in disbelief. I didn't think it could have gotten any worse than this.

"Time for y'all to go," I said, pointing toward the door.

They started picking up their clothes and shoes.

"Hell nah, that shit stays here."

They both looked at me with surprise on their faces. There was no way I was letting them just walk out of my place with respect when they had just disrespected me.

"Nah, man, you can't do this to me," Ronald said as he walked by me.

"Bitch, move it," I said, poking him in the back with the gun. Darius said nothing as he too made his way down the steps and headed toward the door.

Ronald turned around one last time. "Come on, baby, let's sit down and talk about it. Maybe we can even have a threesome or something. I know you like that freaky shit." He looked at me with a smirk on his face.

"Uhhhhhhh." I hummed, acting as if I was thinking about it. "Not! Now get outta my shit." I hated to be ghetto, but liars and cheats brought out the worst in me. I'd had some bad situations but this had to be the worst of them all. "Yeah, lame-ass muthafuckas."

They slowly walked out the door and onto my stoop with their dicks cupped in their hands. I laughed loud as I headed back into my kitchen. And just for good measure I called the police and told them that I saw two naked men on my block. The police would be in my neighborhood in seconds. I lived in a predominantly white neighborhood. That would serve them just right for messing with me. The blisters on their bodies were damn good reminders as well.

My laughter turned into tears as I walked in the bedroom and replayed the scene in my head once again. But they too would not last long. I was done with men for a while and I meant it this time. No relapses. I immediately cleaned my kitchen and bedroom, and afterward I went online to order me a new mattress set from The Room Store. There was no way I was going to sleep on the one they fucked on. It just wasn't going to happen. I grabbed me some blankets and a pillow from my closet and slept on my living room sofa. Tomorrow would be the beginning of a new way of life for me. A fresh start.

Chapter 8

Lewis

One Step at a Time

"What the hell have I done to deserve such loneliness?" I mumbled to myself as I sat inside of a Starbucks. Shit, I didn't have anyone else to talk to and I couldn't have cared less who thought I was crazy right now. A few nosy neighbors at other tables looked at me curiously as I nursed my white mocha chocolate coffee, but all I did was stare at them back until they looked in other directions. I was not for it. I looked around the room at all of the people who were with, I assumed, their dates or significant others, and I sighed in disgust.

I was on my lunch break and all I wanted to do was get out of the office for a few minutes and get my mind off of men. But like drug addicts, men were everywhere. Tall, short, thick, sloppy, muscular, white, black, Asian; I'd fuck any one of them in a bathroom stall if it meant that it would lead to a promising relationship. But I knew that was the thinking that got me in situations I had previously been in and gotten out of.

I guessed all the good men were in jail or straight. And the ones out here all wanted sugar daddies. I wasn't about to father any man. I wanted a man who was readymade, not a Mr. Potato Head I had to put together when I got him. Hell nah!

"Can I sit down here with you?" a strong and masculine voice spoke from above.

I almost looked up and asked, "Is that you, Lord?" but I knew better. "Huh?" I looked up at him, confused and caught in the smell of his bodacious cologne. I knew the scent well; it was The One by Dolce & Gabbana. It was one of my favorites. He was a very good-looking guy. Well dressed, tailored suit. Close-cut hair. Dark, dark chocolate skin. My eyes drifted closed as if I were lulled by a sweet song or dream.

"Excuse me, are you okay?" His voice brought me back.

"Oh, Lord, you must think I'm crazy." Embarrassment covered my face like a snug blanket in the winter.

"No, for a second I thought you were high. I was about to ease on over to another table and act as if I didn't say anything to you in the first place." He laughed a little and so did I.

"Yes, you can have a seat." I watched as he took a seat and scooted close to the table. He had a drink and a scone in his hand. They too smelled good. "I'm sorry about that. It's been a rough day for me."

"That's no problem at all. We all have rough days. And sometimes Baltimore doesn't make it easier." I lingered on his every word like a snake being hypnotized by a snake charmer. I even liked the way that he formed his words when he talked. He was a thoroughbred for sure. "Sometimes a quiet moment away from it all is all that is needed to get back some sense of wholeness, even in a crowded room."

"Yes, that is true." I still spoke with a little bit of gloom in my voice.

"So what has gotten you sounding so gloomy today?" he asked as he sipped on his coffee. His pinky finger didn't stick out like I hoped it would. It was one of those Gaydar triggers. A Pinky in the air says he just might be sticking his ass in the air. I didn't know why I automatically thought a man wanted me or was gay whenever he paid me the slightest bit of attention. I needed to calm the hell down and just enjoy his company and not have any expectations.

"I don't want to be rude but, why are you asking me about my problem like you really care?" I looked at him sternly. I didn't mean to turn the tables on him or even blindside him. I was just curious about his motives.

"Well, I was genuinely concerned about another human being and I am a therapist for a living. I know the signs of someone in need of help."

"Oh, okay." I looked down for a second, embarrassed again because I was always shooting off my mouth without thinking.

"It's all right to be defensive, but it becomes a problem when you choose to stay that way. We all need help in life. We just need to be strong enough to accept that help or ask for help. Many people are crazy out here now because they didn't and wouldn't seek help when the small signs showed up."

"Yeah, it's some crazies out here now." I chuckled a little.

"Yes, and now all you have to do when you are alone is ask yourself if you want to go crazy because of pride, or seek the help that you need." He looked at me seriously.

"I hope you don't think you are getting paid for this session in Starbucks." I laughed. He did too.

"No, this is on the house. God gave me a gift and pays me for that gift. I am going to share it with anyone paid or unpaid."

"I do . . ." I spoke.

"Excuse me?" He looked at me, confused.

"I said, 'I do.'" I laughed.

"I do what?" he asked.

"I was just practicing for my wedding day. . ." I smiled.

"So that is what you are worried about . . . relationships?" he asked.

"Well, yeah. Isn't that what we are all looking for: love and companionship?" I asked.

"You are missing one important ingredient: friendship. All relationships begin with friendship but most start with lust and sex. Following the steps in life is the key to a successful and meaningful relationship, both plutonic and matrimonial," he answered.

"You really got all of this down don't you?" I sat back in my chair, folded my arms, and waited for his answer.

"No, I'm human just like you, and I know that it is trial and error for each encounter we have with potential mates. But I do follow those guidelines as a way to navigate through life. But I get it wrong, too. I just don't stop there though; I learn from my mistakes and try again. Just like you should when you are looking for a potential mate."

"So you are saying I should be friends with someone first and then move on gradually in the process? No sex first?"

"That's what I'm saying." He nodded in agreement.

"So what evidence do you have to back this up?" I asked him.

"Turn toward the door," he instructed me. I did as I was instructed to do. "That was my reward for patience and starting out friends. She is my life and all I need. Today I am about to propose to her and move forward," he said as he got up out of his seat to greet her.

"Hey, baby." She kissed him on his cheek and then looked at me. "Who is this well-dressed young man?"

"Oh, baby, this is . . ."

"Lewis, my name is Lewis." I stood up and shook her hand. She was statuesque and gorgeous. She was beautiful. She had on a nice business suit that hugged her curves but gave enough room for movement. He had his hand around her waist. They looked like Barack and Michelle Obama standing in front of me.

"Well, Lewis, thank you for keeping Arthur company while he waited on me to get here."

"No problem at all." I smiled while jealousy enveloped me. "He is a very knowledgeable and helpful person. It was my pleasure."

"The pleasure was mine as well." He reached out to shake my hand.

"Thank you for the help. I will take what you said into consideration. One step at a time."

"No problem," he said to me and then turned to his wife-to-be. "Honey, can you find us a table by ourselves while I go to the little boys' room?"

Like magic a table opened up, and she was seated, waiting for him to return. It didn't take long for him to get back to her, and pretty soon she was screaming yes to his proposal to be his wife.

Sitting there watching gave me hope for my future, and now all I had to do was be patient and wait for my future to show up. Just like anyone else though, me and patience didn't get along, but I was willing to try it out again. One more time.

Chapter 9

Kardell

Back to the Basics

It took me about a month to mourn the death of my love life. If that is what you want to call it, because there truly was no love involved. During this period of mourning I had moped around work and at home. I was like a dog with a limp and a slight whimper, totally helpless. I tried my best to focus on work and hope that the pain that I was feeling would subside. I also tried to numb it with eating out and intense shopping sprees. Just to return home alone. Well not completely alone; during my bereavement I would take walks during my lunch break. And while on one of my walks I passed a pet shop. Desperate for some kind of companionship I hesitantly went in to only "look" at a prospective furry roommate. After about an hour I was walking out of the establishment with an orange-colored kitten. He was adorable and we took to each other like magnets.

But he too was a temporary fix. I loved him (Grey), but I still longed for someone who would share my life. He had to cherish me and himself. He had to have self-respect and respect for others. A good job and be a family man. Was I asking for too much? For him to smother me with love and affection? Surprise getaways and gifts? Spontaneous lovemaking? Was that too much to ask? I didn't think so. There had to be someone out there who could fill these qualifications. Where was he? I was bendable with some of these requirements, but I was tired of settling for less. I was not perfect, but I came from good stock. It was the American dream to have a prosperous career, own property, and having a decent, loving family. I had the career and I owned my home, but where in the hell in the world was my man at? Was he lost in traffic or on the other side of the country wondering where in hell I was? They say there is someone for everyone. I was beginning to believe that only people in relationships believed that shit. Because I had gone through at least a dozen and a half of no-good losers. And none of them came even close to being my "someone"; they were only "something" for the moment.

I thought on these things as I sat at a table eating alone at a Mexican/Latino restaurant, Pollo Lantern, in Fells Point, that I had been hearing about a lot lately. I was nursing my plate of Peruvian spiced chicken, which was a new yet exciting taste for me. I probably would be enjoying this meal even more if I had someone to share it with. I looked around at all the couples eating—male/male, female/female, and male/female— and immediately felt out of place. I was the only one there alone. It was as if everybody was staring at me so I hung my head in shame. I almost cried in my plate as I contemplated my loneliness and why I just couldn't get a man and keep him.

"Is everything okay?" I heard a voice as I stirred my now-cold food. I slowly looked up, annoyed, and saw the most beautiful eyes staring back at me. Blue as the ocean on a Hawaiian coast. "Are you enjoying your meal?"

"Um . . . Ah . . . Yeah . . . It's okay," I stumbled and mumbled in an entranced gaze.

"Just okay?" he quizzed me with a hopeful look. "It's our signature dish and it is just okay!" He looked offended. I looked at him like he had lost his mind. I was about to lose mine as well.

"Excuse me?" I said looking him up and down in what looked like a waiter's uniform. "I think you need to move it to your next table before I make you eat your "signature dish." I was not mad at him or offended, just not in the mood for anybody's arrogance today.

A wide smile came across his face. He had the most beautiful smile a man could have. What was he smiling about? I was damn near breathing fire and his ass was standing here smiling like I said something funny. He pulled out a chair and sat down. *Okay, I see what I am dealing with. It's about that time. Time for my idiot of the month to show up and he's about right on time.*

"I am sorry if I offended you," he said, still smiling. "I noticed you sitting out here all alone just playing in your food and I couldn't take it any longer. I had to come over and see if I could get some kind of emotion out of you. Anger wasn't the one I was going for, but it will do for now."

"Ummm . . . humph," I mumbled under my breath. He must have thought I was going to fall for his line. "My emotions and I are just fine and if you don't mind we would like to be left alone."

He chuckled as he got up and pushed the chair back under the table.

"You are so handsome and it is a shame to have to leave you here all alone."

"Oh really, let's see how it goes as you take a walk to your next table. I am sure I'll be just fine. Good day," I said, sending him on his way. He just shook his head and walked away. *Good riddance. Another jackass bites the dust.* I was getting a knack for reflecting off the losers.

I stayed around for another fifteen minutes or so and watched the waiter and the way he worked his tables. He was very attentive toward his customers. Refilling cups, bringing fresh rolls, and other various tasks. He now had me feeling like I was the jackass. Maybe I should have been a little easier on him. Just taking a look back on the past month I was taking my anger out on any stranger and it was not called for at all. I snapped at the coffee house guy about two weeks ago for not putting cinnamon in my cappuccino. And a couple of days before that, I was getting ice cream at Baskin-Robbins and told the cashier off because she was moving too slowly. She broke down in tears right then and there. I was out of control and I needed to get a grip.

As I got up and left I saw the waiter coming my way. I waved him over. He still had the smile on his face. He couldn't be this happy all the time.

"Was everything okay here at Pollo Lantern and will you be joining us again?"

"Why yes, I will . . . And . . . ahhh . . . I just wanted to apologize for being short with you earlier." I had a regretful look on my face. "It was so unnecessary for me to treat you that way when you were only doing your job."

"Ahh, no problem," he said, waving his hand. "We all have our bad days."

"Also," I continued, "I run an advertising company and if your boss needs any marketing done I would love to help him out, at a discounted rate of course." I said, pulling out one of my cards and handing it to him, "Your service skills were phenomenal and I will be sure to tell my friends."

I shook his hand and as he shook mine he started to rub his thumb across the top of my hands. It had been a minute, but I knew he was flirting. I pulled away quickly, knowing I was off of men for a while and any longer I would have making out with him in the bathroom or something.

"I'll see you later," I said, letting out a slight smile. "And don't forget to give your boss my card."

"He'll get it. I'll make sure of it," he said, smiling again, showing that spectacular smile.

Chapter 10

Lewis

Home Again

It was the weekend and I was in Philadelphia today visiting my family. It wasn't a holiday, but once in a while my parents would call us all to come home and have a family evening getting caught up on each other's lives. Basically, they wanted to be nosey and they wanted us to spill the drama that was going on in our lives. We all knew what the deal was when we got there so we each played our parts and gave our parents a nice good scare. It was all in fun and we usually told the truth at the end if we could hold in the laughter from the looks on their faces as we supposedly spilled our guts. They fell for this every time we did this. You would think they would have caught on by now. My parents were so plain and boring that it made no sense.

This evening my brother and sister went first and second, and now it was my turn, and I was ready to go all out and give my charade the best that I had.

"So, Lewis, honey, what's been going on in your life? Your father and I worry about you the most. You don't call us like you used to do when you first moved away." My mother was a beautiful lady. She was plump around the middle and her height was about the same as mine. She was soft-spoken most of the time but when she gave a directive you had better follow it to the T. My parents weren't physical discipliners. They both were very vocal in their approach to how we as children, their children, needed to act and be in private and public settings.

But, like most children, we had all tried our hand and were dealt with swiftly.

"Well, Ma . . . Dad . . ." I paused for dramatic effect. "I don't know how to say this. I just don't know . . . how. I mean I still can't believe it today. I am just at a loss for words," I stammered effortlessly.

"Find the words and spill it out, son." My father spoke sternly.

"Well . . ." I put my head down for dramatic effect. I heaved a little and let my shoulders slouch. I was giving it my all. "You're going to be grandparents . . . twice."

"What? . . . But I thought you were . . ." My mother's voice trailed off as she turned and looked at my father in bewilderment. I could almost see a smile creeping up at the corners of his mouth.

Then it came, the sounds of thunderous laughter from my brother and sister. My parents looked on in confusion.

"What's so funny?" my father asked in total seriousness. I almost regretted going through with it. When I discussed this with brother and sister on the way up they both agreed that I would be pushing it with this prank but that they would go along with it while I performed the joke as long as I went along with theirs. My brother told them that he was dating my mother's oldest and dearest friend and she might be pregnant. My mother's friend was over fifty and recently divorced. The look on my mother's face was priceless. And my sister told my father that she had slept with a few of her college professors to get the A's that she had gotten. My father was so pissed that he got up from the table and walked out of the dining room. He was gone for at least ten minutes before he came back in and she told him it was all a joke and that she only did one professor and that it was a female. She eventually told him it was all a lie and my brother and I laughed it off, but we knew that my father was going to investigate if he could.

"Dad, I was joking." I looked at him and then my mother.

"So this is what you all call a good time? A good laugh? Well it just isn't funny. Very callous it is. Yes, that's what it is. We have taught you three better than to joke in that manner. Where is the respect in those situations? They are not funny. Not at all." There was a silence in the room as of now.

"I'm sorry," I apologized. "It won't happen again. But I will ask that you two let us live our lives and come to you in our time and when we feel it is urgent enough to come. We know you love us but we have to make mistakes and learn from them." Both my brother and sister nodded their heads in approval of what I just spoke.

"You all can kick rocks if you think we are going to stop being interested in your lives or even asking questions. It is just not going to happen. We are the parents and you all are the children. And as all of you young'uns say, 'Play your part and we will definitely play ours.' Understand?"

A few hours went by and me and my sister had us some alone time. We were the closest of my parents' children and we talked when we weren't busy with our own lives, which wasn't often. We were sitting outside in a gazebo that my parents had built in the huge backyard they owned.

"So what's really been going on with you, Lewis, since you moved to Maryland? You find that man of your dreams you're always looking for?" she asked as she sat Indian-style in one of my parents' wicker chairs.

"So you are a ventriloquist for our mother I see, with all of these questions you are asking." I laughed lightly and smiled hard. Even though there was an age gap between us we still got along as if we were only a year or two apart. "Wellllll, I'm not looking for anything at the moment, I'm really just going to keep it chill for now. See what comes my way without pursuing them."

"So you saying you're not going to give up the bootie until someone put a ring on it?" She laughed.

"Yes. I am going to try a whole new approach for this finding-a-mate thing. It's too much. It consumes me more than my full-time job and that's a no-no." I looked at her intently.

"Please don't tell me you have given into the hype and read Steve Harvey's *Act Like a Lady, Think Like a Man* book? You didn't sell out to that ninety-day rule thing did you because I don't think you can go that long without . . . well, you know?" She laughed again. "Plus, you had that 'act like a lady, think like a man' down long before Steve did. I believe that was your mantra during your high school years," she added and then she burst into a fit of laughter again. I just sat there and watched her get her giggles in on me. When it was my turn she was going to regret it.

"You finished?" I looked at her.

"Actually, I am now. Go ahead and explain yourself."

"Well, since you being nosy and all. I had a brief conversation with a therapist the other day and it was suggested that I try something different. Like being friends first and then taking it one step at a time with the next person I met."

"Oh, really." Her eyebrows rose in curiosity.

"Yes, and I decided why not give it a try, you know, see if it works. It couldn't hurt me to try somebody else's way."

"That is true." She nodded her head in agreement.

"It's like, what do I have to lose to try something different?" I shrugged my shoulders.

"Let me ask you this though, why are seeing a therapist?"

"I didn't say I was seeing one, even though as fine as he was I would have played depressed just so I could be in a room with him, because he was fine. But alas, he was engaged to be married. Anyway, we had a conversation while he was in Starbucks waiting on this fiancée."

"Oh, okay. I was about to say. I know you not in Baltimore letting those boys get the best of you and having you going to see a therapist and all of that." She looked a bit concerned and then relieved.

"No, ma'am. I was just in deep, thinking about the state of my life and what I needed to do to fix it and he just happened to be in the right place at the right time. That's all."

"Good. So everything else is good in your life? You healthy?"

"Yep, I am very healthy. Thanks for asking."

We continued to talk a little more before we went into the house and began to watch a few movies together until we drifted off to sleep.

The whole weekend went pretty smoothly, as it usually does. My mother cooked the most delicious meals and we all enjoyed each other's company until it was time to go back our separate ways.

Chapter 11

Kardell

Professionally Personal

The following weeks were a breeze at work. I was no longer focused on men like I used to be. My clients were getting supreme service by my company and they were recommending me to other businesses. My clientele list was getting longer and I was happy to be in my field. And one can't help but like the money I was pulling in. I gave a meeting and congratulated all of my staff with hefty bonuses. I believed in happy help. I liked to work in a positive environment.

"Hey, boss man." Lewis, one of my coordinators, walked in my office and stood at my desk as if I was supposed to ask him to have a seat. He was gay as well, and not ashamed to show it. He was the flamboyant type. I really didn't care for his total "I'm here and I'm queer" attitude. But, I hired him because he had an impressive resume and I knew he would be a great asset to my team. Those were the only reasons I tolerated him. "You find that man yet? Because I got the perfect candidate for you. He is so—"

"No, thank you," I said, cutting him off. "I'm doing fine, alone." I truly felt that way as of this week and it was so liberating. "Is there anything that I can help you with?" I asked, changing the subject. He had a tendency to want to relate since we were both gay, but I chose to keep it strictly professional, despite his constant prying. "Are you finished getting those color schemes ready for the Gordon House of Noodles campaign?"

"It's all squared away, boss," he said, pulling out a chair and sitting down. "Boss, you have been looking really lonely lately," he said, crossing his legs, letting it bob up and down. "I know you like to be private, but we bitches got to stick together and I want to listen if you have anything you want to get off your chest. You know, if you wanted to vent about these sorry-ass men who be floating around B-more."

Bitches? Did he just call me a bitch? Last time I checked I had a dick and two balls and no breasts. I just looked at him like he had lost his mind. Yet he still stared back at me like I was about to spill my guts. It was not going to happen. He was the last person I would confide in. My business would be all over the office in minutes and I didn't need anyone to feel sorry for me. I was happy and couldn't care less what everybody else's standards were on happiness.

"Lewis, first I want to thank you for your concern. It is greatly appreciated," I said, lying, then getting up and heading toward my door. "Secondly, your hard work here is appreciated, but I need you to leave and get back to work so I can do the same."

He got up and walked toward me. He quickly grabbed me and hugged me, catching me off-guard. He patted me on my back as if I was in need of a cry. He then walked out of my office. I shut my door and went to my desk to continue working on my current project, ignoring the last few minutes.

The buzzing of the phone let me know that Janice was letting me know I had a call. I pressed the intercom button to allow her to speak.

"Mr. Spencer, you have an unscheduled appointment waiting to see you. He said he was referred by someone." Janice spoke through the intercom with proficiency.

I shook my head. I was not up for surprises today. It was close to the time to go home and I was ready to soak in the tub, curl up with a good book, and then count sheep. "Okay, Janice. Instruct him to have a seat and I will be with him in five minutes." I spoke, buzzing Janice back, as I rearranged my desk so it could look somewhat organized. I still had not gotten my organization skills together at work like I had at home, but I was a work in progress. After about ten minutes I buzzed Janice and told her to show the prospective client in.

I got out of my chair, preparing to meet the new client as professionally as possible. I also wanted to make this quick so I could get out of here ASAP.

In walked the client and my mouth hit the floor. It was the gorgeous waiter from the restaurant I visited a few weeks ago. *What is he doing here? Please don't tell me I just let a stalker find out where I work. Oh, God, no! I can't shake these crazies.*

"Hello, it's nice to see you . . . again," he spoke, reaching out his hand to shake mine. I hesitantly reached out, but did so to show professionalism.

"Is everything okay?" he asked as he read the shocked expression on my face. "Are you shocked to see me?"

"Well . . . Ah . . . Ah," I stammered, trying to find a way to ask him why in the hell was he here and not his boss. "I thought you said you were going to make sure your boss was going to get my card?" I was baffled. *Why are the sexy ones always the psychos?*

"He did get the card!" He smiled, showing that knee-buckling smile.

"Oh, so he sent you instead?" I followed up.

"No," he said as he reached in his wallet and pulled out a card and handed it to me. "I am the boss."

I looked him up and down as I read the card he'd just given me. He was fine and well dressed. Groomed to the T.

"Oh, really?" I said, looking at him doubtingly. "And you wait tables?"

"Ohhhhh . . . That . . . Nooo . . . That is just something that I do at all of my restaurants from time to time. I like to go back to the bottom so I will never forget where I came from. It keeps me grounded."

"Umm . . . humph," I said, nodding my head, letting all that he was saying sink in. He was fine and humble. Two qualities I liked very well. Very, very well. "Please have a seat," I instructed as I walked around my desk and did the same.

He had on an expensive suit that had to be Versace or something like it. He took off his suit jacket and hung it over the armrest. He sat patiently as I opened up a new client file on my computer. I was stalling for time. He was fine and I didn't know how I was going to make it through this meeting without jumping over my desk and into his visibly muscular arms.

"Sooooo. Mr. Lopez," I said as I turned around to face him. "What can I do to you?" He chuckled slightly. I, on the other hand, tried to recover from my fumble. "Um . . . um . . . umm, I mean what my company can do for you?"

"Well first you can call me Mateo. I was hoping that you could run a statewide campaign that features all my restaurants."

"That is no problem," I said, turning back around and facing my computer again. I could see him out of the corner of my eye and he was looking at the various pictures and degrees on my walls. *Ummmmmm-*

mmmmm. My loins hollered out. It had been almost two months without a man and I was going through some serious withdrawal if you know what I mean. I wanted to back that thing up and now. But I had to stay focused. He was a client and I had to keep it strictly professional. Strictly.

"Ooookayyyy," I said, turning back around toward Mr. Lopez. "This is what I propose: a television commercial featuring you, a couple of full-page ads in at least ten of the state's premier newspapers and at least the re-launching of two of your weakest restaurants."

He looked at me for a second and said, "It's a go."

"Great," I said, getting up and walking around my desk. He stood up as well and I reached out to shake his hand. Again as he shook my hand he rubbed it feverishly with his thumb. "How much is this going to cost me?" he asked with a smile, letting my hand go and putting his in his pocket.

"Tentatively about seventy grand," I spoke with a smile. "I can have my secretary get a contract out to you as soon as Monday with the figures and projections."

"Thanks for seeing me on such short notice." His eyes pierced mine as I fought to stay focused. He was so fine my pants threatened to unbuckle themselves and fall to the floor.

"It was no problem at all," I said, staring back.

He turned to leave the office, but quickly turned back around. "I have a condition on signing the contract that will be sent to me."

"And what is that?"

"You have to let me take you out on a date."

"I'm sorry, Mr. Lopez, I don't mix business and pleasure," I stated matter-of-factly. *Shit! Who in the hell was that talking?* I knew I wasn't turning this fine-ass man down.

He looked at me with disappointment. "Well, I can easily find someone else to do my marketing campaign if that is all it takes to get you to go out with me."

"No . . . No, that won't be necessary," I stated quickly. "I will disregard my stance this one time, but don't take this as a sign of weakness. I don't need your money. I just believe in equal-opportunity dating." I chuckled and so did he.

He turned and exited and I watched his walk as he exited. He was confident and I liked it.

As I walked back to my desk I was hoping I had made the right decision in agreeing to go out on a date with him. I sat down in my chair and turned toward the window and watched him get in his car. He turned and looked up and waved at me. A smile crept across my face. I knew he was going to be a keeper, the one who would treat me right. I could feel it.

I turned around and was startled by Lewis standing in front of me with a wicked smile and his arms folded. "Who was that strapping piece of meat?" he said, licking his lips.

Bitch! Back off! He's mine! You vulture! That was what I wanted to yell, but I kept it professional as usual with Lewis. He was the reason I didn't have any gay friends. From the looks of things he probably did half the men in Baltimore. But I had no evidence of it.

"His name is Mateo Lopez and he's a new client who just came on board," I spoke, ignoring his lustful gesture.

"You're trying to get a piece of his Mr. Goodbar, huh?" He snickered. I didn't find it funny.

"Excuse me!" I looked at him, offended. "Lewis . . ." I shook my head. "He's just a client and needs to be treated as such at all times," I said sternly. "Now, if you are finished . . . and you are . . . you need to be going," I said, darting my eyes toward the door. He got the hint and stepped out of my office with quickness.

I shook my head. He was plucking my nerves to the max. I just didn't have the patience to deal with him today. I was glad I was not one of the over-the-top gays like him. He was smart and creative but a full-fledged ho. Shit, I been around the block but his ass been around the state. I could count who I slept with on my two hands. Some might not say that is around the block but to me that was more than a few good men in a lifetime. His ass probably needed to start counting hairs because his hands and feet weren't enough.

Chapter 12

Lewis

Fresh Meat

"His bitch-ass gets on my nerves," I mumbled to myself as I walked back to my work area. I knew Janice probably heard me, but I didn't give a fuck. I was just trying to be nice to his ass. I was just trying to have a conversation with him and develop a friendship, but he wanted to be all uptight and shit. *Fuck him. I hate stuck-up gay men who think their shitty fuck holes don't stink.* "He knows his fucking ass wanted to fuck that man. He just keeps that shit on the low." I knew a ho when I saw one because I was trying to be a re-formed one.

"He acts as if he's too good to talk about dick out in the open." I continued to talk to myself in a grumbled tone. "Bet you his ass take it good behind closed doors . . . pun intended." I laughed to myself and continued to organize the rest of my day at work. I looked at my watch to see what time it was. It was only one o'clock. I had a few more hours of work left, but I didn't plan on staying all day. A crazy plan instantly popped into my head and I laughed to myself. I was so crafty and sneaky that I scared myself.

Fast-forward an hour and a half and I was in my car, in traffic, on my way home. I wasn't feeling good. Well, at least that was what I told my boss as I put on the act of sheer "I'm sick and can't make it." I even went into the bathroom that was near the main work area to add to my performance. I heaved and hacked loudly enough so that everyone could hear me. I walked out of the bathroom with a wet paper towel over my forehead and leaned up against the doorpost for emphasis. Somebody helped me to desk because 'I just couldn't make it'. I laughed at myself in my head. I was giving them the performance of my life. When my boss saw me he gave me permission to go home. One bitch offered to take me to the emergency room and I almost lost it with a "Bitch, get out of my face with that shit," but I told them that all I needed was some rest and I should be fine. I walked out of there as slow as a seventy-year-old in a diaper. I thought I was giving it too much, but I kept it moving right toward my car as I left the building.

I hopped in my car and sped out of the garage as if my life depended on it. I was home in less than a half hour. I showered, shaved, and dressed to the nines within an hour and a half. I had a mission to fulfill and get on the hunt for some fresh meat. By fresh meat I mean a new face and potential new romance. I was going to stick to my "no sex before friends" stance.

I ended up driving all the way to Cockeysville, Maryland in hope of a new life and love. I hoped that this was the final time I had to do something like this. These capers to find "the one" were exhausting to say the least. I eased out of my car at the valet station and handed the attendant my keys. I gave him a fresh twenty for incentive and "the look" to be extra careful with my car. I didn't play when it came to my car. Dings and scratches were a no-no and I just might have flipped out on someone if it happened, especially a valet.

I was dressed to kill: black slacks and a simple black V-neck that made me look like a *GQ* fashion model. I also had on a very thin black scarf wrapped around my neck for accent. I carried my man-bag under my arm and casually made my way to the front door.

"Good day, sir. Do you have a reservation?" a nice-looking Latino guy asked me. He was a fine piece of meat, too. But he was the help and I wanted the owner, not the help. He was working his way up the ladder. I wanted the one who was in charge of the ladder.

"No, I'm sorry, but I don't," I said as I looked at him and smiled. "I am here on business with the owner. Could you tell him that I am here?" I was making this stuff up as I went along. I was quick on my feet. You had to be in this meat market called life.

"I'm sorry but our owner is a very busy man, he doesn't like to be disturbed for anything." He spoke confidently.

"Listen . . ." I read his name tag. "Juan is it? This is very important business that I am handling here and I don't think that this is the right time to be holding up progress. This could get very ugly very fast." I cautioned him as I looked at him dead in the eyes. He didn't flinch. I needed to come up with another way to approach him because he was being such a hard ass. There were a few people lined up behind me and their impatience was showing on their faces as I glanced behind me briefly.

Before I could get another word out of my mouth, someone who I assumed was his boss walked up to see what the holdup was about. "What is going on here? What is the holdup?" he asked as he looked at Juan and then at me.

"This guy here wants to see the boss and I told him it is out of the question." He looked at me sternly and then back at his boss.

"Sir, you are going to have to come back another time. This is a business and the owner doesn't meet with anyone, and when he does he leaves specific instructions for us. I have none for today, so I need you to move out of line and exit this establishment." He looked past me and waved a couple up as if he was dismissing me.

"I am here on the behalf of the advertising company that is doing a major campaign for Mateo Lopez, and I don't think he would be too pleased to get a phone call from my boss if I step out of line and make a call that could end both of your jobs." I looked at both of them sternly.

And then it happened. Mateo appeared out of nowhere. He was fine as I remembered seeing him and that was briefly.

"What's going on?" He looked at his two employees.

"This guy here says he's here on business to see you and we had no record of it."

"Nice to meet you, Mateo." I reached out to shake his hand." My name is Lewis and I am here on the behalf of Bankable Advertising to get a feel for the color schemes and marketing angles we are going to be taking with your campaign." I smiled brightly as he shook my hand back.

"Well, all right then. I am glad that you are here. Sorry about the hassle. I run a tight ship at all of my establishments and these two great fellows were just doing as I asked. I hope they didn't offend you." He was so fine that I almost couldn't concentrate on what he was saying.

"I understand." I held on to his hand a little longer than I should have. "We all have our jobs to do."

"True. Let me get you a table so you can be seated."

"Thank you," I replied.

"Juan, please give these nice folks who are in line complimentary bottles of wine with each of their meals. Sorry for the wait, ladies and gents," he said as he turned back toward me. "Mr. Lewis, follow me right this way."

I was seated within a few seconds and I was already enjoying myself. I was so glad that I snuck and Googled his name on my cell phone, and got information on a few of his restaurants. The information superhighway was something else. Pictures of him at a few local events popped up as well. He was definitely a good catch.

"I'll send the waiter over to assist you as soon as he is finished with another guest." He smiled.

"If you don't mind I would like to have a few words with you. Maybe you could be so nice as to have a seat with me so we can chat about business." My eyes darted from his eyes to his crotch within a split second. I did it in a way so he could notice me doing it. I was serious about what I wanted. He looked like he was a keeper.

"Well, sure." He smiled. "Give me a few minutes to handle some business in the back and I'll be right back."

"Sure. I have all the patience in the world," I said and then he walked away.

"Wine, sir?" a waiter said as he walked up to me.

"Yes, which one is the one that you would consider the best?" I inquired.

"Our Cabernet Sauvignon is quite good, sir," he remarked.

"Well, I'll take that, sir." I nodded politely.

"I'll be back shortly." He walked away.

I am so glad I did this. Since my boss's stuffy ass didn't want him I am going to snatch him up and keep him for my own.

A few moments went by and pretty soon the waiter had brought me my wine and Mateo was heading my way.

Damn his ass is fine . . . And he knows it. The way he walked, it demanded attention. His employees looked as if they feared him. I was sure he was about his business. He was in control. I wouldn't have been surprised if he was into some illegal activities. *I better not say that to him or even imply it though.* I didn't want to ruin any of my chances with him or perpetuate a stereotype or something.

He took a seat and then spoke. "I am glad you came down so quickly to get to work on my campaign. Your boss runs a very good company. I am impressed."

"Yeah, he's good," I said, faking a smile. I didn't hate my boss, just his "too good" attitude. I needed to prove a point and taking Mateo for myself was going to do the trick. I was a go-getter and Mateo was now on my "to get" list. "But I'm here to get to know more about you so I can get a feel for what you really want out of this campaign."

"That is great. What did you need to know about me?" he asked.

"What does the name Mateo mean?"

"It means gift of God." He smiled. "What does that have to do with the campaign?" He followed with another question.

"Nothing, it's just a unique name and I was wondering what it meant. Is it true?" I smiled.

He laughed before he spoke. "Yes, it's true to me."

"I love confidence." I spoke wholeheartedly. "It's very sexy to me."

"Oh, really?" He smiled again. He was very handsome and he had dimples, too. I had to have him.

"Yes, really. I love gifts of God and from God," I answered.

"Me too, especially good-looking ones." He was now openly flirting with me.

Got him! I know that was a flirt. It was time to reel him in. "Why thank you." I blushed. "Let's cut to the chase, are you seeing anyone? I'd like to get to know you better." I spoke and looked him straight in the eyes.

"Straightforward, I see." He chuckled. "I'm not attached at the moment. And I would love to get to know you better as well."

"Well, I think my business is finished here." I took one last sip of wine and slid my chair backward.

"Wait . . ." He stopped me in my tracks. "Here take my personal number. Give me a call so we can get together." He winked.

After that I got up out of the chair and he did as well. He walked around the table and gave me a very strong hug. I almost didn't let go. I could have stayed in his arms forever. He was so strong. His scent was strong and masculine. It made me weak.

I walked out of the restaurant feeling like a million dollars. I knew one day that I was going to be calling shots in his empire. I was going to win him over and then take over.

Chapter 13

Kardell

Moving On

As soon as I got in the house my house phone started ringing off the hook. It was my father. I so didn't want to answer it but I hadn't talked to him in a minute so I picked up. "Hello."

"Hey, son, how is life treating you?"

"Everything is good, and you?"

"Well, son, your old dad needs a favor."

"Sure, Dad," I answered, unsure of the favor.

"I need a couple hundred bucks to pay some bills off. I'm in between money right now."

"When did you need it by?"

"Tomorrow would be fine."

Tomorrow I scheduled myself late so I just told him I would meet him for breakfast at one of my favorite eateries. We hung up the phone within seconds. Again, as I said before, my father and I didn't have a real relationship. He was in and out of my life as a child and teenager, which was very hard for me to handle. Having only my mom to go to when I had issues that only a male figure could help me out with didn't help me get through my teenage years easier. Sometimes I'd felt that I wouldn't be gay if he had been there to guide me when I needed him the most. I now knew that him not being in my life had nothing to do with me being gay. From what my mom told me, which was very little, my dad had some issues and she had some self-esteem issues. She said that was the reason she took him back and put him out on numerous occasions. I felt like she was hiding something because my mom was a very vocal person and she said what she had to say and moved on. I assumed, like a lot of people, she was vocal about what she wanted to be vocal about. She never went into detail when talking about their issues and she always managed to detour conversation into something else when the topic arose. I was sure the truth would come out eventually. It always does.

Enough about my parents and my issues, it's time for me to go to bed. I have an early day and a busy one indeed. Thank goodness it's Friday and I am the boss, because I'm getting in late and leaving early; a wonderful advantage to being the boss. I didn't do it or get to do it often so I was going to enjoy it.

I noticed I had a few messages on my answering service, but I decided I would listen to them when I got out of the shower and prepared myself for bed. I turned on some Anita Baker and soaked in the tub for about a half hour before retiring to my bed. I was exhausted, and it seemed like as soon as I toweled myself off and put on my pajamas I was in my waterbed, savoring the softness of my satin sheets.

I quickly rolled over and picked up my cordless phone, and dialed the code to retrieve my messages. The first one was from my mother, telling me she loved me and that I needed to call her more because I was going to miss her when she was gone. She did this to make me feel guilty. It worked every time. I'd call her tomorrow while I was at work. The next one was from Ronald. Yes, he was still calling me. I listened to the message. He missed me . . . He was sorry . . . Could he come over . . . yadda yadda yadda . . . Delete. That was enough for me to hang up, roll over, and go to sleep.

I woke up Friday morning totally refreshed. I decided I would dress down. Blue jeans and a button up would suffice. I was only going to meet my father and head to work for a few hours. Showered, shaved, and dressed, I headed out the door after feeding Grey. I hopped in my Volvo and sped off toward my destination.

I arrived downtown at about nine-thirty in the morning and was anxious to get this father/son gathering done and over with. I was curious as to what "bills" my father had to pay, but I was not going to ask because as an adult and as a man I didn't like to be questioned, and I was sure my father didn't like that either, especially by his offspring.

I parked my car a block or two away from the restaurant and walked until I could see my father sitting in a chair with one of his legs folded on top of the other, and he was in deep conversation on his cell phone.

"Yeah, Lee, I'm about to handle some business, so I am going to get back with you in a little bit. Yeah . . . Yeah . . . Yeah." He nodded his head while he talked. Then his voice began to escalate. "I *told* you I got you. Now give me some time." I sat down as he hung up the phone and set it down on the table.

My father was an enigma and to this day I still didn't have him figured out. I didn't know where he lived or worked. I'd never seen anybody he'd dated nor had he talked about anyone. He would pop up from time to time at my house or my mom's house and hang out and disappear just as fast as he came. When I looked at my father, I could see where I got my handsome features. He was a shade lighter than me, same height with brown eyes and a medium build. He had sprinkled gray hair in his beard and head. I wished he and I could have the relationship that my sister had with my mom.

"Hey, son, come give your old man a hug." He got up as well as I and proceeded to hug me. His hug was one that was genuine and I could feel the love. Or maybe it was that I wanted it to be genuine.

We both sat back down and looked at the menus, avoiding conversation. What did we have to talk about? Where would I start? *I can't just come out and ask him where the hell he has been and why he hasn't been there when I needed him. I really don't know what his reaction would be and I may not be prepared for the answers that might be given.*

"Son, I just want to say thanks for coming to my rescue." he said, putting his menu down and focusing on me. "I know I don't call you as much as I should. And I don't come by like I should, but I will get better at it, okay? I promise." He looked sincere, but so many men in my life were deceivers that I could not be sure if he was telling the truth. *This could just be an empty promise like he has done before.*

He continued, "I just want you to know I am proud of you. I know I might not say it like I should more often, but I am. And um . . . I love you, son. I couldn't have asked for a better son than you." He was smiling a big, beaming smile. I was beginning to believe him. A tear slide out of my eye and I quickly wiped it away, hoping he didn't see it.

"Anytime, Dad," was all I could blurt out, trying to get past the moment. There was a small pause, so I decided to break it. "Well, Dad, let's get something to eat, because I have to make it to a meeting at work in about forty-five minutes." Yeah, it was a lie, but I couldn't handle the tension at the table.

We ordered some light breakfast and chitchatted a little bit in between bites. He asked me how I was doing and how the "man in my life" was treating me. That was one thing I could say, he never ever showed judgment or shame because of me being gay. I still couldn't get used to him asking about it either. It was just weird. My sister and mother rarely discussed it, but he was nonchalant about it. I guessed he really did care. I shared with him about my recent breakup and quickly changed the subject. I asked him who he was seeing. He said he had no one special in his life.

After about a half hour of breakfast we went our separate ways. I decided to walk to work since I was already downtown and it was only a few blocks away. It was a bright and sunny day; the breeze was blowing through my dreads. It was late spring and I loved the cool, crisp air. It was good to be alive.

I popped my earphone from my iPod Touch in my ear. Sounds of Whitney Houston's *I Look to You* album played in my ear as I made my way to work. It was one of my favorites.

I was walking at a good pace, enjoying myself and loving the single life. I had a tendency of not watching where I was going and walking into people, which I happened to do as I rounded the corner to my office.

"Excuse me." I shuffled to the side. I was watching a cutie across the street, too, and was paying no attention to who I had bumped into.

"Yeah, Excuse you," a familiar voice spoke.

I focused my eyes and they landed on Ronald. *I can't duck dude for nothing!*

"Ump . . . ump . . . ump." He circled me, looking me up and down simultaneously. I took my earplug out of my ear in irritation.

"Damn, you still got it!" He walked up to me and breathed on my neck. "You miss me?" he whispered in my ear. His hot breath eased down the inside of my collar. I looked around, embarrassed. He had on a wife beater and some Capri jeans with tan sandals that showed off some of his taut calf muscles.

"Yeah . . . like I miss having pneumonia." I laughed and walked past him toward my job. He didn't let it go as he ran up to me a few short feet away.

"How come you didn't call me back?" He softly pushed me up against a wall that was near my building. The look in his eyes was intense and wandering over my face. He always made a scene when he came around. I looked around to see if anyone was looking. As usual, the Baltimoreans were looking, but no one said anything. He could have been beating my ass and no one would have done a thing. At times, I was one of them, so I couldn't really get mad at them for just looking on in anticipation. They were always waiting for something to pop off and spread around the office. *This city is so backward.*

"Ronald, what we had was over weeks ago." I pushed him off and moved toward my office again. I was not for this mess today. "I've moved on."

"You moved on, huh?" He looked a little hurt. I felt sorry, but not sorry enough to take him back. "It was that easy, huh?"

"No, it wasn't that easy!" I huffed. "It took some time, but I'm over it. I forgave you and then I moved on."

"So you really over me?" he posed. His hands were stuffed in his pockets. I could have sworn I saw a tear in his eye.

"Yes, sir," I answered.

"Well, okay then," he grumbled. "If that's what you want. I'll see you around." He turned and walked off as fast as he came. I sighed in relief. I was finally rid of him.

I walked into my office building, spoke hello to the building security and then made my way toward the elevator to my floor. My office was on the fourth floor, so on the ride up I took a minute to let out a few needed tears. *Am I really over him?* was what I was really wondering. I hated myself for being so weak.

I walked off the elevator into the lobby before my set of offices. I breathed in and out, and then put on a happy face as I walked in the door leading to my office.

"Good morning, everyone!" I bolstered a cheerfulness I did not feel down deep. Everyone was crowded around Janice's desk, talking.

"Good morning, Mr. Spencer!" a few of them replied.

"Is everything okay?" I asked in concern. It was unusual to have people gathered in one spot and unproductive at this time of day. There was always something to do. I made sure of it, even when I took days off. Janice looked at me with eyes stressing a need of relief. She was all about work at work.

"Yes, sir," Lewis spoke out with a wicked smile on his face. "I would have to say so. Somebody must have put it down on someone last night." He laughed loudly.

I looked on with an expressionless face. Everyone else looked at me to see what my reaction was going to be. I was no-nonsense when it came to work. I let him slide, but glared back at him a warning with my eyes.

"What?" He acted as if what he said was not inappropriate for the office. "I was just saying what y'all was thinking. Damn." He looked at the other workers, huffed, and walked away in his all-about-me sashay.

"Is there no work to be done?" I looked around at the rest of my staff. They scrambled off toward their work stations and left me standing at the front desk with my secretary Janice. "So what was all that about?"

"Sir, you received a very large delivery today and I had to fight off the vultures to keep them out of your office." She looked around with her glasses hanging on the tip of her nose.

"Do you know who was it from?"

"Sir, I have worked for you since the beginning and you know how I feel about personal business. It is not my place to get into your business, whatever business that it may be." She smiled, politely, adjusted her glasses and then stood up out of her chair. "Here are your messages for the day. Would you like something to drink?" She looked at me and smiled, again. She was on point most of the time and I loved it.

I smiled too, the first real one since I stepped foot in my office. "Orange juice, please." I walked into my office to see what could cause such a ruckus.

A fifty-two-inch plasma television, wrapped in a big red bow, was sitting in the middle of my office. I walked around it and surveyed the monstrous gift. I pulled a card that was attached to the top of it, walked around my desk, and sat down. I set the card down and turned on my PC. I was anxious to see who the card was from, even though I already had a clue.

Knock . . . knock . . .

"Come in," I called out.

Janice walked in with my juice in hand. She darted her eyes at the lavish gift and continued to my desk. The only way she was going to talk about it was if I started the conversation.

"Thank you, Janice." I set the juice to my left and smiled.

"You're welcome, sir." She smiled back. She walked out, closing the door behind her, leaving me with the card and my curiosity bubbling.

I looked around my large office to see where I was going to put my gift, and then it dawned on me. I was jumping the gun. I was going against the rules that I set. I didn't even know who it was from and whether I was going to accept it.

I picked up the card and opened it.

Mr. Spencer, it was a pleasure meeting you at my restaurant and then again at your office. This gift is a small token of my appreciation. Just wanted to say thank you, because I know it is going to be a pleasure working with you to promote my businesses. I will also be waiting on the call from you to schedule our personal meeting as well. Until we meet again,

Mateo Lopez

"Wow," I said and then I closed the card, put it in my desk drawer, and turned to my computer to begin working on his marketing campaign.

Buzz . . . Buzz . . .

"Mr. Spencer, a Mr. Lopez is on line one. Do you want to take the call or should I tell him to call you Monday?"

"I'm available to talk. Put it through." A smile crept across my face. I knew I should not be this anxious to hear his voice. I was exhibiting all the same habits that I did with all the men I dated. I was moving too fast in my head. I needed to slow this down before it got out of hand on my part.

"Mr. Spencer speaking," I answered as professionally as I could. The smile I had earlier was gone.

"Hello, Mr. Spencer. I hope that you liked the gift I sent you." His voice was so calm and soothing. I was picturing him with his shirt off, naked in bed with his dick hard and lying on his thigh. I shook my head in shame. I needed to get a grip.

"Yes, the gift was nice, but as I told you before, we need to keep this strictly professional. Me . . . accepting this gift would not look good to my staff and I like to maintain the standards set by me, for me and my employees. I will need you to come and retrieve the television as soon as possible."

"I'm sorry if you feel threatened or if I stepped over my bounds. I just thought that it would be a nice gesture on my part. I will send for it immediately." He sounded a little disappointed.

"Mr. Lopez, I'm not threatened at all. I just thought that it was a little too soon for it. If you're going to give a gift make sure it is for the whole office and not just one person. I like to keep the drama here at a minimum." I laughed and so did he.

"Well, that is fair and easy." Again, he spook smoothly and calmly. "I'll make sure that someone comes and get the television within the hour."

"Thank you, Mr. Lopez."

"Call me Mateo."

"Okay, Mr. Mateo." He laughed and so did I.

"I see you have a sense of humor. I like that. I hope I get to see more of it when I get to take you out."

"Maybe, maybe not. I guess you'll have to wait and see." I laughed.

"Have a good day and don't keep me waiting long."

"Okay and I won't. I promise. Have a good day, sir." I hung up the phone and buzzed Janice.

"Janice, there will be someone coming to retrieve the television in my office. Let me know the moment they arrive please."

"Yes, sir," she replied.

Just like Mateo had promised, the movers were in my office retrieving the plasma television within the hour. And again, my employees were breaking their necks to get a peek at what was going on, especially Lewis. He was eyeing the two large Latino men like they were next on his "to do" list. One of them even looked at Lewis like he wanted to "get done." Lewis stood in the doorway to my office as they hoisted up the television and carried it off.

"Ump . . . Ump . . . Ump . . ." He softly moaned under his breath, but loud enough for the men to hear. He had no shame.

"Lewis," I slightly yelled. "Work!" I pointed toward his work area. He pouted and walked off like a scolded kid. I felt like a babysitter sometimes.

I walked up to my door and shut it. I wondered if I made the right decision. *I hope I didn't offend him by sending it back,* I wondered. *Yes, I did the right thing,* I reassured myself.

I sat back in my chair and looked out the window and watched the two men load the television into a truck and pull off. I had to admit they were handsome men to say the least. I saw why Lewis fawned over them. I never really looked at Latinos as a part of my dating pool. I never really had any of them come on to me. They had their section in the city and that was where they partied and lived. I never really ventured out to their neighborhood, unless I was getting something to eat, and that was usually when I was on a date or something. I didn't know why I waited so long to try dating one of them. I guessed I was going to give Mateo a try. What harm could come from it? *He's a man just like anyone else I have dated.* He owned his own business, he was giving, he was very attractive, and he didn't mind going after what he wanted. All of what I was looking for in a man. Who would have known that all this time I was dating the brothas, here on the other side of town were guys just deserving of a chance at dating me? I felt kind of like I cheated myself. It was official; I was going to give Mateo a try.

I turned around to my desk, called Mateo, and scheduled a date for tomorrow night. He said he would pick me up at my house so I wouldn't have to drive. I wasn't too keen on letting people know where I lived, so I told him to meet me in front of my job instead.

Chapter 14

Lewis

Flying High

"What's up, ho." I was greeted by my best friend, Dennis, as I sat down in front of him. I met up with him in one of our favorite restaurants in Mount Vernon. "You look extra flamboyant today. Like you got an extra good piece last night."

"Why can't I just be happy to be happy? Why does it have to involve sex for me to be happy?" I said as I gave off more attitude than I should have given.

"Damn, I was just joking. You don't have to throw shade," he snapped back.

"No shade, just some T," I stated and smiled.

"Anyway, why is your ass so happy then, if it's not sex?" he asked.

"If you must know, I met someone who just may be the one."

"Oh, really?" he spoke doubtingly.

"So you throwing shade now?" I asked. I wasn't really serious. But I was curious as to what he meant.

"No, it's just that you have been at this place before and—"

"And what?" I cut him off.

He didn't say anything for a second. Like he was prepping what he was going to say.

"Well, are you going to hold on to what you are going to say like you do when your man cums in your mouth or are you going to spit it out?" I asked. He gave a "don't go there" look, but I didn't care.

"How long have you known him?" he finally asked.

"What does that have to do with anything?" I asked, insulted. I didn't come here to get unwanted attitude.

"A question with a question," he muttered.

"What?" I asked in confusion.

"Why do you do this to yourself? You get all worked up the first week or two of meeting a man just to find out that you were just a notch on his bedpost."

I was pissed off. No, I was infuriated. I wanted to flip the table over and storm off. But I didn't. He was my best friend and he was just running me through the ringer to get me to think with a clear mind.

"You're right. I have done this before. I have advanced the relationship before it has even begun."

"Yes, that you do. We've all done it." He looked at me with love in his eyes. He was telling me to slow down and let it take its course.

"I know you think this will end up like it has all the other times, but I really think that he is the one," I said confidently.

"Okay. If you say that he is then he is." There was still an undertone of doubt in his voice but I didn't push the issue.

"Anyway . . ." I shifted to something else before I said something I would regret later. "How are you and Charles doing?"

"Chile, Charles is the best. He's talking about marriage and adopting a baby. He is really gung ho for this family life he's always wanted." He smiled brightly as he talked.

"Is it what you want as well?" I asked.

"Yes, but I don't know. I'm kind of scared to move that fast. You know if things don't work out I will be more than likely a single parent raising a child."

"So you already at the end of the relationship?" I asked; then I picked up my drink and sipped a little through the straw. "You have doubts? Has he been unfaithful?"

"No." He paused. "You know I—"

"Think too much." I finished his sentence for him. He always thought too much. "I mean it is all right to have some doubts, but trying to tell the future is crazy. Give it a chance before your nagging ass gives him a reason to do so."

"Well, I guess you right." A light smile came across his face.

"You know I'm right about this. Besides you will be the perfect housewife. You'll probably give Martha Stewart a run for her money." I laughed. Truth was I was a little jealous of him, but he was a good guy and he deserved his due. *I am going to get mines, I know it. I just have to be patient and keep it cool.*

"Yeah, I know Martha Stewart don't have shit on me but a prison record, and I don't do time I tell time." We both burst out laughing.

"Look, is this man on the up and up? I mean can you trust him? It is a ton of crazy folks out here disguised as sane," he asked me seriously.

"No, he cool and I can handle myself. You know that. I am flying high right now and I truly believe he is the one for me."

"I sure hope so."

"I don't need hope . . . I got this." I spoke assuredly. "Trust and believe."

Chapter 15

Kardell

Prince Charming

I stepped out of the shower and grabbed a towel off of my towel rack next to the shower. I pulled it around my waist and turned around to spray/mist my shower with some shower cleaner and walked out of the bathroom. I grabbed my remote off of the dresser and turned on some Anita Baker. She always got me in the mood when I was going out on a date.

I swayed my body a little to Anita's sultry voice as she belted out "You Bring Me Joy" as I applied my lotion and deodorant. I was in the mood for romance and to be wined and dined. I felt good. Real good. I looked over at my ensemble for the night and marveled. It was the beginning of summer, but a little breezy, so I picked out ocean blue linen pants and a long-sleeved, white linen V-neck pullover. I pulled my locks back in a loose ponytail and let a few fall free in the back for effect. Finally, I sprayed myself with one of my favorite colognes, Burberry Touch. I turned off the music, and scanned my room to make sure everything was in place. I was out of the house by six-thirty on the nose, because I had to make it downtown to meet Mateo at seven o'clock. I exited my house and jumped in my car with hopes of newfound love.

***

I pulled up to the parking garage that was half a block from my office, parked, and made my way down the street to the front of the building my office was located in. It was a little breezy as the wind blew my loose dreads around. I was nervous, to say the least. I wondered if I was making a mistake going out on a date with a client. I wondered if he was going to be like all the other men I had dated, but just a different shade of "loser." There were rich, classy losers. I wasn't naïve about that at all.

I think I need to stick to the brothas! I can't do this! I think I gave up on the brothers too easily. I mean they weren't that bad. What am I doing? I'm perpetuating racism. Dating "outside of my race" wasn't illegal, but I was taking a chance at being talked about by "my" people if they ever saw me with one of "them." I didn't think I could handle that; besides, my mama always said "Pick ya men like I pick my chicken, dark meat only." I laughed when she said that, but I guessed I mentally took heed and never crossed that line.

I had to do this, if only to see if it was or wasn't for me. They say Mama knows best, but my mama wasn't perfect, and she had made her share of mistakes, and I needed to find this out for myself. *Shit! I can't let my mama know about this either.* She would surely have some words for me and I definitely couldn't bring him around my family. That was a no-no. *That's it, I'm going home. I don't need all this pressure!* My mind had talked me out of the date. In a matter of seconds, I was giving up and going home.

I turned and started walking toward my car and I moved fast, hoping Mateo wouldn't pull up.

"Hey, beautiful, where are you going?" I heard his strong accent call out to me. I turned to see him pulling up in a black limo, and not one of those funeral-type ones, but one that looked too expensive to even touch. The ones rappers and "ballers" rode in.

"Um . . . uh . . . nah . . . I just left something in the car and I was headed back to get it before you arrived." I was not a good liar and I hoped he believed me. "But since you're here, I can let it be. It wasn't that important anyway," I said as I walked up toward the car.

He proceeded to get out and open the door for me. As he got out I noticed how distinguished he really was. Black slacks and a tight black short-sleeved muscle shirt. He had a presence about him. One would say cocky, but I knew it was just confidence. That was something I lacked a lot of the time. He smiled and stepped to the side as I made my way into the limousine. After making sure I got in, he followed suit and sat across from me when we got in. I looked around and noticed that there was champagne on ice and what looked like a thirty-inch plasma television that sat catty-corner to the both of us.

I sat back and smiled. Mateo signaled the driver to pull off.

"So where are we headed tonight?" I asked.

"Somewhere very special. One of my favorite places." He smiled. I smiled back, but I wasn't comfortable with not knowing where I was going with a stranger. "Don't worry, you are safe with me. I promise to treat you with the utmost respect and honor your handsome self deserves." He got up and sat next to me and after a few more minutes he pulled me closer to him. I was impressed that he could tell I was uncomfortable and immediately tried to put my tension at ease.

"That still didn't answer my question." I sat up and looked him in the eyes with seriousness in mine. *I am not going to roll over for any man anymore.*

"Do you want to go home?" he said with just as much seriousness in his eyes.

"No, I'm not saying that I want to go home. I just want to know where I am being taken to."

"Look, Kardell, I don't know what the problem is. I am being a gentleman and I think you are ruining the mood for us with these twenty questions. You are a beautiful man and I wanted to surprise you and share my world with you. I get the feeling you have been hurt and that you don't want any more drama in your life. I understand that very well, but I am not going to hurt you. I am very fond of you and was hoping that we can build a friendship and possibly a relationship down the road. I am not taking you anywhere to kill you or rape you. Do I look like I would rape you?"

"No, but—"

"But what? If I were going to rape you, I would have done it by now. I need you to trust me, because I already trust you and I don't do that often. I have been hurt before too and I know how it feels. I was hoping that you would be a welcome change to my life. I guess I was wrong, so I'm going to ask you once more. Do you want to go home?"

I looked at his face. He was so handsome and his cleft chin was absolutely gorgeous. And I looked at his lips and they were beckoning me to them. But I didn't want to be too aggressive so I just said, "No, I trust you." I trusted him because I saw the hurt in his eyes when he spoke and when he spilled his guts about his hurt, I knew then that I would be safe with him.

He leaned over and gently rubbed my face, and I let him. I felt all of the uneasiness go away and I allowed myself to be free with him. The whole ride to wherever he was taking me was filled with talking and nothing more than that. He never once pressured me for sex and he was a complete gentleman the entire ride. I still had some hesitance and would be a fool to completely let my guard down. That indeed would take some time.

"Are you ready?" he asked with a smile on his face that made me weak. The limousine had come to a stop after about an hour and a half of constant driving. I was still a little hesitant about trusting him.

"Yes, I'm ready." I smiled back. It was an uncertain smile, but I smiled. I didn't know what was going to happen next. What was it that I was getting ready for? Was it love? I could only hope. Was he the one? The one I prayed long and hard for? Only time would tell.

He got out of the car and opened the other door for me, like a gentleman would. I stepped out of the car, one leg at a time, just like I was a star. He treated me as such as he grabbed my hand and helped me out. As I got out, I looked around to see where it was that he had taken me. It was almost nightfall and I could see the sun setting on the horizon. It looked like one of those scenes out of a movie, almost fairytale like. I was in awe. We were at the ocean. On a beach. Out on the ocean the water sparkled and twinkled. On the sand there was a tent set up with a table with candlelight. There was a waiter patiently waiting for us to come to the table.

"I can't believe you did all this!" I was floored. I had never been treated with such opulent care and sponta-neity. I was always the one who gave. I almost couldn't believe I was here.

"It's all for you," he whispered in my ear as he held me from behind. His breath on my neck made me moan in bliss. My head drifted back on his shoulder and we swayed as I listened to the ocean and the hum-ming of his heartbeat for a few seconds. "I knew I would like you from the moment you walked into my restaurant. I knew I wanted to be the one to mend your broken heart."

"Oh, really?" I reversed myself so I could face him. He was a little taller than me and I looked into his eyes and he into mine.

"Yes, really!" He pecked me on the forehead. "Now let's get moving. Our supper awaits us!"

I took my shoes off before we stepped onto the sand. I loved the way the sand felt between my toes as we walked across it. When we got to the table, it was exquisitely set. Glass flutes and champagne chilled on ice. One of Celine Dion's romantic classics lightly played through the air. I could smell what I knew was lobster bisque located on a serving cart next to our table. It was one of my favorite dishes. He pulled my chair out for me and let me sit down before he made his way around to his chair. We were briefly interrupted when he had to take a call. He excused himself and walked away from the table and several feet from where the elaborate setup was.

In those few minutes, I pondered again if I was doing the right thing or if I was being too uptight. I decided to go with the flow and see how things went. If things didn't progress the way I thought they would then I would just get out and move on. I prayed that I wouldn't get too emotionally invested and lose my mind and fall too easily again. I laughed to myself, because even I had wished myself good luck on that one.

"What's so funny?" Mateo came back and sat down at the table, breaking me out of my own thoughts.

"Oh nothing." I waved my hand. "I was thinking about something one of my silly employees said to me at the office."

"I love the way you smile." His eyes intensely focused on mine. "And your laugh is infectious, too."

"Thank you." I blushed and looked down at the table for a second. Compliments weren't always easy for me to take, but his seemed so sincere that I ate it up.

"I feel really honored to have you here with me. This evening is a perfect evening for getting to know someone better. You agree?"

"I do."

"Hopefully those words will be spoken before a magistrate one day." He looked at me seriously. I knew he wasn't assuming what I thought he was. Getting married wasn't at the top of my list of things to do.

"We'll see." I knew it was an indefinite answer but I wasn't about to commit to someone and not know a thing about him.

"We shall." He smiled. You would have thought I just had said, "Yes, I'll marry you," or something.

"Are you ready for supper?" he gently asked as he rubbed my hands as they comfortably rested on the table in front of me. I nodded my head yes and he signaled the waiter with a snap of his finger.

The dinner was delightful and we had the best conversation during and after our meal. He even had a violinist playing lightly in the background. It was simply a marvelous evening. After the dinner there was a blanket laid out on the beach for us to lie on. We lay there and fed each other fresh fruit along with some crème brûlée. After the help cleaned up our dishes we both lay face to face and chatted. His scent was rich and it lingered on me even after we had gotten up and made our way back toward the limousine.

The ride home seemed much shorter than before. After, he waited for me to get in my car and pull off toward home. I tossed and turned in bed all night because I had never had a man touch me the way the he did. It was with such care and patience. I was glad that I didn't give in and give him some right on the beach. I was very proud of myself. Proud indeed.

Thoughts of the possibility of being in a steady and fulfilling relationship with someone who could carry his own weight financially and success-wise was an extreme turn-on to me. It wasn't all about money and success to me; he was a nurturer from what I could tell. He wanted to take care of me. I wanted to be taken care of in every aspect. He looked and acted as if he was willing to be my knight in shining armor, and I was willing to ride off into the sunset with him. I still wanted to have my company but I was going to hire someone else to run it, and I could be a consulting board member. I didn't want to be totally inactive but at the same time I could leave and fly off to faraway lands and enjoy the lap of luxurious living at the hand of my lover. Who could ask for more? I couldn't, and that was why I rolled over and slept well.

Chapter 16

Lewis

You Got It Bad

"'You got it . . . you got it bad . . .'" I sang along with Usher as he sang one of my favorite hits by him. It was a very true statement. I was excited even after the conversation I had with Dennis the other day. He kind of pissed me off with his negativity and all. Here he had close to everything he, I, and most other people wanted, and he was BSing about it. I had to admit I was a little envious of him and all that he had, but I had a feeling that my future was going to change for the good very soon.

I hadn't even known Mateo for a couple of days—and I use the word "known" loosely—but I knew I was infatuated with getting him to be mine. I thought I deserved it. True happiness was for everybody and I was going to get mine come hell or high water.

I was making my way back from the beach where Mateo took me on our first date. It was so majestic and tranquil for a first date. He picked me up at one of his restaurants and whisked me away in a fancy car; just the two of us. His driver didn't count because he was quiet most of the time as if he weren't there anyway. We talked the whole way there and I got to know about him.

"So where are you originally from?" I asked him. Looking into his eyes just sent me over.

"My family is from a small town in Brazil."

"Are you an only child?"

"Yes, it's just me." His eyes wandered away from mine for a quick second.

"So where are we headed?"

"I'm taking you to a special place for just me and you to be alone. I want to be alone with you. No interruptions." He then caressed the side of my face with his hand. He then cupped my chin and leaned in, and waved his nose in front of my lips like he was savoring a sweet smell.

"You smell so good." He smiled.

"I do what I can." I smiled and blushed. I had on some sweet cologne that I knew would drive him wild.

It took us awhile to get to our destination. I had to admit I was a little nervous being driven in a tinted vehicle to an unknown location with a guy I just met. But I didn't let on. I just enjoyed the ride and the moment I was having right now. I couldn't say a guy had ever treated me this well before. Mateo looked like he adored me. It was what I was waiting for.

"I know you are going to love this place. We are going to bask in the stillness of Mother Earth." He continued to look at me intently.

My heart was swooning in anticipation. He was saying all of the right things. All of the things I was waiting to hear.

I assumed we were at our location when the car stopped.

"Wait right here," he said as he eased out of the door of the car on his side.

Seconds later, he opened the door and motioned for me to get out. But before I could fully get out he got on his knee and removed my shoes and socks one by one. His hands were so gentle and smooth. He wasn't rough at all. His touch sent shivers up my spine. Normally I would have given him the blow job of his life in the back of the car after he smelled me but I didn't want to ruin this moment. I didn't want to mess up a potentially great thing.

He then pulled me up by one hand and helped me out of the car. I wanted to "accidentally" fall just to see if he would catch me, but I knew that would be too much. I just went with the flow of things as they were going right at that moment.

I looked out to the beach that we had pulled up to. It was a beach that I had never been to before and it was a private one; I could tell by the signs scattered around. *He must own this beach.*

"Give me one second." He touched the point of my nose with his finger. He then went to the back of the car where his driver was waiting with the trunk open. He pulled out a decorated basket and his chauffeur retrieved other items from inside the trunk. We all made our way across the cool sand. The crashing sound of the ocean against a few rocks scattered near the shore made for a perfect scene. The sand felt really good in between my toes as we walked.

Mateo found a spot and instructed his chauffeur where to set up our picnic. The chauffer laid down some thick foam and then covered it with a blanket. The area was about the size of a large living room area rug. There were trays for our food, champagne, flowers, and even an iPod playing classical music for us. We both sat Indian-style as he fed me nasty expensive cheese and wine. Mateo was so smooth and gentle. He touched me quiet a few times. All gently. He never once made a move for intercourse. I was a little shocked by that because most of the guys I dated were only looking for one thing.

Finally he had the chauffer, who stood by and watched the whole scene quietly, clean up the food and wine and then Mateo opened up his legs and pulled me in between them as we both looked out into the ocean. His arms were wrapped around my upper body. I was totally relaxed. I closed my eyes and my head drifted back to his shoulder. I could hear his heart beat against my chest. I felt his warm, un-aroused manhood resting against me. It struck me as odd, but I just brushed it off. I was with a new breed of a man. He was older and more mature than the guys I regularly dated. He could control himself around me. I took it as him not wanting to move too fast. I had even more respect for him.

I still wondered in the back of my head if he was dysfunctional in that area or something. I mean he looked to be about forty years old. I didn't know what age a man would start having problems like that but I thought forty was a tad bit young for that. But again, I took it as a sign for taking things slow and easy. I liked it. I liked him.

We didn't stay out there much longer and soon he dropped me off at my car, and here I was driving home with sheer excitement and optimism running through my veins. *I just might be in a really good mood for work. I just hope my boss doesn't ruin it with his attitude. I don't want to have to curse him out and tell him where to stick his job until I am sure that Mateo will be taking care of me forever.*

Chapter 17

Kardell

Happy Days Are Here Again

I woke up the next morning feeling a little more optimistic about life. I wasn't going to be a fool and think that because of a successful first date I had found "the one." I would only be setting myself up for disappointment. I jumped in the shower with a little more pep than usual. I even hummed a little. It wasn't a particular song, just a simple hum. A hum I knew all too well. I tried to ignore it but I wasn't clueless to my problems.

After about fifteen minutes in the shower I exited, wrapped a towel around my waist, and went to my closet to pick something out to wear. My cat was following me around the house like he needed desperate attention. I kneeled down briefly and stroked his coat, letting him know I was paying attention to him. He was attached to me and me to him. After a few more seconds of appeasing him I was off to get dressed for my day.

I grabbed what I wanted out of my closet and made my way back in to my bedroom. I laid the clothes down on my bed and walked to the bathroom to brush my teeth. Just as I finished brushing my teeth I heard my phone ringing. I walked to my dresser, picked up the phone, and looked at the caller ID to see who it was. A smile radiated my face as I saw who was calling.

"Hello," I answered with cheer. It was Mateo. He sounded like he just had woken up. He still sounded smooth though. I walked over to my bed and sat down next to the clothes that I was going to wear to work that day. My cat jumped up into my lap as I talked.

"How are doing this morning, sir." His voice glided over his words. His accent was thick, but low. I tried to find something special to say, but it didn't happen.

"God is good." I smiled. The vision of us on the beach flooded my mind. It was so nice to be treated like a person and not like a piece of ass.

"That He is," he concurred. "I know it is early, but I just wanted to tell you that I had a wonderful time with you and I can't wait to do it again."

"I had a great time as well. We'll have to see about a next time." I had to show him that I was sticking to my guns when it came to business and play remaining separate.

"Oh, I have a feeling there will be one."

"Oh, really?" I got up and walked toward the window in my room. I peeked through and looked at the passersby. "How do you know that?" I was curious to know how he thought I was going to give in so easily to his request.

"You answered the phone when I called you this morning. I know that you like me, all evidence of a next date."

"Oh, really?" I walked back over to my closet and pulled up some shoes that I was going to wear and sat down on the bed. "Again, I guess we will have to see about that. You know I have rules about work and play."

"This I know. But I have ways of persuasion that you have not seen yet."

"We'll see." I lightly chuckled. I was a little curious as to what he could do to get me to go out with him again. I was up for the challenge, to tell the truth.

I turned on my Bluetooth and got dressed as we continued to talk back and forth. I made my way down the stairs and to my kitchen to fill the cat's water and food dishes. I checked myself out in one of my mirrors and exited my house to my car. I told Mateo that I would call him later because I did not like to talk and drive, even with a Bluetooth on my ear.

I pulled into the parking garage, turned off the music I was listening to, and exited my car. I grabbed my briefcase out of my trunk and walked across the street to my office building. Before I could get to my building I was approached by a woman handing out fliers.

"Excuse me, sir, have you seen him?" she said anxiously as she handed me a flier. "He's my son and he's missing."

"No, ma'am," I spoke after I looked at the flier for a brief second.

Disappointment enveloped her. Her weariness in her eyes made her look like she had been up for days. "Well could you show this to your friends and see if they have seen him? Please? I'm desperate. Any help would do."

"I sure will." I smiled, hoping it relieved some of the anguish I knew she was feeling. I walked into the building a little disappointed that I couldn't help her.

I was hoping today would be a very productive day for me and my staff as usual. I walked off the elevator and toward my office door. This time I didn't have to pretend that I was happy. I was. It wasn't because of Mateo, believe it or not. I was just happy with the thought of "maybe." Well, maybe Mateo did have a small part in it.

"Good morning, everyone," I spoke out as I walked up to my secretary's desk. There were a few people moving around swiftly, just like I liked to see it. It was nice to know that your company was moving and functioning like a well-oiled machine.

"Good morning, Janice. Are there any messages for me today and is my itinerary for the week ready?" I asked as I walked into my office.

"Yes, sir." She followed me. "They are already on your desk." She pointed to them as I made my way around the desk and sat down.

"Thank you, Janice. How was your weekend?" I asked. It was a Monday ritual that we went through every Monday morning.

"Sure, it was quite wonderful. Just me and the grands." She smiled. She was proud of her grandchildren. She was a mother of three successful children: one doctor, a lawyer, and a schoolteacher. She had four grandchildren she loved dearly. She really didn't have to work, but she did because she said old people sit at home and die.

"That is great, Janice." I started up my PC and logged on to Microsoft Office.

"Sir, would you like the usual juice and bagel this morning? We have some lovely Danish pastries that were delivered this morning."

"Who ordered pastries?" I looked at her, confused.

"Well, sir, I thought that you did." She looked a little confused as well.

"No, it wasn't me." I got up and walked into our small kitchenette, and looked on the table to see a tray of pastries set out with a note on the top.

"To all of the staff at Bankable Advertising, Inc." I read the card out loud. Janice was standing beside me as I read. I smiled, because I knew that this was the work of Mateo, but I played it off.

"You know what, I forgot all about ordering these."
I smiled and put the card back on the table. "I thought
you guys would like these. I tried one in Lexington
Market and thought that it would be a nice treat for the
office."

"Sir, that is so sweet of you."

I hated to have to lie about something so small. I just
didn't want people in my business. It was a major pet
peeve. "I thought it would be." I turned to the coffee
machine to get my own coffee since I was already in
there.

"And I see that some of the staff has already taken
advantage." I spoke as I reached to grab me a cream
cheese–filled pastry.

"Well, that is expected, sir." Janice snickered and
turned to leave me standing by myself. That was short-
lived though.

"Hey, boss." Lewis walked up and reached for a
pastry. I assumed that he had one before my arrival to
work. "These are sooo good."

I looked at his attire and smiled. Some people probably would say I was throwing shade, but I wasn't. It
was just that he was always overdressed. Bright colors
were always his style. He had on a basic suit but he had
on purple and gold. I was no hater. I just thought that
men should wear certain colors and leave the rest for
women. I was an earth-tone type of guy, but I wasn't
afraid to mix in a red or green every now and then. He
dressed like he had every color of the rainbow in his
closet. I had even seen him in colors that I didn't even
know existed. He did wear his clothes well, but his
flamboyant personality and loud clothes were a lot to
handle at times. But that was why I hired him. He had
an eye for color and fashion, which made him an asset. One of my business teachers in college always told

us that a business requires a team. One person wasn't enough to successfully run a company and you were foolish to think otherwise.

"Staff your weaknesses," was something he drilled into our heads. It was one of the best things he could have told us. I took that advice and ran with it.

"That they are, Lewis," I agreed.

Something was up with him and I didn't know what. *He's being too nice. Not like his regular racy self.*

I followed him as he left the break room. He was almost skipping. It wasn't that I didn't want him happy. I just didn't want a "phony happy" working in here. *I don't need a postal employee killing folk in here, especially me.* I was just at the breakthrough point and I didn't want a happy crazy taking me out before my time.

"Everything all right with you today, Lewis?" I stood at his cubical as he sat and looked at his screen.

"I'm doing super, boss." Still no eye contact. He was a good worker, I'd admit that, but his ass wasn't this dedicated. "Life is grand."

"Did you have any of the work done for the Mateo Lopez campaign?" I asked with a small attitude.

"For the most part." He looked at me briefly and then turned back toward his PC monitor.

"I need the specs on my desk by close of the day," I instructed. My voice was firm.

"Whatever you want, boss." He turned and the smile on his face was spread wide. "Will that be all?"

"Are you shooing me away with an attitude?" I asked to see if his "happy" face was an act. Lewis was defiant and I knew that if I pressed him he would press back.

"No, I was just following orders, like you like them to be followed." He got up and walked past me and back into the break room. I followed him again.

"Lewis, is there something you need to say to me?" I knew that I had taken it too far with that question. A boss really shouldn't care what an employee thinks. Especially to this degree.

"Nothing at all, boss." He smiled. The corners of his mouth twitched a little. He was going to blow. I knew it. I needed people to stay the same in the workplace. I knew people changed but this was a drastic change. He was just snappy and flamboyant a few days ago. Now he was quiet and happy. Plus, I could have sworn I heard him humming this morning as I walked past his cubical. *Crazy folk exhibit these drastic mood changes.*

"Okay." I turned to leave the room, but turned back around for one more stinger. "Oh, and stop calling me boss, my name is Mr. Spencer to you." His mouth dropped. I left him where he was standing. The rest of my day was going smoother. Everybody was in line and I received several calls from Mateo to brighten up my day.

Chapter 18

Lewis

Heavenly

His muthafuckin' ass is pushing to get beat down beside his car in the parking lot. That was the thought I was thinking as I walked back to my desk. His ass just didn't want to see anyone happy because he wasn't happy. They say misery loves company, but I didn't want an invite to that type of party. I was just getting close to happy and loving every moment of it. I loved it so much that I decided to treat myself to a massage and a manicure/pedicure after work.

My day just about zoomed by as I thought about the prospects of Mateo and my future with him. I was excited. More than I should have been probably. I walked out of work with a smile on my face, even with my boss pressing up on me a few more times that day.

"Excuse me, could you take this flyer?" A beautiful black woman gave me half a smile and a frown as she handed me the piece of paper. She looked like she needed some sleep. I looked at the picture of the cute guy as she continued to talk. "It's a picture and bio of my brother. He's been missing for a few months. We just trying to find him and get closure. Call us if you see anything."

"Okay," I said as I walked away. I felt terrible about someone losing someone and then having to hand out fliers to people who really didn't give it a second thought unless it was someone close to them.

I got to my car, got in, and looked at the flier briefly. He was my age, size, and as good-looking as me. It looked like he could be gay, too. I shook my head in shame as I opened my glove compartment box and shoved it in with all of the other loose fliers and pamphlets I get handed on a day-to-day basis. I pulled off toward my destination.

I pulled up to the massage/pampering spot and got ready to get the treat of my life. I was so ready to get myself pampered. I thought every man should treat himself to a good time by himself every once in a while.

I walked up to the establishment that was in a quiet little area in Baltimore County. It was new to me and I was just ready to get "done." I needed and wanted it.

"Hello, sir, how may I help you?" the pretty Asian woman spoke from behind the counter.

"Hello, I am here for the Heavenly Maximum pampering deal." I smiled politely.

"Sure, follow me right this way." She opened a door beside the counter where she worked and I walked through behind her. "Have a seat here and your specialist will be with you shortly." She exited the room back to the front.

I was so glad this was an establishment that let you pay after the service. I thought that it was unique. I guessed they were confident in their services. Services that I was getting included a nude massage, with a towel on the lower part of the body, of course. They had a pretty nice setup; a few doors were spread around this medium-sized waiting room. The music, small running fountain/pond in one of the corners of the room, and television on one of the walls kept me very entertained while I waited for my specialist to come and get me.

I picked up a magazine that was on one of the tables beside my chair and thumbed through it while I waited to be called in to my room. I couldn't wait to get undressed and let someone work over my body. I wasn't really a stressed man, but a good massage and pampering always did the body good.

"Good day, sir." I was greeted by a familiar voice. "You ready for session?"

The person before me was a person I was familiar with and surprised to see. I never had a conversation with him so knowing he worked here was a surprise and a gift. My Asian lover looked at me and smiled.

"Why yes, I am." A smile crept across my face too. I knew I shouldn't do what I was about to do but one last time couldn't hurt. After this only Mateo could have my body.

"We hurry. My wife back soon." He turned and walked to the room where he was going to give me a "massage."

I got up from my chair and practically ran into the room. I was undressed and on the table in minutes.

He did the typical massage. I was face down on a soft table and there was soft music come from a small Bose radio in the corner just like in the waiting room. He worked over every muscle with precision. He started with my shoulders and then my upper back. He was a master at this. Before, he never did any of this; it was just fucking, sucking, and then him sneaking out of my apartment and back to his place.

He then worked my back area with that karate chop–type rhythmic massage. I was ooohhhing and ahhhhhing involuntarily. He was doing the damn thing. Then he moved on down to my calf muscles in my legs. He worked them over by kneading them like they were balls of dough. I didn't know that I could feel this good.

The whole time he was working me over I was thinking, *why didn't I get to know him any better?* Because if I did, I could have been getting this heavenly treatment on the regular. Shit, he had my toes curling and he didn't even get to fuck me yet. I was feeling good. Then it dawned on me that he was unhappily attached.

"You like?" he asked as he even worked over my feet with some hot oil.

"Yessssssssss," was all that I could get out in a moaning type of way. A few times while massaging my feet he made me laugh because I was extremely sensitive on my feet, more than the average person.

He then lifted my towel up so he could work on my thigh muscles. My dick and balls were spread out in between my legs and he touched it a few times as he worked over my thighs. It didn't take long for me to become aroused. He noticed this and he touched it a few times, making me get harder.

"Turn over," he instructed. I did as I was told.

Now that I was turned over on my back my erection stood up quite noticeably.

"Ahhhhhh, I see he happy to see me." He smiled and then licked his lips. Never during any of our sessions did he ever once go down on me. I guessed today was a different day. He took some heated oil and poured it onto my dick and watched it slowly make its way down to the shaft and then he took his hands and started to pump me like he would do me if he was fucking me. I thought he was enjoying himself because the smile on his face never left. I just closed my eyes and let him do what he wanted to do. After few more minutes of him just jacking me he took me into his mouth. Now I wasn't a well-endowed guy. I was a little over average, about seven inches. He had no problems in deep throating me and taking it down to my balls.

"I see someone has been practicing," I spoke with my eyes still closed and my hand at my sides, clawing at the table a few times. He was good. As I said before he was an ass guy. He tried to suck me off once and scraped his teeth against my dick. And any guy who's ever experienced that knows that is painful.

"Yes, me have," was all that he said as he went back down on me. A couple of minutes later I was clawing at the table again as he brought me to a climax.

"You like?" he asked as I opened my eyes. I just nodded my approval. I was spent and needed to take time to get myself together. But that didn't take long, because before long he was ready to get his rocks off as well.

He went to the door and made sure it was locked, something he should have done at first, but I guessed he was too excited to see me and so was I. He then retrieved a condom from a duffle bag in the corner that I assumed belonged to him. It also let me know that I wasn't the only one he was doing.

"Turn on your side," he instructed me again. I followed the instruction. He pulled me over to the edge of the table so that my rear end hung off a little and then he oiled up two of his fingers. He eased them inside of me slowly, one at a time, until he was able to get them in me easily. I watched over my shoulder as he unzipped his pants and eased his dick out. He then stroked himself to a full erection and put the condom on. Once again, he shattered the small-dick Asian man stereotype. He was working with a whole lot of meat. I tensed up when he slid himself into me. It didn't hurt but his size wasn't to be fucked with. I was a power bottom so I took it like a champ. At first he slowly stroked me and then he worked up a good pace and fucked me with ferocity. I was taking him blow for blow. This was going to be a good last time with him. I had to make sure I was getting a good fucking because I didn't know when I was going to take that step with Mateo. I had to get one for the road. It didn't take him long to get the nut he was fucking me for. He pulled out, wiped himself off, and tucked it back into his pants as if it never happened. He and I were both satisfied.

I got dressed and then I pulled out some cash from my wallet to pay him. He walked out of the room to get me change and then he returned.

"This one was the last one for me," I said as I put my coat on. "I can't see you anymore."

"Okay," he said nonchalantly. If he was hurt I couldn't tell nor did I care. He opened the door and walked out and I did the same. I didn't get all that was offered in my pampering session, but I didn't care, because getting what I just got was good enough for me. We ran into his wife as soon as we walked into the front room. The look on her face was that of pure hate. I smiled as hard as I could.

"Thanks for the massage, boo." I kissed her husband on the cheek and then walked out of the door before she could say anything to me. I laughed all the way home.

Chapter 19

Kardell

We Can't Be Friends

Today I wasn't doing something I really wanted to do. I was spending the day with my family. It was a Saturday and I wanted to be with Mateo, but I had this planned before I met him. Sucks to be me, right? I, my mother, father, sister, her baby daddy, and a friend of his were doing the family dinner thing that my mother wanted to do for a while now. My nephew was with his father's mother for the weekend so it was all adults. I usually used my nephew as an excuse to escape the adults, but this time I was left to fend for myself.

I listened to one of my favorite CDs by Deborah Cox on the way over to my mother's house. When "We Can't Be Friends" came on I sang like the song was written for me instead of the lead singers. I wasn't a singer and needed to stick to my day job.

I pulled up to my mother's house and exhaled a few times before I opened my car door and exited the car. "It's only for a few hours and then you will be home free," I coached myself as I walked up the short walkway to her house and put my key in the door.

As I opened the door and entered the house the smell of my mother's lasagna filled my nostrils. It immediately made it worth the trip for me. I was immediately greeted in the hallway by my mother, who had an apron on and a smile on her face. Her smile made me happy. She embraced me in a tight hug that seemed to last for a few minutes. You would have thought that she didn't see me a week ago nor talked to me every other day.

"How's my baby doing?" She put both of her hands on my cheeks and wagged my face from side to side.

"I'm doing great, Mama," I said as I took off my coat and hung it on the coat rack by the door. "How are you doing?" I asked.

"Mama is doing great."

"That's good."

"Angela is in the kitchen helping me finish up the food. Your father, Alex, and his friend are downstairs watching some type of sports game. You know Mama is going to have to turn the sucker over to get them to eat." She laughed and so did I. We walked as we talked a little bit more. As soon as we got close to the kitchen she stopped me and warned me in a hushed tone, "Be nice to your sister."

"Mama, if she don't start nothing it won't be nothing." I spoke in the same tone and chuckled a little.

"Boyyyy!" She raised her hand and acted as if she was going to swat me. "Don't make Mama break out the belt."

"All right, Mama, I'll be good." I was serious about both. *I'll be nice as long as my sister doesn't get it twisted.* My sister and I had a good relationship; it's just that we could get on each other nerves at times, her more than me, in my opinion. But when it came down to it we stuck together like siblings should stick together.

"Hey, Angie." I walked up to my sister as she stirred something in a pot that smelled really good. "What'cha cooking?"

"Hey, Dell." She turned and we embraced. It was a tight hug. It felt good to do it and mean it. "Just some jambalaya."

"It smells good," I honestly complimented her. She was a good mother and cook, just like my mother.

"Y'all need any help around here?" I asked, wanting to get busy so I didn't have to go downstairs with the guys and fake like I was interested in sports. I also didn't want to see my sister's baby's daddy either. My episode with him flashed back in my head and it made me cringe on the way over here.

"You're not going to go down and say hi to dad and Alex?" My sister looked at me curiously.

"I'll do it a little later, right now I want to spend time with my two favorite ladies." I was a good manipulator and today I was going to put on my best act.

"There's no time like the present," she said in a singsong manner as she turned back around to stir her pot.

"I said later," I replied with a snippy tone.

"All right, you two . . . cool it." My mother stepped in before it could get out of hand. "Kardell, come over here and pinch the edge of these three pie crusts for the apple and sweet potato pies that have to go in the oven soon."

"Okay," I agreed, sitting down at the small kitchenette table and doing as I was told.

"So . . . ah . . . Dell, who have you been dating lately?" my sister's nosy ass asked me as she sat down across from me and looked me dead in my mouth waiting for me to answer. I didn't really talk to her about who I dated.

"You know I don't discuss that type of business with you." I looked right back at her.

"Kardell, you act like we don't know you take dick. We know you be letting dudes take a trip down your Hershey highway. You're so stuck-up. I knew you were gay when I found you making two of my Ken dolls do it when you were six years old." She had a vicious smile on her face. That was a secret she promised to keep. I cleaned her room and waited on her hand and foot for a few weeks to keep her quiet. And now here she was spilling the beans.

My mother's mouth hung open in shock. I didn't have a rebuttal right away. I was too shocked.

A few seconds went by while a lot of things swirled around in my head. The first thing that popped into my head was blurting out the fact that her baby's daddy was bi-sexual, but I kept it to myself. I wasn't going to stoop to her level. And that probably would have shut the house down for sure.

"What's wrong, dick got your tongue?" she asked and then laughed. I got up from the table and opened the door that was in the kitchen to the backyard. I walked to the back of the yard and leaned on the fence and cried a little as I hung my head low. It was what I did as a kid, and now as an adult when someone made me mad and I didn't have the guts to retaliate and hurt them the way they hurt me. I heard the screen door open and shut, so I knew that someone was coming out in the yard with me.

"Son, your sister didn't mean that. She's just going through a rough time right now." My mother rubbed my back as she spoke. I wasn't really crying about my sister's remarks; it was the emotions and thoughts of my past that she triggered when she said what she said. I, like many other gay guys, had it rough growing up different. School wasn't easy for me so I had to stay to myself to get by. I wasn't stuck-up. I just stayed to myself as a defense from being hurt. It didn't really work because people teased anyway, but I continued to close myself in as a defense.

"I know, Mama. Hurt people hurt people. But why does she have to be so mean?"

"Son, I don't know. She doesn't get from me or your father. Then again we not really her parents so maybe it was from them."

I spun around as quickly as I could and looked at my mother in shock. "What?"

"Just kidding son, I'm afraid she's all ours." She laughed. I laughed too. "See, son, it's not that bad. Now get back in there and make up with your sister. Life is too short for the drama."

I did as I was told. I hesitantly made up with my sister. Best believe I owed her one though. We worked and talked for about another hour before the food was finally done and the desserts were in the oven.

"Angie, go get the men and tell them that the food is ready, and don't make me have to come down there. And say it the way I said it and look the way I looked when I said it." She smiled.

My sister followed instructions and went downstairs. My mother and I went into the dining room and set the table and arranged the food. Not long after we finished the guys and my sister filed into the kitchen to eat.

They came in one at a time. First it was my father. "Sooonnn." He held out his hands as he waited for me to hug him. I did and it was a nice tight hug like he hugged me when we had breakfast a few weeks ago.

Then Alex came into the room and I just looked at him for a second before I reached out to shake his hand. He had fear in his eyes.

"H . . . hey, Kardell. Long time no see." He smiled nervously in front of everyone in the room, which was me, my sister, my mother, and my father. "Nice to see you, man." He gave me one of them strong-arm hand-shakes and then pulled me to his chest and patted me on the back. He had "please don't let today be the day I get outted" written all over his face. This was the reaction I got every time I'd seen him since he groped me in the club.

"Nice to see you too," I replied. He took a seat on the opposite side of me and two chairs down. It was a wooden dining room table that sat six. My sister sat down beside him and then my mother and father sat beside me.

"Baby, where is Ron?" my sister asked Alex.

"Oh, he had to make a call. He said he would be right in when he finished."

"Oh, okay. We will start when he comes in and sits down," she said.

My phone began to vibrate and I looked at it and then put it back in my pocket. It was a call that I didn't recognize so I let it go to voice mail. I knew it wasn't Mateo because I had his number programmed in my phone and he said that he would only call me from that number. A few seconds later my phone vibrated again and let me know that I had a voice mail. Curiosity got the best of me and since we were waiting for Alex's friend to make his way to the table I decided to check to see what the message that was left said. I almost never let a voice mail linger for too long without listening to it. I retrieved the phone from my pocket and pressed my voice mail button so I could listen. I wasn't surprised to hear Ronald's voice on the voice mail, but I was surprised to see Ronald's face as he walked in my parents' dining room while my phone was still pressed to my face.

Chapter 20

Lewis

Simplicity

Waking up in a good mood on a Saturday morning and walking out the door to find the word FAGGOT spray painted on to your car is not a good way to start the day. I couldn't even get mad. You might even say I deserved it or worse for fooling around with a married man.

I had a date with Mateo and wanted to go and get my hair cut and then get the manicure/pedicure that I didn't get a chance to get the other day. But here I was sitting at the Maaco car paint shop getting my car repainted. They said it was going to be a couple of hours to strip the paint off of the left side of the car, repaint it, and let it dry. I called Mateo and told him of the dilemma and he said he would send a car for me. I was going to be pissed if I didn't get to see "my man-to-be" today.

Sure enough not fifteen minutes after I made the call I was picked up and whisked away to meet up with Mateo.

This is the life! I thought as I chilled in the back of the limousine where there was a bottle of wine chilled for me along with a long-stemmed rose. My ass felt like Julia Roberts's character in *Pretty Woman* when she finds the man of her dreams. I dropped my head back and enjoyed the peaceful ride to my destination.

I must have drifted off to sleep because I awoke just as the car came to a stop. The door opened just as I got myself together.

"Greetings, Mr. Turner." A guy with a very nice suit on nodded his head at me as I exited the car.

When I fully exited the car , I thought I was going to fall out from the sight I saw in front of me. It was a mini mansion. I mean it was huge and beautiful. The lawn was immaculate and the few people I saw looked like they were happy to be working for him.

"Greetings sir," I nodded my head back at him. *Mateo must treat his people well.*

"Would you please follow me? Mr. Lopez is awaiting your arrival." He walked me up to the door and then he opened it. When I slowly walked in I was in awe once again. I felt like Little Orphan Annie when she met Daddy Warbucks. Except there wasn't anyone singing and flipping off of shit in here. It was quiet as shit in here. I was afraid to even walk. I admit I had some ghetto ways and didn't want to do or say something that might mess up my chances to "move on up" like the Jeffersons did. I mean I loved my job and all but who wouldn't want to live like this?

Kardell's stuck-up ass missed the boat on this one. You snooze you lose. Bitchessss! I thought and almost laughed out loud at myself.

"Please follow me," the butler, I was assuming, requested of me. I followed him to the back of the house and out to a luxurious pool area.

"Mr. Lopez, sir." He greeted Mateo as he sat under an umbrella while he was stretched out on a wicker lounger. "Mr. Turner has arrived." He stepped back and bowed once again.

This shit is unreal, I thought.

"So nice to see you today, Lewis." He spoke as he got up from the lounger. His voice commanded attention even with an even tone. He wasn't a huge guy but he was thick and somewhat muscular. He didn't have a shirt on and he was glowing from the sun hitting his slightly sweaty body.

I wanted to lick one of his pecks just for the heck of it, but I kept my cool and said, "Thank you, it is nice to see you as well."

"I'm sorry to hear about your car." He looked at me in disappointment.

"Yes, it is unfortunate, but I have a feeling things will work out." He looked at me in the eyes the whole time he looked at me. Almost as if he were looking through me.

"You have the most beautiful eyes."

"Thank you." I blushed.

"Here, have a seat." He pulled out a chair that was at a table and chair set near his lounger. "Do you want something to drink or eat?"

"Yes, I'll have some ginger ale if you have it."

"Sure." One wave of his hand and a member of his staff was standing in front of him, awaiting instructions. "Our guest would like a glass of ginger ale, and bring him a bowl of fresh fruit while you're at it." He then turned his attention back toward me.

"Would you like someone to come and rub your feet or something?" he asked.

I actually was speechless for a moment. I couldn't believe he was treating me this good after only knowing me for such a short amount of time. "Yes, that would be nice." I accepted because I didn't want to offend him. Or maybe I should have said no because he might have thought I was a gold-digger looking for a free ride. *Shit, I hope I didn't just fuck this up.*

"Great." He smiled.

Not long after that I had a nice cool glass of ginger ale and fresh fruit to nibble on. My feet were propped up on a small ottoman as a nice lady went to work on my feet and calves while another guy was working over my shoulders and arms. Soon after they had my hands and feet in paraffin baths and cucumber mask on my face. This was better than the massage I received at Asian parlor the other day. I was in heaven. Simplicity was the order of the day. I could do this every day.

Mateo sat nearby and watched all of this go on and he smiled as if he was enjoying me getting pampered. I was glad he was enjoying this because I damn sure was enjoying it too. I was now at the point I would fight someone tooth and nail for this spot. But I had a feeling that it would never come to this. The way he was treating me only showed me that he didn't have interest in anyone else but me. He was a perfect gentleman all of the time and I know he was the best man for me and I for him. It was just that simple.

Chapter 21

Kardell

One Mo' Time

My mouth hung open like I was waiting for a big dick to suck. He came in the room and sat down like it was his second home; like he had been here before. I couldn't believe it. Alex and Ronald were friends. This was truly a small world.

"Dell, this is Alex's good friend, Ronald, or Ron as we call him."

All I could think was, *damn, why is this happening to me?* "Hi, I'm Kardell." I reached my hand out to his and he shook it.

"Nice to meet you." He shook my hand back and then took a seat right in front of me. He was as good-looking as I remembered him. His hands were still soft, too.

"Nice to meet you too." I almost couldn't breathe and I didn't know why. I was over him. At least I thought I was over him.

"Are you okay, Kardell, baby? You look a little flustered," my mother asked me.

"Ahhh . . . yes, Ma. I'm fine. I was just thinking about something I had to do," I lied.

"Well could you pray for us so we can eat and stop ogling the man? He doesn't want you." My sister offered an unsolicited comment. I wanted to jump across the table and fuck her ass up.

"I wasn't ogling. I just thought I knew him from somewhere, but I was mistaken," I countered like I was six years old again and then lowered my head to pray over the food. Trying to keep my eyes on my plate and not on Ronald was a task in itself. For some odd reason he was so good-looking right now. Just thinking about how he used to fuck me made me hard as a brick. I fidgeted in my seat a few times to keep from publicly rearranging my erection.

"You look familiar too," he spoke after he finished fixing his plate. "But I'm sure I've never met you before."

"Isn't this nice . . . having family and friends together for dinner," my mother commented. "Family is everything I love. I love my family; even as crazy and dysfunctional as we are." We all laughed.

We all ate and enjoyed our time together. Ronald and I played our parts as best we could. After we all had dessert we all piled into the living room to watch a movie like we always did as a family. The movie was good, or at least the parts I saw because all I could do was think about Ronald. What was also good was the fact that Alex was putting on the performance of his life. I watched in seething anger on the inside as he pretended to be so into my sister. Even though my sister and I didn't always get along, she was my sister and I didn't want anyone to hurt her or lie to her. I wanted to bust his ass right now in front of everyone. But I kept it cool and formulated a plan to out his ass without being involved. I just hoped it worked.

It was getting late and even though it was a Saturday I wanted to get home.

"Well, I guess it's time for me to get going. I'm a little tired." I stretched my arms for effect.

"Yeah, I need to go too. Got some things I need to get done tomorrow." Ronald spoke up as well.

"Kardell, why don't you take Ronald home, since he is on your side of town?" my mother suggested. "Alex and Angela have to go get my grandson and he is on the other side of town. No need for them to go all the way out of their way to take him home and waste gas."

If I didn't know any better I'd think my mother was trying to set me up.

"Mrs. Spencer, I'm good. The bus stop is a few blocks from here and it takes me straight home. I'll be good," he countered.

"Are you sure?"

"Yes, ma'am, I'm sure."

"Well, let me at least make you two some plates to go so neither one of you will have to cook tomorrow." She walked off toward the kitchen.

"Okay," Ronald and I said almost in unison. We waited for a few minutes and sure enough my mother had some healthy plates ready to go. I left the house, as did Ronald, and my mother and father waited until I pulled off and Ronald started walking toward the bus stop before they went into the house.

I drove a few blocks down the street and then turned the corner on a secluded street and waited for Ronald to show up. Since I knew what bus stop he was going to from catching it as a teenager I just waited for him to show up. When I spotted him, I tapped my horn to let him know that I was waiting for him. I did all of this because I didn't want my parents nor my sister to be in my business. I enjoyed my personal business being personal.

He hopped in and before we pulled off I had a few things to say to him. He tried to kiss me, but I put my hand up to stop him.

"Ronald, how long have you known Alex?" I asked.

"I've known dude a couple of months. Why?"

"Have you and him ever messed around?"

"Nah, he's not even like that. He doesn't even know about me," he answered.

"Well, he is like that and I need you to do me a favor."

"What am I going to get for this favor?" he asked as his hand made its way onto my thigh. He was always thinking about sex. I mean I was too but at least I keep it cool.

"You don't even know what I want you do to and you asking me about sexual favors."

"Baby, I been missing you. You know that," he said as his hand made its way up to my chest and he squeezed one of my nipples. I almost forgot what I was getting ready to say. It felt so good to feel his touch on me.

"Ronald, it's over between us. I told you that," I stated.

"Then why did you wait for me? Why am I sitting in your car? Why couldn't you keep your eyes off of me the whole time I was in your parents' house? Look me in the eyes and say it over."

"It's over." I looked him dead in his eyes. "But I do need one last favor from you. It's important to me." I gave him the softest look I could muster up. Yeah, I was good at manipulation.

"You need a favor?" He then looked at me for a second and said nothing. "Why should I help you if you don't want me?"

"Because I really need your help with this one."

"What about my needs?" he asked.

"Okay, but one last time. That's it."

"Okay, so what do you need me to do?"

"Alex is putting my sister's life on the line, because he is on the down low. I can't tell her because she won't believe me. I need someone to do it for me."

"And tell me how I am supposed to do this?"

"I don't know. Get him drunk, take him to a gay club, and take some pictures of him getting it on with a guy or something. And then send the pictures to her anonymously. I don't know. I know you're smart enough to get it done."

"I'm going to need two or three rounds with you for all of this work." He laughed. "You lucky I didn't really like him like that anyway. He was an obnoxious little fucker."

"Okay, then that should make it a little bit easier," I added.

"So let's go so I can bust them guts open. I've been thinking about you a lot lately, and who would have thought that I would have caught up with you the way that I did?"

"So you have, have you?" I looked at him salaciously. I was horny too. *I might as well get me some before I start my new journey with Mateo.*

We made it to my house in less than a half hour. We were fucking within fifteen minutes of our arrival to my house. My phone rang but I didn't answer it because I knew it was my mother making sure I got home safe. Ronald's phone rang too. *I guess we both will have some explaining to do in the morning.*

Chapter 22

Lewis

Men At Work

I was a little groggy when I woke up from my slumber this morning. I jerked off twice before I went to bed last night just thinking about Mateo's hard body pressed up against mines in the near future. He looked like he could passionately make love to me for hours, unlike the losers I had dated in the past.

Now I was back at work and feeling myself for sure. I walked around with my head in the clouds. Everybody got a smile and a hug today. I got some strange looks back, because I wasn't the touchy-feely type on the regular. But today was a new day. I was going to enjoy the prospects of my future. Mateo had texted me this morning, wishing me a great day and that he was looking forward to touching my soft skin and looking into my hypnotic eyes. I blushed and almost giggled as I texted back that I couldn't wait to see him again as well. I was falling for him I was sure. I didn't want to and I knew that it could possibly end up like the others before him, but I was very optimistic and looking forward to a future I knew I was going to spend with him.

"Lewis, I need you in my office for a quick meeting about Mr. Lopez's advertising campaign," Mr. Spencer said as he walked into my work area. I was just sending another text to Mateo as he walked up and startled me.

"Okay, give me a sec," I said as I placed my phone in my front pocket. He walked away. I then got my work folder for the project and made my way to his office.

When I walked into the office I found out that I wasn't the only one in the office. The love of my life was sitting at a table looking fine in his well-tailored suit. I could say that I was kind of shocked that he was sitting there and didn't tell me he was coming to the office today. I assumed he was just here on business and not on a pleasure call, even though it was my pleasure to see him. He smiled when he saw me and I sat down at the table across from him. I had to practically force myself from smiling so hard.

Kardell was sitting next to me and two other office workers were sitting on opposite ends of Mateo. We had meetings like this all of the time, but this one was different; it was one when I was going to have to really show off and show Mateo that he was getting a hard-working guy to share his bed and life with. I didn't want to be just a piece of eye candy to him. I wanted to be someone who he could trust and come to about business.

"Good morning, everyone." My boss smiled as he looked at everyone at the table and lingered a little too long on my man. Mateo smiled and nodded his head. He was so smooth. "I just want to open up the meeting and thank everyone for their hard work on this campaign, and I know for myself that this is one of my favorites. I hope that Mr. Lopez will enjoy working with us and getting the best out of us. I am sure we all will do a fabulous job because it is all about teamwork and we are a wonderful team."

Everyone at the table was smiling brightly, mainly because we knew that Mr. Spencer would be handing out some nice bonuses if the campaign was as successful or even more successful as former campaigns.

The whole meeting went by so smoothly and even during the meeting Mateo was texting me messages about my smile and appearance. I tried my best not to smile too hard but it was hard. My boss's phone chimed a few good times and he would momentarily glance at Mateo and then everyone else in the room. It was probably his mama texting him since he was a mama's boy. He needed to get a man like I had and I was pretty sure he would have a smile for all the right reasons.

"Well, everyone, let's call the meeting to a close, since I see that everyone is bringing their A game to the table. Mr. Lopez is looked forward to billboard placements in a week or two and we will start filming your television spots in the next couple of days. Everyone have a great and productive day."

Everyone got up and filed out of the room. I made sure I was the last one to leave so I could get to give my man a handshake and a sweet word.

"Mr. Lopez, I'm so glad that you chose to use this company to work with to get a boom back into your business. I will do *all* that I can to make this a huge success. Just let me know what to do and I *will* do it. And I do mean *anything*." I knew it was a little shameful but I had to show off a little bit in front of Kardell.

"I sure will." He smiled and then shook my hand. "Thank you for your hard work."

I smirked as I looked at my boss and then walked out of the door. I almost said, "Who gon' check me, boo," to my boss but that would have been too much. I walked back to my desk and prepared the rest of my day. *I am going to have dinner with my bestie Dennis tonight and I'm going to be looking fabulous tonight.*

Chapter 23

Kardell

Spoiled Rotten

During the whole meeting I couldn't help but notice how strange Lewis was acting. His random texting and giddiness was a small distraction and I tried to pay it no mind because I was beaming with pride and excitement because the man I was dating secretly was in the same room with me sending me love notes via text. I was so glad I had everyone talk about their progress so I could text in between nods and "excellent work" comments to each individual after they spoke. I had to admit I wasn't truly there in total capacity. I was stealing glances at Mateo every chance I got. I thought I was falling for him. We were having our second date tonight and I was so excited. Work was the furthest thing from my mind. I just knew that Mateo was going to surprise me and spoil me rotten again like he did on the first date.

After everyone had left, it was just me and Mateo in the office. I wanted to run up to him and shower him with kisses, but I had to keep it professional in the office. The people you set rules for can't see you break the rules because then they will lose respect for you and the rules.

"It was so nice to have you come by today." I shook his hand and then walked over to the area where my desk was. I sat down and watched him come and take a seat in front of my desk. He looked so distinguished. His body language was poised with confidence. He sat up straight and he didn't slouch and I never saw his hand go limp, if you know what I mean. I really didn't care about it, but it was just something I noticed.

"Yes, I can say that I enjoyed the meeting and all of your staff."

"We aim to please." I smiled again. I couldn't help it. I was ecstatic about the possibilities of finding love once and for all. No more looking. No more dating losers. No club hopping. I'd have a true love life.

"Can you come over here for a minute?" he asked. I had to admit he threw me with the question, but I got it together and made my way around the desk. He got up at the same time.

He gently pulled me close to him with one arm around my waist. I almost went limp.

"You smell so good." He sniffed the side of my neck. "What do you have on?"

"I . . . I don't have anything on but my bath soap," I answered.

"Your skin is so soft . . . so smooth." He looked at me in the eyes as he rubbed the side of my face with the back of his hands. He was so gentle.

"Excuse me, Mr. Spencer, but. . ." Janice walked into my office. She usually knocked but she must have forgotten today. *Out of all of the days to forget today is the day she forgets to knock.* I jumped out of Mateo's embrace as fast as I could, but I was sure she saw us. I was so embarrassed.

"Oh, I'm so very, very sorry. I forgot to knock. I'm so sorry, sir." She turned and hurried out of my office.

"I'm sorry . . . I just couldn't help myself," Mateo apologized.

"It's no problem. She won't tell anyone. She is very professional, unlike me right now." I nervously chuckled.

"I'm sorry for this. Let me get going. I will see you later?" he asked.

"Yes, most definitely," I answered and then walked back behind my desk.

He didn't linger long, but I could still feel his arm around my waist like it belonged there. Like in his arms was where I was supposed to be and stay. There was no way I was giving him up now. Any man who wanted him was going to have to climb over my cold, dead body.

Chapter 24

Lewis

Questions

"You sure you don't just want to get fucked really good?" my best friend asked me as we sat in a nice quaint restaurant on Charles Street in Mount Vernon. I was shocked, and for me that was hard to do. "I mean if he is all of that why hasn't he made a move on you yet? He didn't try to finger you or anything?" He looked at me in all seriousness.

I'm not going to lie, he made me think. Why didn't Mateo ever make any advances toward me? I mean he'd pampered me physically without any advances of a sexual nature. It felt good, but it made me wonder why he hadn't tried to get in my pants. I had just chalked it up as him taking his time and wanting to get to know me first.

"I am trying to build a friendship before it goes that far and I am sure that he is doing the same," I said and then sipped on some chai tea I ordered.

"Okay, so what do you know about this guy, besides the fact that he has money and owns a few businesses?" He looked at me curiously.

"You don't want me to be happy do you?" I asked. "You want to be the only one of us to be happy and well off."

"See, you are being stupid right now, and coming for me is not going to solve the fact that you don't know anything about this man you are seeing. The fact that I am asking you these questions should let you know that I care and that I want you to be happy. How can you say such a thing to me?"

"I'm sorry." I apologized and then looked out of the window for a few seconds. There were a few tears threatening to fall but I blinked them back. I was embarrassed for acting so stupid. I was going to be strong and keep my head up.

"I don't know what you about to cry for because you know I'm right and if you don't remember you gave me this very same speech more than once, especially when I met Charles."

I silently nodded my head because words escaped me right now. I was being haunted by my own words at the most inopportune time. I hated that.

He continued, "Just promise me you will get more information on this guy and I don't mean his dick size." He laughed after he said that and I chuckled a little. He was trying to lighten the mood and he did for a second.

"You know what, you are right and I didn't think about any of that," I admitted.

"That's because you are used to getting in bed with anyone and then letting them walk off in the morning. You didn't want to get to know them. Now that you are trying something different you need to work smart and get as much information about him as possible. I'm not saying do a full background but get to know him and his family. Things like that."

"Okay," I said as I made some mental notes. I couldn't believe that I didn't think of this myself. I couldn't even say that I didn't hear this before, because the counselor I met in Starbucks awhile ago said some similar things. I guessed I didn't really let it sink in.

"I'm proud of you for even trying to do something different, so don't even think in the tiniest part of your mind that I'm not. You deserve happiness. You know I knew tons about Charles before I even let him hit it and he wasn't having it. We had many a fights over this here booty." He laughed as he tapped the side of his butt cheek. "But I held firm and now look at us, we are going strong as ever. You can do the same."

"Thank you." That was all I could say as all he said sank into my head.

"Don't thank me . . . pay me, bitch." We both burst into laughter. "Shit, or at least buy my food. I'm not a starving artist but I will play the part for a free meal." We laughed together again. We did that all evening until it was time for him to go home to his man, and me to my list of questions for Mateo.

Chapter 25

Kardell

Check Yourself

"Hello," I picked up the phone. It was a Saturday morning alone in my bed and I was extremely happy from the date that I had with Mateo the night before.

"Are you asleep?" she asked. It was my sister, Angela. I didn't know why she was calling me this early in the morning or at all for that matter. We didn't talk on a regular basis and she was always insulting my lifestyle in one form or another and today I wanted no part of it.

"I was," I answered dryly.

"Oh." She paused for a few seconds.

"Did you need something . . . some money?"

"I need . . . I need . . ." She burst into tears before she said anything else. I mean she was crying like somebody died. I quickly sat up in bed with a nervous energy running through my body. I was scared of what she might say next. Like somebody *had* died.

"Angela, what's going on?" Legitimate concern filled my voice.

"Alex is on the DL . . . He's fucking a man." She burst into tears once again.

It didn't take a genius to tell me that Ronald did what I asked of him. I had to admit a small piece of me wanted to enjoy her pain when I thought about her finding out. But now that it was happening I didn't feel a twinge of excitement or joy. All I felt was her tears and sobbing as she cried into the phone. It was gut-wrenching as I sat on the side of the bed and heard her mourn a loss.

"I can't believe it." She finally calmed down and spoke. "How could he do this to me? . . . To us?"

"Are you sure?" I asked.

"Yes, somebody sent me some pictures in the mail this morning. I got them spread out all over the kitchen table. I'm so glad Jonathan is in school and not home. I don't know what I would do if he was here and I opened these pictures up in front of him."

"Yes, that would not be good," I agreed.

"Kardell, did you ever think that Alex could be this way? Did he ever exhibit any signs?"

"Angela, being on the down low is just that, down low, people are good at keeping their business their business." I purposely answered the situation but not her question. "No one really knows what someone else is doing until they find out. Gaydar is a myth and a lie, honey."

"I mean he just loved . . . um . . . pussy," she almost whispered. "He was good at it. I just don't understand."

"Angela, it's not a science, he could actually love both, but only exhibit the thirst outwardly for one and secretly for the other. And just for the record not all men are like this. That's the problem, people put it in a box and paint pictures of DL men when in truth it could be anyone. You find out when you find out. Sad but true. It's a cruel, cruel world out here. Not everyone is who they seem to be."

"Wow, I'm just so out of it right now. I don't know if I'm going or coming. And he's upstairs, asleep. I'm in the basement talking to you."

"So what are you going to do?" I asked out of extreme curiosity. "Don't do anything that you will regret."

"Actually, I'm going to post this picture to his Facebook page and then put him out." I could see a big, bright smile on her face on the other side of the phone.

"That's a little extreme don't you think? With social media being what it is today you could go to jail for that."

"Really?" she asked.

"Yes, sweetie, you don't want to do that. Just ask him to leave and then you go get yourself tested for STDs," I counseled.

"Right. I can't believe this. I just can't. How can I make him pay for this though?" she asked.

"By truly letting him go and treating him like a man in the process. Kill him with kindness. Guilt will eat him alive," I answered.

"Very true . . . That is very, very true. I never thought of that." She seemed surprised. "Not to change the subject . . ." She paused for a minute. "But I'm sorry for not treating this sensitive subject with sensitivity until now. I guess it takes something like this to gain perspective."

"I accept your apology and I understand because I do it as well," I stated matter-of-factly.

"Can I ask you something?" she began. "Have you ever been in a situation like this before, where you thought you knew someone but it turns out that you didn't know, but it was too late before you found out?"

"Well . . ." I paused and thought for a second because I really didn't know. "I really can't say that I have, but it's not a situation that I want to be in either. This is kind of crazy for you to go through this."

"Are you dating someone right now?" Angela asked.

"Yes, I'm seeing someone right now," I answered.

"Do you know everything you need to know about them?"

"To be honest I'm just starting to see this person and I'm not really sure where this is going to go, but I want it to go somewhere."

"That's good, but don't end up like me. Get to know the person, ask questions, follow suspicions and pay attention to the red flags. I wouldn't want this to happen to anyone, even my worst enemy. I feel so crazy right now because I didn't know."

"Well you don't have to feel so crazy about it because you didn't know. We all have situations or put ourselves in situations where we really don't know what is going on, but it's by taking away from those situations that we learn important life lessons. "

"What lessons can I take away from this?" She chuckled for a minute and then paused. "This is such a mess."

"What you can learn from the situation is the fact that you can't make someone love you when they don't love themselves or they don't know what they want in life. Alex wasn't a bad person, it's just that he didn't know what he wanted in life and he decided that he wanted to do what he wants to do and not really care about the situation or the people. You can learn to love yourself more and you can also learn to forgive people because we all have problems and we all might not be as strong as the next person to deal with them and deal with them right away."

"You know what, little bro, you are absolutely right. I guess this is one for the books. Shit, I might as well write a book about it and maybe I'll call it *Both Sides of the Fence*." She laughed. She sounded a little bit happier than she did before.

"You can do that and maybe you can use a couple of chapters out of my life." I laughed a little bit myself. "Well, big sister, I can't say this will be easy to get over because almost nothing is easy to get over when you put your heart into it, but you can call me if you need to talk again and only if I'm not getting it in."

"I hear that. You are right about that. It was actually really nice talking to you. I know I can be a smart ass at times but it's only because I love you and sometimes I don't know how to say it and sometimes I can be hurt and want to hurt someone else. They say that you only hurt the people you love."

"Angela, we all are guilty of doing things that we regret so let's just let bygones be bygones."

"Okay, that's a deal."

"Well, Angela, it's time for me to get off the phone and get back to my beauty sleep."

"Rest easy, sir. Rest easy."

I hung up the phone and rolled over, glad that that situation was over and finished with. It would be something now that I could scratch off my list but was also now something that my sister would have to deal with in the days, weeks, and months to come. She did give me some things to think about. I really didn't know anything about Mateo. I guessed I was going to have to do some research and get some questions answered.

Chapter 26

Lewis

Masterpieces

"I think I'm falling in love with you," I practiced in the mirror in my house as I was getting ready to go out on the town with Mateo. We were going to another one of his fabulous outings that I was sure was going to be a super luxurious time. It was always a surprise with him and I loved surprises.

He said it was going to be very low key and I could dress comfortably, so I threw on some cute jeans and a really cute V-neck shirt I got from Nordstrom the other day. I had some cute loafers that were very comfortable and stylish for this summery spring weather. My haircut was fresh and my skin was soft and glowing. Mateo was a touchy-feely guy and he loved my skin and touched me almost compulsively. I adored the attention.

We were headed to the museum. At first when he told me I was like, *huh?* in my mind, but my mouth said, "Great." I am not going to lie and say that I was a museum kind of guy because I wasn't. It wasn't that my parents didn't teach me culture or anything, it was just that it spelled out b-o-r-i-n-g to me. We would go all the time in Pennsylvania and I hated it then and now was no exception. I'd rather have gone to an amusement park and ride roller coasters and things like that but now I was a responsible adult and I had to keep it adult. Adults did do theme parks; they just did it when they had kids. I didn't think that it was kosher to go to the theme park without kids, but that is just my opinion and I didn't think that Mateo would go for that anyway.

I was dressed, fresh, and ready to pretend like I was having a great time. It would be one of the only performances that I would have to put on with Mateo because I enjoyed everything else we did, except this and maybe sexually if he wasn't well endowed or didn't know how to perform. I was hoping his ass didn't have erectile dysfunction or something like that. That was the flaw in my plan of dating before sex and not the other way around. The way of the world now was sex first and everything else later. I guessed sex was high on the list of priorities now and getting to know the person came later on. I could see now that was a flawed plan. Getting to know the person was now top on my list and then sex. Since we were going someplace where talking was ideal it would be a great time to get some more information about Mateo and even pass on some information about me, because, come to think of it, he never asked me any information about myself either.

I jumped in my car and made my way downtown toward the Walters Art Museum where he said he would be waiting for my arrival. I arrived downtown in good time, parked my car in a garage a block or two over, and walked to the museum.

I was a little nervous when I walked in and saw all of the people walking around talking and pointing at the artwork pieces and smiling. It was a little intimidating that I didn't know anything about art. I hated to be in situations where I was out of the loop or the odd man out. But this was a part of life and in life we have to do things we don't like nor understand to gain knowledge. I stood at the entrance of one of the sectional galleries and wondered where Mateo was in the museum. My palms were a little sweaty. I quickly checked my breath and then reached in my pocket to text Mateo on his location in the museum. But before I could get a single letter in I felt a tap on my shoulder.

"Nice to see you today."

I turned to see Mateo in jeans and thin polo shirt. He looked really nice. He looked like I wanted to take him in the bathroom and get on my knees and . . . well, you know the rest. "Nice to see you as well." I spoke and a smile gleamed across my face.

"Your skin is glowing I see," he remarked as he ran the back of his hand down the side of my face like he did always.

"Thank you." I blushed.

"Are you ready to look around?" he asked.

"I'm ready as ever."

"Good, there is so much I want to show you."

"Well, let's go and enjoy this day." I spoke gleefully.

The first room we entered was filled with a few couples walking hand in hand as they admired the different art pieces. I had to admit I felt a little twinge of jealousy because most of them were holding hands while Mateo and I weren't. Then, while standing in front of a black woman's beautiful picture of her holding a bright baby boy, Mateo clasped his hand into mine. There was a spark as if we were standing on carpet. A smile was instantly smeared across my face. My insides felt like I was hit with a jolt from electric paddles that brought back a person from the brink of death. My heart was racing.

"Look at her. Look at the definition of the face, the smile. The artist got it all in this picture," Mateo said as he admired the picture.

"Yes, that is so true," I agreed. I really didn't care about the picture or the woman. His hand in mine was enough for me. I could get used to this. I would fight for this. This was a public display of affection. No, it wasn't a kiss, but it was a great start. Actually a kiss may have been too much for me at this moment. I probably would have been compelled to reciprocate in the bathroom on my knees or something. But that was my conditioning and that was the old me. This was new to me. I could say that I had never dated a guy and had him treat me so gently and kindly. Mateo was what I was looking for and needed in my life.

"Her skin looks as soft and glowing as yours does right now." He looked at me in admiration. He then took the back of his hand and gently rubbed it against my cheek. "Do you know you're a masterpiece of God? A beautiful work of art."

I blushed and then I closed my eyes for a brief second, taking in the moment. I knew we were in the middle of a room with other people and this was not the place for this, but when I opened my eyes there were a few eyes on us, but to my surprise there was no condemnation in them; instead theirs were smiles of admiration looking back at us. I too smiled back because they looked happy for me and for us. It was a nice feeling to be adored as a couple by others. This must have been what celebrity couples felt like in the limelight.

We moved on to other pictures and even to a room with sculptures and various other things. Piece by piece we admired the artwork. Mateo complimented me more and more as the day went on and I inhaled each one as if it were the fresh air my body needed to survive.

"Are you hungry?" Mateo asked me as we headed out of one of the exhibit rooms.

"A little," I answered.

"Well, let us go to the café and get a little something to eat. I can't have you wasting away."

With that we made our way into the café and found us a table and waited to be served. After we placed our order we made small talk while waiting for it to come back. While chatting we had an unexpected interruption.

Chapter 27

Kardell

Outed

After getting off of the phone with my sister I just couldn't go back to sleep. I tossed and turned in my bed for a few more minutes before I decided to get up and do something. I had nothing to do today since Mateo said that he was going to be busy today. He did mention that he wanted to take me to the museum on our next date. I had to say that I loved them. I was just out of touch with them. I hadn't been to one in such a long time that it would be like going for the first time for me. I needed to go do some research and there is nothing like hands-on research.

So that was what I decided to do. I decided to take a trip downtown and go to the Walters Art Museum. I was going to get a heads-up and impress him at the same time. Mateo looked like the type of guy who liked a well-bred man and that was what I was: well bred.

I cooked myself a small breakfast, showered, primped myself, and was out of my house in no time. It took no time to drive downtown and park in a garage a block or two over from the museum. I had a feeling that I was going to have a good time today.

The sun was shining and I was smiling as I walked down the block to the museum. I had to say that my life was good. I also figured today to be good to figure out something to ask Mateo about himself.

I walked into the entrance of the museum, and there was a nice-sized crowd in there. It was a Saturday and admission was free so I should have factored that into my visit today, but it was all good. I was going to enjoy the day nonetheless, and nothing could bring down my joy today . . . nothing.

I took my time and walked around the different rooms and exhibits. One of my favorite exhibits was Revealing the African Presence in Renaissance Europe. It was very enlightening and informative.

After about an hour and a half of looking I got a little hungry and decided to grab a small bite to eat at the museum café called Café Q. As soon as I walked in the café and surveyed the room for a possible seat, a nauseated feeling attacked my stomach. It was instant reaction to a sight that I was sure I should not have been seeing. I knew my eyes were playing tricks on me. I couldn't believe it. I just couldn't believe it. So I did something that I had never done before. I caused a scene.

"What the hell is going on here?" I walked up to the table where my man and my new enemy sat across from each other, talking, one hand covering the other's hands. It was a sign of affection to them but a sign of betrayal to me. There was a few people staring at me and the scene going on, but I didn't care at the moment. I had completely forgotten my reputation as an upstanding, law-abiding citizen and my senses. I was seeing red. I wanted to flip the table over in a tirade. My man looked at me calmly and the "enemy" had an evil smirk on his face. I wanted to smash his head into the glass window and watch the blood run down the side of his face and then do it again. This was my man he had his hand on. He had his filthy, hoeish hands on my man.

"Hello, Kardell. How are you?"

No, this bitch didn't just ask me how I am doing while he is sitting across from my man. I didn't answer him at first because I wanted to retain my dignity and some of my reputation as an upstanding citizen; but, as they say, shit was about to get real.

"Have you lost your fucking mind?" I couldn't believe I was speaking in such language in front of my man, but I was seething hot and didn't care at the moment.

"My mind is great right now. It couldn't be better. I'm out with my man and we were having an almost quiet meal together before you showed up and showed us your ghetto side." He looked at me and then at my man and then smiled slyly, like he was winning.

"Your man?" I asked, looking at my man, waiting for him to answer.

"Did I stutter? You have a degree or two and you mean to tell me that you haven't grasped all of the English language?" Lewis said sarcastically. "How could he be your man if you didn't want him?"

"You're in my business and I'm about to be in yours," I threatened.

"Like I said, my man and I are enjoying ourselves and we don't want the interruptions, so we would appreciate it if you found you a man, if you can, and leave us two lovers alone."

"Are you forgetting the fact that you work for me and not the opposite?" I stated matter-of-factly.

"Is that a threat? . . . Are you threatening me?" He turned toward me in his seat as if he was about to get up.

I took a step back just in case he was about to swing or something. I can say I wasn't planning on this shit happening today. I guessed there was something that could change my mood today. I never thought in a million years that it would be this.

"It is what it is," I replied.

"Excuse me is everything okay over here?" A male and female member of the museum's security walked up to us. The male asked the question.

"No, everything is fine . . . Just a little miscommunication." Mateo finally decided to talk by answering the officers. "Kardell, have a seat so we can discuss this rationally." His smile, his calming voice was all I needed to hear, so I hesitantly pulled out a chair and sat down at the table. I was breathing hard, and looking at Lewis's ass was not making it any better.

"Okay, any more profanity or arguing and we will have to ask you to leave the grounds. This is a family-friendly environment and we like to keep it that way. Have a great day at the Walters Art Museum, fellas." They walked off and left us to hash out the mess that we were in.

"Gentlemen, this is entirely my fault. I wasn't being honest with either of you. I like both of you and couldn't decide on which one of you to see exclusively. You two are very good-looking guys and it is hard to decide when two guys meet my standards. I like you both." He looked at both of us, one to the other, intensely.

I was shocked at what I was hearing. *Here I am thinking I am the only one and he is dating Lewis and me.* I wanted to get up and walk out and leave them both here looking stupid, but that would only make Lewis the winner and I wasn't going out like that. I found him first. The truth is I probably fucked myself by seeming uninterested in Mateo when I first met him and denying that attraction to Lewis. His fast ass swooped right in and made his move. I had to give it to him: he was a go-getter. I guess he was looking for love too. It just happened to be the same guy I was interested in.

"Mateo, it's okay," I spoke up first. "It can happen to anyone."

"Yes, I forgive you," Lewis stated, and then reached his hand across the table and placed it on Mateo's hand that was resting on the table. I reached over, knocked it off, and placed my hand on his. I knew it was petty and downright childish, but I wasn't giving up that easily. Pretty soon we were pushing each other's hands off of Mateo's before he finally pulled his hand back.

"No need to fight, fellas. I have a great way to solve this dilemma." He looked at both of us and smiled. "Since I can't possibly choose between the both of you I propose a contest of sorts to see who the best man for me is. I love games; and why shouldn't life be interesting?"

"A game?" I spoke hesitantly.

"Yes. I know it is totally unconventional, but I think it would be fun to have a little friendly contest. Think of it as *American Idol* for dating." He laughed lightly.

"I'm game if he's game." Lewis looked at me sharply. I eyed him back in the same manner.

"But you can't take it out on each other at work."

We both nodded our heads yes even though I knew that it was going to be hard to keep this from spilling over into the work atmosphere.

"Great. It will take me a few days to think about what I want to do, but expect a text with the first challenge," he said, getting up from the table. "I'm looking forward to this. Have a great day, gentlemen."

We both watched him walk off and then we looked at each other in silence for a few seconds.

"May the best man win." I stuck my hand out to shake Lewis's hand.

He hesitantly did the same before he said the same: "May the best man win."

Chapter 28

Lewis

Sewed Up

"A contest?" I laughed to myself after I said that out loud on the side of my bed. "I got this shit sewn up." I believed that wholeheartedly. I was a winner by nature. Spelling bee, cooking, style, and poise: I had all of that shit on lock.

"Kardell's stuffy ass doesn't stand a chance against me. He is in over his head." I danced around my room like I was Muhammad Ali jabbing into the air like I was "like that." "I'm up for the challenge . . . any challenge."

All kinds of thoughts raced through my head as I made myself busy around my house sprucing up this and that. I looked around several times and thought, *I'll probably be moving into Mateo's house pretty soon, especially after I whip Kardell's ass in this contest.*

After finishing off the cleanup of my home, I sat on my couch and wondered what in the world could be on Mateo's mind when I came to this contest.

My thoughts were interrupted by the ring of my phone.

"Hello," I answered.

"Hello, son," my mother spoke in an even tone. Both of my parents showed little emotion as I grew up. I mean they loved us no doubt and they encouraged our school life but when it came to emotions and talking about how you felt, that was off-limits. It was school and more school to them. "Be successful" was their motto. I was successful. I was bred to be a winner. *I will win.*

"Hello, Mother." I was happy and full of joy. "What can I do for you today?"

"Nothing, son, I was just calling to see how you were faring in life."

"Mom, things are actually very good right now. I have a home, friends, steady employment, and an awesome wardrobe, all the things a successful man could ask for." I was saying hopefully what she wanted to hear. I was feeding her ego.

"Son, all of those things are great, but are you dating someone or just sleeping around with every Tom, *Dick,* and Harry that comes along?"

I gagged for a minute because I knew my mother didn't just come for me. *Did she just call me a whore on the sly ?* I pulled the phone away from my ear and looked at it to make sure it was my mother I was talking to on the phone.

"Mother, are you feeling well?" I asked, confused at the sudden interest in my love life.

"Lewis, I'm worried about you. You never call and you never discuss what is going on in your life besides work and projects you are working on."

"You never seemed to care." There was a lump forming in my throat after I said that. I was nervous about her response. My parents both have low tolerance for what they may see as foolishness.

There were a few brief seconds of silence on the phone. *What, my mother speechless for once?*

"Hello," I spoke into the phone to see if she was still on the line.

"Yes, I'm still here." She paused again. "You know, Lewis, your father and I did our best when raising three children. Yes, we missed some things and some steps making sure that you were successful. I see the error of my ways now and I'm trying to correct it. I know it may be too little too late, but I am sorry for not sharing with you and just talking *to* you. I know now that there is a difference between the two. Do you forgive me?"

Now I was the one who was speechless. I didn't know what to say. What does one say when a parent asks for forgiveness?

"Are you dying or something?" That was the first thing that came out of my mouth. It was like she was making her peace with me or something. It was really weird having this conversation out of the blue.

"Lewis," she said sternly. "I'm not dying. I'm apologizing."

"I'm sorry. I was just caught off-guard by this whole conversation. I do forgive you, Mom."

"Thank you, sir."

"No problem, Mom."

"Lewis, you never answered my question."

"And what was that?" I asked, playing dumb. I even snickered a little away from the phone. Teasing my parents was a hard habit to break easily.

"I asked if you were dating anyone."

"Mother, I'm at the beginning stages with someone."

"Okay, are they successful?"

"Yes, they are very successful."

"So when do we get to meet them?" she asked.

"At the appropriate time," I answered.

"Okay, Lewis, I'll accept that answer for now, but don't be surprised if I pop up at your home to introduce myself."

"Okay," I responded. I knew that she was dead serious about coming down. My parents were the popup type. "I promise to introduce you the moment it gets serious."

"You better. And get to know them, son. Take your time. Ask questions. Investigate and then fall in love. In that order."

"I sure will."

"All right, son, your father and I love you so take care of yourself."

"I will, and thanks, Mom. Talk to you later." I hung up the phone before she wanted to do any more digging. I knew for sure that she wouldn't approve of having a contest to win a man. She bred a winner and I knew that I would win this contest as well. *I have it sewn up tighter than a fat woman in a small dress.*

Chapter 29

Kardell

And It Begins . . .

The text that I received this morning put me in a state of sheer shock. It was really mind-blowing for me. I read it over and over again to make sure that I had read it right.

"This just can't be." I sat on the side of the bed and shook my head from side to side in bewilderment with a few tears glistening on the sides of my eyes. This was the first challenge and I almost changed my mind and let Lewis win. I couldn't let him win. I would just bite the bullet and accept the first challenge.

I got dressed and ready for work but I made a detour before I stepped into the office.

When I pulled up to my destination I sat in my car for a few moments and I thought really hard about what I was getting ready to do.

I exited my car on shaky legs and opened the door to the establishment. The smell of alcohol and cologne hit me as I browsed the area against the wall where two other people were waiting to be served. If you haven't guessed by now, I was in a barbershop. No, I wasn't getting my hair shaped up. I was here to complete the first challenge.

Fifteen minutes went by before I was called.

"Shape up?" the barber asked me as I took my seat.

"Cut it off." The words stammered from my mouth. I wished I could suck them back in.

"Cut it all off?" He asked me if I was sure. Now was the time I could have gotten up out of the chair and exited the building, but I stayed planted in the seat.

"Yes . . . All of it," I said, wanting to slide down in my chair and onto the floor.

"If you don't mind me asking, how long have you had these?"

"Six years," I answered. I tried to focus on a picture of Obama on the wall and then the sport on the television to keep from thinking about it but it didn't work. I loved my hair; it was a part of me as if it were an appendage or something. I put work into them and cutting them was not on my list of something I wanted to do. I thought that they made me look more distinguished. My hair got me most of my attention, along with my cute face.

"That's a long time to have these and cut them off." He stated something that I didn't need to be told.

"I know." I huffed, disappointed in what I was about to do.

"Bruh, what would make you want to cut them off all of a sudden, if you don't mind me asking?"

I minded him asking but I answered him anyway. "Cancer," was all that I could say knowing very well I couldn't say that I was doing this to win a man. I prayed a silent prayer of forgiveness to God for that lie. I didn't want to make fun of a cancer patient or even get diagnosed with it.

"Damn, bruh. Sorry to hear that."

I felt some type of way lying to a stranger, somebody who probably didn't give a shit about me or my hair.

"It's okay, I'll beat it."

"I sure hope so. I really do," he said as he cut the hair with clippers he had in his hands. The humming sound made me nervous. My heart was beating like an African drummer beating a drum to an exotic beat. It was rapid.

I couldn't believe I was going through with this. It hit me all of a sudden how drastic this actually was. But I sat still and put on a brave front. I jumped the first time the cold steel hit the nape of my neck and made its way up my head to the front. I watched as my six years of hard work fell onto my shoulders and onto the floor. I wanted to shed a tear for each one of them that hit the floor. On the inside, I cringed as each lock of hair hit the floor. What was I going to tell people about this sudden change in my appearance? How was I going to react when I looked in the mirror for the first time without my locks? I silently wished I had jumped up out of the chair and said I had changed my mind.

When he finished he asked me a question I wasn't ready for. "Do you want to take them and hold on to them as a souvenir of your diagnosis? I have had a few women who came through to do that and some even donate it to a cancer society or something."

"Yes, I'll take it." He gathered them together and placed them in a plastic bag for me.

I got up out of the chair and looked at myself in the mirror. I smiled on the outside but I was still really unsure of myself on the inside. My hair was a part of my confidence. This was a strong leap of faith for me. I smoothed my hand over my head for the first time in a long time and felt very little hair. It felt weird and awkward. I didn't feel like myself. I knew now that there was no turning back for this contest. It was all or nothing now and I wasn't ending up another broke Negro.

Chapter 30

Lewis

Speechless

When my boss walked in the office the other morning all eyes were on him. I couldn't help but say I was super shocked at his appearance. I was actually speechless for once. I thought he was too. He had his business satchel over his shoulder and he had a clear plastic bag full of his hair in his hand. The look on his face was one of a fake smile. He looked happy but the eyes never lie as they say. He wanted to fall out and cry. I knew I would've been a mess if I had to cut my hair off. Especially the way Kardell loved his hair. He *loved* his hair. He would flip it and twirl it in his finger unknowingly. To be honest his hair was a great fit for him. Now that he was like a hairless kitty (pun intended), it just looked weird. He was still cute, but as drastic a change as this couldn't be good for one's psyche. I trembled a little bit as I walked back to my seat and sat down.

I suspected this to be one of Mateo's challenges because Kardell loved his hair like it was a limb. I had no clue as to what he was going to choose for me since I was next. I had been in anticipation all night every day and up until now I was excited; now I was a bit nervous. If Mateo was going after drastic changes to physical appearance then what would he ask me to change?

Because I had no hair on my head to cut. I kept my hair cut close.

I tried my best to concentrate on my work, especially the closing minor details for Mateo's campaign, but I was consumed with what I was going to get in the text that he was going to send me.

I was finished with my day and ready to go home to my nice warm home when I received the text that would rock my world. I mean I literally gasped when I read it. I couldn't believe that he wanted me to do this.

This was what the text said: Would you give up everything for me? If so this is your challenge. Spend the next two days homeless in downtown; take only five dollars in cash, no cell phone, and no identification. You can't take a bath and the location I want you to stay at is the park near the main post office downtown. I have someone watching you, but you won't know who. It's just to make sure you are not cheating.

"He can't possibly expect me to do this. This is outrageous. He hasn't even hit me off with any dick for me to be going to these great lengths to be with him," I grumbled to myself.

It was a Friday so I didn't have to be around anybody I knew but that only made me feel better momentarily. I had never slept outside in my whole life. Even when I clubbed and stayed out late it was only to around 3:00 A.M. at the latest. Yes, once I was so drunk I slept outside in my car but that was a far cry from on a park bench. I passed that park many a time feeling pity for the people who slept there and even had makeshift living areas.

"You can do this, Lewis. You are a winner. You got this. It's only two days." I coached myself. It was cool weather outside so I didn't have to worry about being cold.

So I did it. I got out of my car and locked everything I had in the trunk except for my car keys. I left my car in the garage that it was in and walked out onto the street. The park that Mateo mentioned wasn't that far from my job so walking there wasn't a problem. I got there in no time. The park was supposed to be closed at dusk but people still migrated there and the police got tired of telling them to leave so it was a packed house; and I use the word "house" very loosely.

I made my way into the park. There was a bench that was empty and I made my way over near it. The smell was rank with body odor and decay. That alone made me rethink this whole contest business, but, again, I wasn't a quitter. I was used to winning and I wasn't stopping until I won.

I had to admit that lying out in the dark night on a park bench wasn't all that bad. Even though I didn't have my cell phone with me or anything to occupy my time I did have time to think about my life and the things I really wanted. I really wanted to win. *My friends have their lovers, my parents have each other, and my sister and brother have their lovers. I'm the only one without one.*

I had finally drifted off to sleep at about one in the morning according to my watch. I was balled up pretty tight on the bench for both protection and heat. I was awakened by the grumbling in my stomach. It was the urge to use the bathroom and I'm not talking about urinating. I had to do the number two and had to do it really bad. I spotted a Port-O-Potty in the corner of the park and I cringed at the thought about having to use it, but I didn't have a choice at the moment; it was the only thing available. So I got up and I looked around to make sure that it was safe for me to go use in privacy. I didn't want to have anybody sneaking up on me while I was taking a crap out in the dark. The rumbling in my stomach didn't help either. I didn't remember what I had for lunch but it was making its way back out now. I almost sprinted over to the Port-O-Potty. Just as I got to the Port-O-Potty it dawned on me that I had no toilet paper.

"Shit," I exclaimed. Now I was pissed off. I prayed and hoped that there would be a roll of toilet paper waiting just for me when I opened this door. I closed my eyes and then opened the door. I slowly opened my eyes with two of my fingers crossed on my other hand. I was hoping really hard for the toilet paper that I prayed for to be there. I needed a miracle. Guess what, there was no toilet paper. There was only a rancid smell that caused me to start gagging, so I covered my mouth and nose and slammed the door shut. The grumbling in my stomach never stopped even though I didn't have a place to relieve myself. I clenched my cheeks together, trying to hold back the inevitable.

What the hell am I going to do? I thought as I paced in circles. I spied a dark corner of the park and that was where I needed to do my business. As I walked to the dark cubbyhole of the park it flashed in my mind that the homeless do this all the time and most of them now do it with ease as if it were second nature. I felt out of sync being outside and now having to relieve myself outside.

I pulled my pants down and did what I was there to do. I can't say it didn't feel good because it did, even if it was outside. I grabbed a few leaves that were scattered around on the ground and wiped myself because I wasn't going to touch my own shit. Thank God I carried some hand sanitizer in my pocket so I could at least sanitize my hands. I started out of the corner and made it back to my bench, feeling like the piece of shit

I just pooped out. This was one of those moments you don't tell your friends about. This was definitely going to the grave with me.

I balled back up on the bench in the same position I was in earlier and reflected on life until I fell asleep. *How could Mateo ask me to do this?* Was he trying to see if I would do anything for him? Or did he think I was a gold-digger and he wanted to see if I was only after his money? I didn't know any of that but I was going to weather this task and be victorious.

I was awakened by another vibrant and breathtaking smell, and it definitely wasn't Folgers coffee or a McDonald's sausage biscuit. I had opened my eyes to the biggest, fattest woman I'd ever seen in my life smiling and rubbing my face.

"Hey, baby." Her face was grungy and her breath was vicious in my nostrils. It smelled like what I did last night in the far corner of the park. I immediately hopped up and back as far as I could. My space was violated and I was defensive about my personal space. "You are new here. What is your fine self doing out here in this park?" She smiled and showed the gateway to her stomach. It looked like her teeth were fighting to get out of her mouth.

I couldn't get any words out. First thing in my mind was to dig in my pocket for some mints and give her some so I could breathe comfortably. I handed them to her and then spoke, "Swirl those around in your mouth and then inhale for a second." She did as she was instructed. I wasn't trying to be rude. It was just not good to let someone go walking around violating people with rancid breath.

"This is only temporary." I answered her question.

"That's good 'cause you fresh meat out here and these here men will try to get at you like you the wife they never had." She snickered.

My eyebrows rose in curiosity and fear as I looked at a few suspect-looking men eyeing me down. Flattery was far from what I was feeling right now. "What?"

"Yeah, honey. One of them tried to get at you last night. But I got them for you. I stayed over here all night while you slept."

"Thank you." I actually wanted to run but I didn't want to be rude again.

"What's your name, honey?" she asked.

"Melvin," I lied.

"That's a nice name." She smiled again. My stomach grumbled loudly and I looked at my watch. It was close to nine A.M.

"You hungry?" she asked.

"A little," I answered.

"Melvin, theys got a food truck that comes by here in about another hour if you don't have any money."

"Okay. Thank you," I said humbly.

"It's not the best but it's good for a day or two."

I remembered the money I had in my pocket but I didn't say a word. It would be really ignorant of me to go to McDonald's or Burger King or something and watch them eat what they eat.

"What's your name?" I asked. If I was going to be out here I might as well be friendly.

"Annie, but everybody around here calls me Tootsie."

"Oh that's a cute name." I smiled for the first time. "Tootsie, how did you end up out here on the streets?"

"Honey, that's a long story where I don't even re-member some parts of, but I will tell you to say no to drugs. That crack she don't play fair and heroin is a muthafucka. I'm straight and sober now. It's too bad that my family won't have any parts of me and so here I am."

Tootsie and I got close over the weekend and she made it a whole lot more tolerable to deal with. Allies in life are important. I couldn't help but think that maybe she was the one Mateo sent to watch me. I didn't think she was because I thought that would be too obvious to me.

I made it, was all that I could think about as I left the park and made my way to work that day. I know what you are saying: why not go home, bathe, and deal with the consequences of being late when I got to work? I wanted to, believe me, but I wanted Kardell to know and see that I would do anything to win, even be filthy and stinky for a couple of days. So, yes, I was filthy and I smelled terrible, but I was happy that I conquered this challenge.

Chapter 31

Kardell

In the Lead

I had briefly come out of my office to see a few of my staff whispering in a huddle.

"He smells like warmed-over puke," I heard one of them say.

"He must be on that stuff to be looking like that. He never looks like that. And he had the same clothes on that he had on Friday. Damn shame." They were so engrossed in conversation that they didn't even see me walk up on them.

"Uhmmm." I cleared my throat to get their attention. "I'm very sure that there is work to be done." I eyed all of them down. They scurried off in different directions. I noticed that Lewis was not among the crowd and that piqued my curiosity. He was always the ring leader when it came to some drama or gossip.

I walked over to his work area to see if everything was okay with him. There was a smell that hit me a few feet before I got to him. It made me curious as to what was going on and especially what the others were whispering about.

"Um, Lewis, is everything okay?" I asked as I walked up near him. I didn't want to get too close because he did have a pungent odor.

"I'm great." He turned, smiled at me, and then turned back to focus on some work on his desk.

"Is there a reason you are, um, looking the way you do today?"

"No." he answered without even looking in my direction. I could smell shame all over him along with all of the other scents he was carrying.

"You don't look fine. Do I need to send you home today? Because this is unacceptable behavior and hygiene."

"I *said* I'm great. Please leave me be."

I didn't like his tone and as his employer I should have reprimanded him on the spot, but I figured that it must have something to do with Mateo's challenge for him, so I left it alone. I did go into one of the utility closets and pulled out the can of Lysol so I could at least temporarily get rid of the smell he was carrying around.

I went back in my office and smiled as I sat down in my comfy chair. It looked like Lewis wanted to give up. I was winning or at least that was what the text from Mateo said after I sent him a picture of my dread-less head. In his words, I was "in the lead." I was hype about it.

Now all I had to do was wait for the next challenge from Mateo. I could admit I was super curious and fearful at the same time about what he was going to have me doing next.

My day went by pretty close to perfect. I put out a few fires work-wise and continued to wait for this challenge. Again, I was anxious to see what was next.

When I got the text message on the next challenge I nearly lost my lunch. I read over the lengthy text several times to make sure I got every detail down. It was close to leaving time and I just sat in my chair shaking my head from side to side.

There was a knock on the door.

"Come in," I called out.

Lewis walked into the office with a smile on his face. The odor was still on him but at the moment he and I weren't focused on it.

"Did you receive the same text that I received?" he asked. I just nodded my head. I couldn't utter a word. I couldn't even look at him. My mind was all over the place.

"So are you ready to be me?" He sat down in the chair in front of my desk. The smell that he had on him was now lingering too close. I pushed back from my desk just a little to put some more space in between him and me.

Ready to be him? I shuddered in my chair. Just the thought was unnerving.

The text that Mateo sent Lewis and me stated that we must switch lives for a week. Yes, I said a mutha-fuckin' week. Excuse the language but I was just that upset. I had to be and live the life of Lewis Turner for the next week and he had to be me. Shit just got even realer. I had to give him my keys to my house, car, my cell phone, passwords to my personal social networking sites: Facebook, Twitter, Instagram, and the others. Lewis had to do the same. I even had to dress like him. Oh God, the agony of thinking about dressing in anything he wore was too much. We also had to tell each other what to wear from day to day. And here is the ultimate kicker: he got to be the boss for the week. That shit didn't sit right with me at all. Mateo also said that there would be challenges inside of this challenge, and I didn't think I could take another thing outside of these specifics that he had already given us. What more could he make us do?

"It's whatever," I finally spoke up and looked him dead in the eyes. "The question is, are you ready to be me?"

"Shit, there isn't much to being you. All I have to do is walk around the world like I have a stick stuck up my ass and I will be just fine. I got this. Humph!" He crossed his leg over the other one and looked at me cocky.

"And replace the word *stick* with *dick* and I'll be just like you," I snapped back at him. I had to admit this contest thingy was changing me. It was bringing out the snappiness and sassiness in me.

He was quiet for a second.

"Whatever." He flung his hand flippantly in the air. "Just let Janice and the rest of the staff know that I'm running shit this week so we can get this show on the road. I already know you are not going to last two days being me." He got up out of the chair and began to unload his pockets on to my desk and then he scribbled his address down on one of the sticky tabs on my desk.

"Lewis, you're not boss material and you barely cut it as an employee. I'll give you two days until you come crying to me to take it back. So let's just face the facts; we are cut from two very different cloths: I'm Egyptian cotton and you're polyester." I got up and unloaded my pockets onto the desk as well and then I scribbled my address down on a sticky pad too. I could see that he was seething and trying to come up with something else to say.

"This is a winner's game, Lewis. A winner-take-all game. I'm moving into position to take all. Get ready, because I'm the best man and I'm going to win. That's all I do." I walked around the desk and stood in front of him and waited for him to speak.

"Please, I don't have any worries. They say all is fair in love and war. You better start worrying because I don't play fair. I play to win. Watch your back because, honey, I'm already in front and I'm about to run circles around you and leave your head spinning. Oh, and I'm going to need you here at seven A.M. instead of the normal eight A.M.; New captain and new rules. Check and mate." He walked around my desk, sat down in my comfy chair, and threw his legs up on the desk like it was his. I was fuming on the inside, but I said nothing. I just gathered his things off of the desk and walked out of my office.

It took some guts but I informed every one of my staff members of the temporary change. Everyone looked at me as if I had lost all of my senses. And my secretary Janice all but had a fit. Well, not a fit but her face sure did wrinkle up quite a bit. She checked my head for a fever and all. Lewis and she were not the best of friends and they had a "working" relationship and that was how it'd always been. She treated everyone with dignity and class, but she also handled Lewis with a long-handled spoon. She told me in confidence that he was too messy for her.

I left the office and walked down to the car garage. I searched for Lewis's car and when I found it I cringed again. I pulled off and started my way to my temporary home for a week. I was totally unprepared for this challenge. It was evident that Mateo was going to get even more drastic with his challenges until one of us gave in and walked away. I didn't plan on it and neither did I plan on walking into Lewis's living habitat. His and my styles and tastes were quite different. I walked into his place and was immediately blinded by the color schemes. It was like nothing I had ever seen before. He had blue furniture, drapes, and carpet in his living room, a purple bathroom, and his bedroom was green and red.

Don't get me wrong, everything was on point, but it was so over the top that at times I had to step back and look at what was really going on. He did have good taste it was just too damn colorful for me.

After I finally settled into his space, I took a shower and looked in his dresser drawers for something to sleep in. He even had neon pajamas. I'm talking about yellow and orange silk pajamas. Ugh! Thank God he wore regular underwear because if I saw anything lace I was going to be flying commando for the rest of the week. I went to sleep after climbing on a California king bed with about ten stuffed animals and pillows. Most of that shit was on the floor by the time I finished.

Chapter 32

Lewis

Normal

After I gloated and got used to my temporary office I made my way out of the office to stares of confusion and hate. Mainly from Janice, but, hey, I didn't give a fuck. *Her ass better be marching to the beat of a different drum come morning time.* I knew she didn't care for me but I didn't lose any sleep over it either.

I left the building and made my way to Kardell's car. I smiled when I opened the door and looked at the nice interior. His car was nice I had to admit. I got in, sat down, and closed the door. I started it up and the radio automatically came on. It was WEAA 88.9 FM, the jazz station. *Um, yeah, it gotsta go.* I flipped that dial to WERQ (Work) 92.3 FM or 92Q as most Baltimoreans called it and was immediately hyped up as Nicki Minaj's "Beez in the Trap" came on. I whipped his whip out of the garage like it was mine. I blasted 92Q jams all the way to my temporary home.

I got to his home and admired the neighborhood that he lived in. It was fabulous. A little too quiet for me but I was going to be livening things up in just a little bit. Yes, I was going to be having a blast up in his shit. For sure.

I parked his car and walked up to the immaculately done mini front yard. It had Kardell's stuck-up ass all over it. He was a perfectionist so now you know I had to mess some stuff up before I left his happy home.

I opened the door to his home and was immediately astonished at the detail of his living room. Everything was clean and neat. He was an earth-tone type of guy: browns, grays, taupe all covered his living room area. It was very uninteresting to me. No color or anything. It was just the way he dressed: plain and stuffy. He had body-length mirrors on the walls and pictures of his family strategically placed over a fireplace. I sat down on the couch and put my feet up on his nice stone and wood coffee table. I put my head back and folded my hands behind my head. I closed my eyes and took in the smell of his house. The smell of lavender and bamboo overpowered the scent that I was still carrying with me.

I was startled back to reality by the meow of a cat. My eyes shot open and down to the cat that was sitting down on the floor looking up at me. I wasn't a cat lover. I preferred a dog to a cat. I didn't do a pussy in any form. I didn't make any sudden moves because I didn't want to startle him and send him on some type of tirade causing me to have to play kickball with him as the ball. I eased up back into an upright position and looked at his needy-looking eyes. He wanted to be rubbed, I assumed. I took a chance and petted his head first. He reacted with no resistance. So I took it a step further and decided to rub his back. He received that as well as the lower part of his body lifted off of the ground and into the air with the front of him lowering a bit.

"Look at that. You a ho just like your master pretend he's not." I laughed to myself.

After rubbing the cat a few more times I decided to go and shower to get this smell off of me. I walked up his steps into the second floor of his house and it was pretty much the same as the rest of the house: plain and boring. The cat trailed me everywhere I went. He was worse than a man who received a good blow job from me.

I found Kardell's linen closet and grabbed me a fresh towel and washcloth. Even that closet was organized to the max. I wasn't a messy person by far but his shit was borderline obsessive. I understood being neat but he was a neat freak.

I showered for a good forty-five minutes, because I had to get that smell off of me. Two days of no show-ering was horrible and I felt like I had to make up for it double time. I didn't know how I did it. It had to be that got-to-win attitude that I had. I was an at-all-cost winner for sure. Yes, I planned on throwing a little dirt around before it was all said and done.

I walked out of the bathroom with a towel wrapped around my waist. I was smelling good and looked for something on his dresser to cause me to smell even better. And as you guessed, his toiletries were all aligned perfectly, too. I picked up some lotion and smoothed that on my already-perfect skin. That was one of the best things that Mateo loved about me and I wasn't going to deny the man the luxury of my soft and smooth skin forever.

After getting all prepped for bed I decided that I was going to sleep in the nude and leave my scent on his bed every day that I was here.

Chapter 33

Kardell

Out of Control

"This is not going to fly with me." I spoke to myself as I stood in front of the mirror and looked at the outfit that Lewis texted me this morning. "Lavender pants and shirt with a turquoise tie and matching shoes. Who dresses like this? This is an Easter outfit or something." I shook my head in embarrassment toward myself. I couldn't believe I was going to walk out of his house like this. I knew Lewis was going to enjoy my embarrassment that I would feel at work with these clothes on. I couldn't even smile. It definitely looked like something he would wear. I was a suit man all the way and I did earth-tone/neutral colors when I dressed for work and most of my non-working attire was the same.

But I did leave the house. I ran to his car like I was Beyoncé and the paparazzi were chasing me. I pulled off and headed to work on my first day as Lewis.

I walked into the building and the lobby attendant looked at me and laughed. He was usually a very quiet guy but today I was a spectacle for him to get his jollies off of. I really wanted to go into hiding.

I couldn't get on the elevator fast enough. I arrived at my floor and exited the elevator. I had to stand in front of the door to get myself together before I went inside the office.

"Good morning, everyone," I greeted them all with a smile. They weren't so kind. The looks of shock were all over their faces. I had to admit that I wasn't shocked. I did the same thing to Lewis from time to time when he wore these clothes.

"Wow," was all that Janice could say as I approached her desk. Her mouth was gapped open in shock. But she never asked me what was going on. I was glad because explaining my current situation would be too hard for me to do. I still couldn't believe I was doing all of this for a man.

I left her desk and made my way back to Lewis's work area. She walked with me.

"Sir, he is out of control already," she said in a hushed tone. When we finally made it to his work area I sat down and looked at his confusingly arranged desk.

"What has he done?" I asked.

"He's just being his overbearing and outspoken self." She looked at me, annoyed. "He wants his coffee at a specific temperature or I have to make it over until it is correct. He wants me to type up senseless memos every half hour. He even put me on a restroom schedule. He even had the nerve to ask me if I had on a bra because my breasts were 'low and offensive.' I don't know if I can take him for a week. And I am not the only one he's offended."

"It won't be for long. Trust me," I tried to reassure her.

"It's only been an hour and that has been too long already." She leaned in and whispered.

"Excuse me, but, Janice, your work area is empty. Shouldn't you be in it? You don't get paid to hold conversations. You get paid to pick up the phone. I know you are over the hill but acting like it can get you replaced." Lewis spoke as he came up behind us like a cat burglar. We both jumped because he startled both of us. We turned to see an all-too-serious look on his face. Janice made her way back to her area while Lewis handed me my work agenda for the day.

"This needs to be done by the end of the work day. No excuses." He didn't even wait for a reply before he walked off back toward my office.

He has lost his damn mind. I shuffled through the pile of work he handed me. It looked like it was going to take me a long time to get this done. If this was going to be his attitude for the next few days then crazy outfits were going to be the last thing I had to worry about. I had to pray that my staff could hold out until I got the reins back to this ship I was the original captain of.

The rest of the day I had a few of my associates pull me up in the break room, bathroom, and even a broom closet about Lewis and his newfound power. I actually laughed at one of them who threatened a beside-his-car beat down. I thought they were serious too, but I talked them out of it.

I had to admit that it was pretty cool to not be in charge for a few days and things still got done in spite of Lewis's antics and attitude.

Like his constant timing of everything he assigned me or another worker. One time he even stood by his desk and watched me work. Also, his nagging comments to me or one of the other workers I overheard like, "You should have finished this by now," "Do this over, it's not good enough," or my personal favorite, "Do I have to hire a monkey to do your job?" I had to admit the last one was funny.

He also called two meetings to tell us and reprimand us about productivity and he even got on a few staff members' wardrobes. The words tacky, horrendous, and trashy were used unsparingly and he even made one of the female workers cry when he said she looked like she was dressed by Ray Charles and her hair was cut by Edward Scissorhands.

This challenge was not as hard as I thought it was going to be. A bit trying at times but other than the persistent ringing of his phone from his family and friends it was okay being Lewis for the week.

It was the last full day of this challenge and I had to say I would be glad to get back into my home and my clothes. I was really tired of looking like a different box of crayons during the week. I just knew that I was going to end up on one of those hotmess.com Web sites with the outfits he had me wearing.

Tomorrow I was going to work and switch back to being me at the end of the day. I was stretched out on one of Lewis's chaises daydreaming about Mateo. I couldn't help but wonder what it was going to be like in a solid relationship with him. I hadn't seen him since the day in the museum and he said his prize to whoever won was a very special place in his life and home. I was antsy to say the least.

The sound of Rihanna's "Birthday Cake" song rang out into the quiet atmosphere, breaking me out of my daydreaming. The first time I heard his ringer I was in the local Cheesecake Factory eating by myself and forgot to turn the ringer off. I was completely and utterly embarrassed. I had only known the song from going to the club a few times and hearing it but having it as a ringtone on your cell phone was a bit much for me. I put it on vibrate immediately. I couldn't wait to give him this phone back and get my simple ringing phone back.

It was a text from Mateo. It was our next challenge. I gasped at what it instructed me to do before I went to bed. For a few seconds I couldn't breathe or think. I was floored once again. This was the first legitimate time I considered bailing out and letting Lewis have Mateo. This was too much: over the top and unfathomable.

Chapter 34

Lewis

Ass Out

Now I was one for loving attention and getting it almost at all or any cost. Right now I was on the edge of Kardell's bed reading the next challenge for Kardell and me. I was beyond speechless. The ramifications of this next challenge were innumerable. I mean who thought of this type of thing? This was the first time that I truly considered calling it quits and letting Kardell have Mateo. This was one of those "fuck it" moments for me. I read the text out loud just to make sure I read it right.

"Two beautiful men and two visions of loveliness. Share your beauty with the world. You have each other's phone and access to each other's Facebook and Twitter accounts. Take one photo of yourself the way you came into this world, tag each other, and enjoy the attention from the world. May the best man win." I threw the phone onto the bed and walked away from it. I walked into the bathroom and looked at myself in the mirror and started to have a conversation with myself. I did this at times when I made a critical decision in my life. It was a secret security mechanism for me.

"I love me but am I ready to let the world see me in all of my glory?" I lifted up my shirt and looked at my magnificent chest. "I mean my entire family is on

Facebook. The backlash from this could destroy me. Or it could make me famous." I laughed a little at the thought of being famous for being naked.

"The biggest question is, is it all worth it?" I cocked my head to the side as I wondered.

"I could have it all if I am willing to show it all?" I pondered out loud. "I mean you see it on television and even in books but when you are in a situation like this one it's real and a wrong turn could mean a drastic change in life, good or bad. What the hell am I going to do? I'm going to fucking do it. You only live once." I pumped myself up.

So I got myself all shined up and glistening for the camera. If I was going to be nude I was definitely going to be fabulous and memorable. Kardell had a top-of-the-line phone so it had a fifteen-second timer and it took multiple shots. I lay across his bed and had the phone positioned on the dresser across from the bed. I was nervous but it was all or nothing and after all that I had done thus far I was not ending up with nothing. I knew that Kardell was too scared to do something like this and this probably would be the winning challenge for me. I took a few test shots and they ended up coming out really good. So I did the real thing and pressed SEND once I found the one that was the most flattering. I made sure I tagged myself in this picture so that I would complete the whole challenge.

It didn't take long for Kardell's phone to start blowing up with likes and comments. I was too afraid to look at the comments so I just shut down the phone and went to sleep for the night.

I couldn't possibly imagine the attention or the kind of attention that I was going to get when tomorrow came but I was ready.

Chapter 35

Kardell

Just Do It

I paced Lewis's floor for what seemed like hours, but in actuality it was only a half hour. I was thinking about giving up on being with Mateo and just moving on with my life. I just wanted to throw in the towel and give in to my destiny to be alone. I was thinking about the consequences of this last challenge. I was weighing the pros and the cons. It was something I did often. Even with which company I was going to do an advertising campaign for.

Quitting was almost never an option for me. Quitting usually gets you nowhere. I was going places in my profession but my love life was on life support and I did want to pull the plug on it now.

The buzzing of Lewis's phone brought me out of my thoughts. I walked over to the dresser where I had it charging to see a quite a few Facebook notifications. There was a picture I was tagged in by Lewis. I clicked on the link and his naked body was strewn across my bed in a seductive pose as if he was doing a shoot for *Do Me* magazine. My mouth gapped open in shock and awe. The number of likes was close to the hundreds and the comments from some were tasteful and some very raunchy and that was coming from some of my friends. Thank God I didn't have that many family members as friends. In fact, I only had my sister as a friend on there. They were asking who he was and what the hell was wrong with him. I could only assume that they were blowing up my phone by now with questions. I knew I would have done the same thing under the same circumstances.

I closed the app and set the phone back down on the dresser. I walked away from the dresser and practically threw myself onto Lewis's bed. This was one of the hardest decisions I had to make in a long time. The first one was coming out to my parents, but this one would overshadow that one by far. All I had to do was do it. Like the Nike commercial said, "Just do it." I wasn't the "just do it" type. At least I wasn't until today.

But after seeing Lewis bearing it all and not looking bad doing it I wanted to be free and wild for a change and not care about what people thought. I wanted the prize at the end of the maze and the pot of gold at the end of the rainbow. I wasn't going to let Lewis win. Mateo had everything I wanted in a man or partner, plus he was patient and caring. I wanted all of that. I even thought about closing up my business and moving on with him into the lap of luxury and leisure. I wanted the good life and the work-free life and I was willing to risk it all to get it.

So I stripped right there in the middle of Lewis's bedroom. I showered, shaved the appropriate areas of my body, and then oiled up like I was a body builder getting ready for a shoot.

"Kardell, you can do this. Just step outside of your comfort zone and do it. Just do it," I coached myself.

It didn't take long for me to do it. I took the picture and then looked at it for several minutes before I uploaded it to Lewis's page. I tagged me in it and then I closed the app. Almost instantly the phone began to vibrate with notifications and then it started to ring like crazy. I eventually shut it off when I checked his inbox and people were asking for my number and giving me theirs. I was flattered at first and then shame came over me. I knew I didn't need to be embarrassed about being nude since I was born nude. I was afraid of what it was going to do to my business. For the most part I kept my business affairs away from my personal page but in this world you never know who knows who.

I went to sleep that night full of anxiety of the impending bombardment of attention I might receive tomorrow, but also pride because of something I wouldn't normally have done. I was glad I did it. *And if anybody asks me why I'll just say I lost a bet.* I was so glad that at the close of business tomorrow I will be getting my life and title back and hopefully beating out Lewis in this next challenge or two. *I am going to sleep a winner.*

Chapter 36

Lewis

Hate Me

As soon as I woke up this morning I cut Kardell's phone back on to see a text from Mateo congratulating me on my completion of the challenge. He again told me that I was in the lead. I was elated by that news. He also said that the next challenge would be coming soon.

Today I walked into the office and everyone was in an uproar. I guessed that my nude picture had everyone talking. I couldn't say I was super excited for everyone to be looking at me but attention was attention. I ate it all up.

"Good morning, Janice," I greeted her as I walked up to her desk. She didn't even look at me in the eye. I didn't know if she had a Facebook page but I was sure she saw my picture from someone in the office. I was friends with at least one or two people here in the office. I still didn't care because I was fabulous and gave them a picture of all of my fabulousness. I wanted to tell them to eat their hearts out but I didn't. I just let them stare and gawk.

"Good morning, Mr. Turner." She spoke in a very low voice as if she was embarrassed for me.

"Listen." I turned around to speak to the few workers that were standing about. "I am proud of my body and live my life for me. Don't feel sorry for me or pity me. Half of y'all don't have nearly as much guts as I do. Well, literally some of y'all do, but that's neither here nor there. I love me and now you'll have another reason to hate on me. Well hate away and while you're doing it print my picture out and paste that shit on your mirror so you can remind yourself of what you need to work toward, because I have most of y'all beat in every category of life. Now suck on them lemons."

I turned, threw my head up in the air, and proudly walked into my temporary office and closed the door behind me. Being in charge this last past week was nice but it has had its cons; being in charge of everything was just that. You had to make sure the workers were working efficiently. I had to make sure that payroll was in on time. I had to know who was late and who was sick. I had to know what projects needed to be done and what order things needed to done in. I had to make sure contractors and laborers got paid on time. I was busy calling this person and calling that person. Work work work. I had to come down harder on the others because this was too much for me. I didn't want them to know that though. I didn't know how Kardell kept his sanity having to all of this. *I will be glad to give the reins back over to him shortly. It was a lesson learned. I will be glad to just be an employee again.*

I was in the office for an hour before Kardell walked into the office. I had mercy on him and his lateness because I knew he was having a rough moment this morning. The look on his face was one of seriousness, but I could see some shame hiding in there, too. I got a look at his nude shot this morning and had to say that he was good-looking naked, too. He wasn't me but he sure did give me a run for my money.

Chapter 37

Kardell

Give It Up

"Good morning, Lewis." I walked up to my desk as he proudly sat behind it. He looked good in one of my least favorite suits. The picture of him nude flashed before me for a second as I spoke to him. It was etched in my mind.

"Good morning." He spoke with a hint of jealousy.

"So I see you went through with the challenge last night," I said as I took a seat in front of him. "Nice job." I was trying my best not to sound condescending. By the look on his face I could tell it wasn't working.

"Yes, as did you." He spoke with a smirk that said "so what." "It was, um, cute." I could tell he was trying to be nice. He was a good actor but he could never win an award for his unsavory performance as a nice person.

"Cute, huh?" I repeated.

"Yes, that is what I said. I see your hearing is leaving you in your old age." He laughed lightly.

"No, everything about me is just fine. But you know that already since you saw my flawlessness for yourself." I smirked and gave him a side eye. "You didn't think I would do it did you? You probably thought you had this in the bag?"

"Kardell, I wasn't the *least* bit worried about you or anything you do or have done. Lewis is a top performer in anything he does in life. Shit, I even got your job down pat in a week. I'm a monster and I devour people like you for breakfast. You should just give it up and retire with a few more cats like the one you have at home. That's what an old maid does right?"

"Old maid?" I huffed. "Don't get this twisted, Lewis. I'm only a few years older than you and much more experienced. They say experience is the best teacher and I'm about to show you better than I can tell you. I think *you* should give it up and move on with your life. Besides, by the response from your picture I think you would do good in the porn business since you got ho written all over you."

"Actually I can say that I'm impressed with how long you have lasted. I didn't think you could or would take that stick out of your ass. I guess you did take it out long enough to take the picture. We all know who the real ho in the room is. If I'm one I know you're one. As they say, it takes one to know one and you called me out first, so hi, ho." He laughed and waved at me.

I had to admit that it was a good one.

"Lewis." I laughed lightly to myself. "Poor Lewis. You don't even know when you are being played. Mateo just feels sorry for you. That's why he didn't let you down at the museum. We both know that you won't fit in his world. You can't turn a ho into a housewife but you damn sure can string them along. You're a puppet being played like you're Pinocchio. You should let me cut the strings now so you don't end up in the box of 'used' toys like the rest of the hand-me-down hoes."

His mouth gaped open for a few seconds.

"Close your mouth, honey, there are no dicks around for you to suck on," I said as I got up and proceeded to walk out of the door. I didn't even leave him time to come back.

That confrontation was long overdue. I tried to treat him like I wanted to be treated and I have encouraged the other workers to do the same even when they wanted to curse him or even punch him in his sarcastic mouth. I'd been taking his craziness with his mouth toward me and toward my staff all week long and I wanted to say something long before now. I just didn't want him to take me out of my character in front of the others. I wanted to keep my reputation as the poised one and the one who always conducted himself professionally in the workplace. It was like he was trying to make me step out of character. I think he wanted me to act up with him in front of everyone, but I held my ground. It wasn't easy to watch him on his power trip. I just couldn't take it anymore. I had to get out on him. I had to admit that it indeed felt good to get a few good quips in on him to put him back in his place. The little bit of power had gone to his head.

Chapter 38

Lewis

How Low Can You Go?

I sat at Kardell's desk, stunned from his last comment. I had to admit I did underestimate him. He was just as fiery as I was on the inside. He just had to tap in. But he didn't know just how low I would stoop to get the man I wanted. *I have a trick up my sleeve to deliver what will make sure that I am the one who wins.*

The rest of the day went by smoothly and I was very happy to give Kardell back everything that was his and go back to my world. That challenge was cute but I loved being me and living my life carefree. I learned some things about me and what I could handle and I was very pleased. I thought I did a good job with this challenge and I was sure I was a better person for making it through.

As soon as I got my phone back I checked my voice mail. There were several messages from my sister and even one from my brother asking me to explain myself and my actions. They sounded like they wanted to have a heavy conversation like I knew my parents would. I was so glad that my parents and most of their friends stayed away from social networks because I would not be looking forward to explaining my actions to them. And I didn't have to worry about my brother or sister blabbing because I had dirt on them that exceeded crazy in comparison to my nude picture on Facebook.

I also got a voice mail from my bestie asking to urgently meet up with me to discuss this "lewd" photo as he called it. So that was where I was headed to after work. I didn't need to explain anything to anyone but being honest with him was something I could do and not be offended when he gave it to me raw (no pun intended).

I also checked my e-mail and found one from Facebook saying that they deleted my inappropriate photo and would delete my account if it happened again. I just laughed and moved on with my day.

"Hey, boo." I kissed Dennis on the forehead as I sat down at one of our usual outside café spots. He was in the middle of a conversation when I arrived and sat down. The waiter came over and I gave him my order. By the time I finished ordering he had ended his conversation on the phone.

He just looked at me and shook his head from side to side in disapproval.

"What?" I smiled, playing like I didn't know what he was gesturing about.

"So this is as low as they go now to get a man. You just throwing random nude photos out there and seeing who you can get. Has it come to that nowadays? Is the dating pool that small now?"

"You have to admit that I looked fabulous," I shamelessly gloated.

"You looked like a hoes-r-us model," he countered.

"Throwing shade I see."

"No shade, just some tea."

"Yeah, okay," I said, brushing him off.

"What were you thinking about doing something so crazy?"

"I'm living my life."

"Lewis, this is not you. I admit you are wild at times and you have diarrhea of the lip at times too but this is way over the top even for you. What would make you do something like this?" Dennis asked.

"I'm doing this for me."

"I think you are doing this because the last man we discussed dumped you and you are crying out for attention."

"Wrong," I snapped, with an attitude. "I didn't get dumped. It's quite the opposite actually."

"You dumped him?"

"No, no one dumped anyone."

"Well, what the hell *is* going on?"

"You wouldn't understand if I told you," I answered. "Plus you are so quick to judge." *I know I've said that I don't mind him being honest with me but sometimes I just want him to listen and not give his opinion.* I wanted him to hear me out.

"I don't judge. I just assess a situation and give my feedback constructively."

"Since when?" I asked rhetorically. "I can't remember a time when I told you something and you haven't given me unwanted feedback instead of just listening."

"Okay, okay, I'll just listen this time and if you want me to give you my opinion just ask."

"For real?" I asked him seriously.

"Yes, my lips will be tighter than your virgin ass at twelve." He laughed. I did as well.

"Okay, so here it goes." I paused to get my breath and thoughts together. "The guy I am dating is fabulous, money, good-looking, charming, and patient. He treats me like a king. He's all that I've been looking for in a man. But there is a catch. My boss wants him too. So the guy says he likes us both and can't choose between the both of us. He proposes a contest and gives us challenges that we must complete to see who the best man for him is. One of those challenges was to post that nude picture of me on Facebook and Twitter."

"So you are saying two grown men are humiliating themselves to get a man?" He looked at me like I was crazy.

"You're judging and it's not humiliating; it's actually quite exhilarating. I feel freer than I ever have in life." I smiled proudly.

"If that is how you feel then okay." He smiled. It was a fake smile. I knew he wanted to respond even further but I didn't give him permission to and I knew it was killing him to keep all he wanted to say bottled up. The expression on his face spoke volumes.

"Go ahead and speak your piece. I know you want to so bad."

"No, I'm good."

"Dennis, please. If your leg shakes any harder I'd think you were a grasshopper getting ready to take off."

"Okay, I think you and your boss are crash dummies in waiting."

"Huh?" I asked, confused.

"So this guy just says 'I can't choose between either of you so let me run game on you and then decide on who the biggest dummy is so I can take him home'?"

"It's not what you think. It's quite entertaining," I rebutted.

"I bet it is . . . for him," he countered. "Both of you guys are very attractive guys. I saw your boss's picture, too. Why would you two allow him to make you guys do things to win him over? Both of you guys have degrees but you are acting quite dumb for a man you don't know fully."

"I know enough. I know what I want." I spoke confidently and convincingly.

"Yes, but what does he want? You ever think about that?" He looked at me intensely.

"He wants the same thing I do: companionship."

"I sure hope so because it looks like he's playing 'how low can you go" to me." He shook his head like he was disappointed in me.

"Man, it's not like that at all." I waved my hand like I was dismissing him and all that he said. "Besides I got this in the bag. Pretty soon I'm going to be moving up and begin to be a kept man just like you."

He just looked at me and smiled. He didn't say anything else to me about the situation. In fact he steered the conversation in another direction all together.

"So guess who is getting married?" He smiled with glee and then he stuck his hand across the table, showing off the ring that was on his finger.

"Oh shit, he proposed." I bounced a little in my chair with genuine excitement.

"Yes, he sure did," Dennis said as his eyes began to get a little watery. He grabbed a napkin that was on the table and dried the corner of his eyes.

"Look at this drama queen over here crying and shit." I smiled as I looked at Dennis having his moment. "When did this happen?"

"About two days ago. We were at the launch of my new clothing line. I had walked my way down the runway at the finale of the show and he surprised me by coming out with a microphone and getting on one knee and proposing to me in front of all of the people in attendance."

"Awwwwww. That was so beautiful. I know you let him fuck you in every hole but your nostril that night," I joked.

"You are a damn fool, but you ain't never lied. He got it good that night." We high-fived each other.

"You guys have a date yet? I asked.

"Not yet but it will be a great event. And hopefully you and your man will be in attendance."

"Oh we will be," I said with confidence.

The rest of the evening went by with us laughing and joking just like we normally did. I couldn't stay mad at him because I knew he was only trying to look out for me, but I felt like I knew what was best for me and I was doing what was best for me.

Chapter 39

Kardell

Just Believe Me

I was exhausted after I left work. I didn't even check the many voice mails I knew I got when Lewis handed me back my phone. I just put it in my pocket and made my way home. I got home at the usual time that I did after work, but there was something different about this time when I arrived at my home. My sister was sitting on my steps waiting for me arrive. To say that I was surprised was an understatement. I immediately went in to high alert.

"Good evening, Angela," I spoke as I walked up on her. "Is everything okay?"

"I was going to ask you the same thing." She looked at me curiously.

"What do you mean?"

"Let's go into your house before we have this conversation," she suggested. "It's not one you want to have outside."

"Okay," I said and then I walked past her and up my stairs toward my door. I opened my door and walked into my house. I was so relieved to be home. There was no place like home. From the looks of things everything was still in place.

"Make yourself at home," I said as I walked toward the flight of stairs that led to my second floor. "I'll be right back."

I went upstairs and checked out my bathroom and bedroom to see if everything was okay. I had some linen that needed to be washed, but other than that Lewis left everything just as he found it. I changed out of the last ridiculous outfit from Lewis's ensemble and put it in a bag to return to him on Monday. I grabbed some sweat pants and a shirt and threw them on for comfort. I walked back downstairs to join my sister, who was patiently waiting for my return.

"So what do you want to talk to me about?" I asked as I got comfortable on my sofa like she was.

"I just wanted to know if you had lost your mind." She looked at me seriously.

"Excuse me?" I asked, confused.

"Kardell, don't act like there isn't a picture of you naked floating around on Facebook. You didn't think I would see it?"

"If it was on my page wouldn't it be apparent that I didn't care what people thought?" I spoke with more attitude than I should have been speaking with. I was a defensive person when you got into my business. That was a no-no and most people who were close to me knew it.

"No need to be nasty, Kardell. I was just concerned and since you didn't answer the phone or e-mail I sent you I thought a house call would do the trick."

"I appreciate the concern, but everything is just fine," I assured her while looking at her in the eyes.

"Kardell, you have been this overly conservative guy all of your life and you want me to believe that everything is all right when I see a nude picture of my brother pop up in my news feed?" She looked at me intently, waiting for me to answer her question.

"I don't care what you believe, but as they say 'seeing is believing.' You saw, now I'm telling you to believe me when I say I'm good."

"Kardell, are you that lonely that you would place a photo like that to get attention?"

"I'm not lonely," I assured her.

"Okay, let's say I believe you." She looked at me doubtingly and then continued to talk. "What other reason would you of all people be doing posting a nude picture of yourself online, especially Facebook?"

"I could have sworn that this was a free country that allowed freedom of expression," I said defensively.

"Kardell, I'm your big sister, cut the crap with me. Be real with me. This shit is not about no damn expression. This is on some desperation type of shit. I know some desperate shit when I see it and your ass is desperate. Either that or it's about a man."

"Angela, I'm not desperate."

"So it's about a man then?" She looked at me curiously. Like I'd said before me and my sister weren't the closest of siblings, but now I felt a little more comfortable with her to share something personal with her.

"Yes, it's about a man," I admitted.

"What kind of man would ask you to do something like that? Most kinky men keep that kind of stuff behind closed doors. But I guess times are different." She shrugged her shoulders.

"He's a very good guy, all that I want in a companion and lover."

"His ass must have laid down the pipe real good to have you exposing yourself to the world."

"We haven't done that yet. He's been the perfect gentleman." I smiled proudly.

"So you're saying you and him didn't get busy yet and you going to these lengths for him?"

"No, it's a little more complicated than that. Let me explain."

"By all means, make me a believer." She sat back and crossed her legs, waiting for me to spill my guts. This was new territory for us. Again, sharing my business was not something I did with anyone. But I guessed it was safe to go ahead and tell her. Part of me wanted to share it anyway. I just hoped she didn't start judging me about my decisions. That was something I hated as well.

"The guy I am dating is fabulous, money, good-looking, charming, and patient. He treats me like a king. He's all that I've been looking for in a man. But there is a catch. My employee wants him, too. So the guy says he likes us both and can't choose between the both of us. He proposes a contest and gives us challenges that we must complete to see who the best man for him is. One of those challenges was to post that nude picture of me on Facebook and Twitter."

"You're joking right?" She looked at me in disbelief and even chuckled a little. "Please tell me you're joking."

"No jokes."

"Okay, let me get this straight. You and this other guy both have college degrees?"

"Yes." I nodded my head.

"Did y'all buy them from Kmart or something? You all can't be letting this guy get you to degrade yourself to see which one he wants. I know it's hard out here to get a good man but has it really come to this?"

"It's not what you think. He's not playing us. He's just seeing who will fight for him and be in his corner no matter what."

"If that's what you believe," she said doubtfully.

"I do believe it and him. Just watch and see when all of this is over you'll get to meet him and see how sweet he really is. Just believe me. I'm going to win and live happily ever after."

"I sure hope so." Angela patted me on the leg.

"You know I am really surprised that you really cared enough to come over here and talk to me about this. You know there is a thing they invented called the phone," I said sarcastically, yet playfully.

"I know, I called, and you didn't answer so I decided to make a person to person visit. I needed to look at you in your face. Eyes don't lie but the mouth will. You have always been quiet and sneaky. Plus I know we don't always get along but I really do care about you and the things that go on in your life." She sounded sincere as she spoke.

"I know you do. And I know that you love me in your own smart-ass way." I laughed and then continued. "And believe me I hear what you are saying. I just need you to trust in me and be there for me when I need you to be. And keep some of them smart-ass comments to yourself."

"Okay." She laughed. "But I can't promise you that all of the time. This mouth has a mind of its own and I can only control but so much that comes out of it."

"Okay, let's take it one day at a time," I said and then smiled. It felt good to be a little closer to a sibling.

"All right, brother, come over here and give me a hug so we can seal the deal and I can go about my business." We hugged for a few seconds and then pulled apart.

"And whatever we discuss stays between us," she said assuredly.

She didn't stay at my house much longer. I was actually happy that we got a chance to interact civilly. I was glad that we brought some type of resolution to our feuding even if it took her seeing me butt-ass naked on Facebook to do it.

Chapter 40

Lewis

Blind Ambition

When I returned home after my outing with Dennis I was just happy to be home. I surveyed my home and for the most part Kardell left everything in very decent shape. I wasn't worried about him being a slob, it was just the fact that someone else was living in my home for a week. His scent lingered on my furniture and I wasn't fond of that. I Febrezed everything I could to get it smelling the way I loved it.

I showered and primped myself for a nice slumber in my bed. I was just getting nice and cozy when my telephone chimed, letting me know I had a text message.

I rolled over to look at the message. I smiled because it was the last challenge from Mateo. It instructed me to get dressed if I wasn't and to wait outside of my apartment for someone to pick me up.

I did as I was told. I waited for about ten minutes before an all-black sedan with tinted windows pulled up. It looked just like the one that Mateo always picked me up in. The back door opened and I hopped in. I was blindfolded and duct tape covered my mouth. My heart was racing because I felt like this was it. I was going to complete this challenge and then walk off with the prize. I was going to leave all of this behind me.

Yes, I was apprehensive about where I was going and who I was with but I pushed caution to the wind and focused myself and my mind on the matter at hand. I was going to win. Besides, Mateo hadn't ever given me a reason to not trust him and I wasn't going to start now.

The ride was yet another long ride and I was getting antsy, and anticipation filled every part of me.

Then the car came to a stop. The back door opened and I was carefully helped out of the car as if I was precious cargo. I was led by the hand to an unknown location and we stopped. I heard a door being opened and I was once again led by the hand. The person leading me never said a word to me, just led me down a long hallway. All you heard was the sound of our footsteps hitting the floor as we walked. It was a warm environment wherever we were. Then we stopped once again. Another door was opened and I was led in once again. I was led to and sat down on what I assumed was a bed. Breathing only through my nose was weird for me. I couldn't speak nor could I see. They say that other senses get heightened when others are cut off. I could hear and smell. I heard only quietness and the smell was of nothing.

"Scoot back and lie still." I heard Mateo's voice speak into my ear. "This one last challenge is for you to do the unthinkable. Something you've never done before. This will prove to me if you are the best man for me. When you hear the door shut again you may remove your blindfold." That was all that he said. I wanted to reach out and touch his face but I didn't want to ruin anything by making any sudden moves. A few seconds later the door shut again.

I quickly pulled the blindfold off of my face. I blinked my eyes as I tried to focus them. When they began to focus I saw that I was in a room with low light and a very romantic setting, but what else I saw was something that blew my mind. There was a completely naked lady standing in the room. She was gorgeous. A vision of flawless beauty.

She walked over to me seductively. "Are you ready?"

I nodded my head but I didn't know what for. She then began to unbutton my pants and pulled them down to my ankles and she did the same for my underwear. Then it clicked in my mind. *He said do something I've never done before. A woman. I've never done a woman before.* Nervousness suddenly enveloped me because I was never attracted to a woman. Ever.

She put her hand on my penis and began to massage it. She was trying to make it hard, but it wasn't working. She tried and tried but nothing happened. In my mind I was trying to conjure up a fantasy with a man, any man, to get the blood flowing to my nether regions. But it wasn't working. All I could think about was the woman with her hands on my manhood trying to raise it from the dead. Then she went down on me and tried to give me a blow job. She was working feverishly but it was still to no avail. It was like working with a limp spaghetti noodle. She looked at me as I frowned in anguish. I began to thrust in her mouth to give some momentum but that too was a failed effort. *I can't believe that he would have given me this challenge.* This was not what I was prepared for. Who could prepare for this? Why would he do this knowing I would fail? Or did he think I would do it and cut me off for fear that I would one day leave him for a woman? I didn't have a clue and I was upset about it now.

I felt heartbroken as she got up and looked at me with disappointment all over her face. I was still duct taped. I moaned for her to try again. But alas it was proven that in the fifteen minutes that she tried it wasn't happening. I was not a happy camper. I was devastated. She placed the blindfold back on and then I heard the door open and close again. Tears ran down the sides of my face and my heart sank because I knew that I had failed the challenge.

I banged my hands on the sides of the bed in a fit but ceased when I heard the door opening again. The person walked to the side of my bed. They pulled my clothes back up and then pulled me from the bed. We took the same trip that I took for me to get here. The entire ride back home I slouched in disappointment. When the car stopped, the blindfold and the duct tape were removed from over my eyes and mouth. The door open and this time I was instructed to get out. The car pulled off, leaving me standing there in front of my place of residence. I felt like a huge failure. I was sick to my stomach.

I walked the few steps to my door and went in. I wasn't feeling my best. I felt like I had lost everything. I felt cheated.

I went to bed that night confused and hurt but I was not going to work that way. I was going to fake it in hopes of another chance because that was what I texted Mateo before I went to bed that night/early morning.

I wanted another chance, another challenge, because I couldn't lose to Kardell and look him in the face every day at work. I just couldn't do it.

It was the Monday after the challenge and I was back at work dressed to impress but feeling like a wreck on the inside. I didn't do anything the whole weekend. I just lay in bed with the covers over my head. I didn't sleep much, bathed little, and I ate very little food. I didn't hear anything else from Mateo for the rest of the weekend and it almost drove me crazy. I couldn't believe that I lost the challenge. I got all the way to the end and lost. I was devastated. I didn't think that it was fair but as some people say "you win some you lose some"; but I didn't care about losing at this moment. Winning was everything and only losers said that shit. I felt so close and then to see it all slip through my fingers was just too much.

I went into the bathroom and cried at least twice today. There was still no word from Mateo. I knew why and it didn't take a genius to figure out that I had lost and it was over for me. I was now stuck at this job to look at my boss and all the rest of these boring people. *I know I am going to have to fuck a few good men to get over this one.* I just couldn't stand losing and then having to look into the smug and fake face of the winner. That shit was for the birds.

I watched my boss work today and he was pretending like he lost and that things were back to normal. I wanted run up to him and spit in his face and walk out of this muthafucka for good. But I didn't do that. I just held my ground and moved on with my life like I was supposed to do. I knew I was going dick hunting as soon as I got off. I was so pissed off that an orgy sounded just like it might make me forget all of this. At least that was what I hoped.

But that was short-lived. My work day had ended and I was headed home to get ready to go out and treat myself to some distractions. Just as I was about to leave I received a text message from Mateo that changed my whole mood. Two simple words: You Win.

I fell to my knees in sheer happiness and joy. A few tears escaped my eyes as I looked around my office.

Another text came through telling me to leave everything and meet Mateo at a specified location. I drove my car to a desolate place in Baltimore County, Maryland. There was a car waiting for me there. I got out of my car and practically jumped into the back of the same type of black car I had been in before. This time Mateo was in the back seat waiting for me.

"I'm so glad to be here." I spoke with sincerity.

"I'm glad as well." He smiled. "I can't wait to show you your spot in my life so just lay back and enjoy the ride."

I did just that. I laid my head back on the seat next to Mateo. The whole ride I smiled in victory. Winning felt good. No, winning felt great.

"We have arrived." Mateo's sweet voice said to me. I stretched a little as he got out and walked around to open the door for me. I got out and looked up at the same mansion that I had come to before. I smiled as I looked at my new home. I couldn't believe that this was all mines.

"Are you ready to spend forever with me?" he spoke as he gently turned me toward him.

"Yes, I was born ready. Here is where I belong." I wanted to kiss him passionately but didn't want to seem like the ho I used to be. But let it be known that I was going to rock his world when we did get to the bedroom.

"Well let's go," he said as he put his hand on the small of my back and we walked toward his home.

"There is something I want to show you." We walked down a small hallway until we got to a room filled with books. He pulled on a book and a door slid open just like in a superhero's house, but this was real life and I was impressed and curious as to what he was going to show me.

The door revealed a set of steps that was surrounded with naked brick walls. As we went down the stairs the temperature changed from warm to chilly in seconds.

The door behind us closed automatically with two clicks following it. Mateo was a rich guy and all that I could think about was the huge amount of money, jewels, and pricey valuables he had stored down here. He was about to show me his secret stash and I was excited. I was going to be, as Rick James said it, "I'm rich, bitch." I floated down the hall with Mateo until we came to a door. He punched a few keys into a keypad near the door and the door slowly slid open. We walked in as the lights fluttered on, illuminating the entire room.

What I saw before me made my heart drop.

"This is where you will be staying." Mateo spoke but my mind was focused on the things I was seeing in this room. "This is where you will be staying as a personal part of my living museum."

"Living museum?" I looked at him like he had lost his mind. This room was filled with tall glass containers with men floating in some kind of clear liquid. They were hooked up to all types of machines that looked like they were keeping them alive. Their eyes were open and it looked like they were looking right at me. It looked like one of those containers they keep the aliens alive in all of the *Alien* movies. I freaked out when I saw the young guy whose flier I had in the glove compartment of my car. *This is what happened to him.* I now wished I paid more attention to the flier and not getting my clutches into Mateo. Now I was sure to be missing.

"You're crazy. You have lost your mind," I said as I inched away from him and toward the door. I wasn't fast enough because he grabbed me by the arm and pulled me back toward him. This time it was not gentle and the look in his eyes was glazed and crazy.

"Let me show you my first lover." We walked over to the first glass container. I was crying uncontrollably. He had an engraved metal plate in front of him that read MARK HUBBARD—2004. I gasped because that meant that this guy has been down here almost seven years. I knew then that the chance of me getting out of here alive was slim to none but that didn't stop me from begging.

"Mateo, please let me go. Please just let me leave. I won't say anything to anybody. I promise. I never even met you. I'll get selective amnesia," I pleaded.

"Mark was my first love," he said, ignoring me. "He was the prettiest, most handsome guy and as you can tell he still is. He wanted to break up with me and leave but I couldn't let anyone else have him. I didn't want him to die so I came up with this way to keep him alive and pretty. I don't get to hold him like before but now I get to see him when I want to; just like it will be with you."

"Mateo, it doesn't have to be this way. I won't leave you. I love you." I reached up and touched his face.

"I know you do. That is why I want to put you on display, to keep that love fresh and alive forever."

The door to the room opened up and two guys walked in the room.

"These guys will now help you with your transition. You will now be a permanent piece of art in my museum. Thank you for fighting so hard to win the spot. You were the best man, but I am the true winner."

I fought and fought the two guys but it was futile. They covered my mouth with a rag and then I felt myself passing out.

Chapter 41

Kardell

Trust

After my sister left my house tonight I was happy to do a little sprucing up and then get myself ready for a non-productive weekend. This week had been enough for me. I drew me a nice warm bath and then climbed into my bed. I had drifted off to sleep when I heard the chiming of my phone alert me to a new text message.

I rolled over to look at the message. I smiled because it was the last challenge from Mateo. It instructed me to get dressed if I wasn't and to wait outside of my house for someone to pick me up.

I did as I was told. I waited for about ten minutes before an all-black sedan with tinted windows pulled up, the back door opened, and I hopped in. I was blindfolded and duct tape covered my mouth. My heart was racing because I felt like this was it. I was going to complete this challenge and then walk off with the prize. Yes, I was apprehensive about where I was going but I knew that Mateo was behind this so I chilled out until we got to the destination. It was a ride filled with thoughts of what was next for me in my life. I figured I might as well do a little plotting about my life after I won this last challenge. The ride was long enough for me to go into great detail about packing my house and storage for the possessions that I wouldn't need once I moved in with Mateo. *I am pretty sure I won't need much. He probably has everything and adding me to his life will complete him.* I knew that was what I was thinking about him. I was so happy that my life would be complete after this last challenge. I felt sorry for Lewis though. *Since he will be the odd man out he'll probably start falling back into his hoeish pattern again and who knows where that will lead?* But that wasn't for me to think about now. He knew the risk that he took when he signed up to go head to head with me.

I was still in my thinking process when the car came to a halt. We had arrived. I sat up in the chair and waited for what was next. My heart raced in my chest again. I swallowed back the nervous lump in my throat as soon as I heard the door open. I definitely knew what Ray Charles felt like when he was being chauffeured around during his musical career. I had to wait to be helped out of the car for fear of falling flat on my face.

Pretty soon a hand reached in and grabbed my hand. It was soft and gentle. I knew Mateo's touch so this had to be his hand in mines.

"Are you ready to complete the last challenge?" Mateo's voice was in front of me. I could feel his breath; he was that close to my face. I nodded my head yes.

"This will tell me all I need to know." When he said that, it piqued my interest and made me nervous all at the same time. *What could he possibly have me do? What could be more challenging than all of the other things that he put me through?* I had watched a few episodes of that television show that made you drink horse semen or eat cow testicles or something far more unimaginable. All of that was swirling through my head. The possibilities were so innumerable in my head that they were all I could focus on as he was now ushering me by hand across some gravelly rocks until we stopped and I heard a door creak open and then we walked in. The door slammed shut, causing me to jump a little.

"No need to be afraid. You are not in any danger," Mateo reassured me. We walked down a long hallway. I counted about two dozen steps and we turned at least one corner. Then we stopped again and I heard yet another door open. We walked through that one and that door too closed behind us. Only this time this one was a lot quieter when it closed.

I was guided from behind by my shoulders a few steps and then he turned me around. "Have a seat and then pull yourself onto the bed and then lay flat with your arms at your side," he instructed me. I did as I was told. I was still a little tense as I lay there, waiting for what was next.

"When you hear the door shut again you may remove your blindfold." Mateo whispered in my ear my next instruction. I nodded my head, confirming my understanding.

It wasn't long before the door opened and closed.

I quickly pulled the blindfold off of my face. I blinked my eyes as I tried to focus them. When they began to focus I saw that I was in a room with low light and a very romantic setting, but what else I saw was something that took me by complete surprise. There was a completely naked woman standing in the room. She was a vision of flawless beauty.

"Hey, fella, is this your first time with a woman?" she asked seductively.

I nodded my head yes.

"Well, I'm going to take it nice and slow with you. Okay?" she said as she looked at me like a teacher did a student. I nodded my head again.

She walked over to the bed with her body moving fluidly with each step. At this point, or maybe before this point, a straight guy would or should have had a full erection by now. But that was not the case with me.

When she got to the side of the bed she gave me another instruction. "Unbuckle your pants and pull them down to your ankles for me." I followed the instruction and then I just lay there with my flaccid penis lying in between my thighs, lifeless.

"Somebody's not happy to see me." She frowned in disappointment. "Well, let me see what I can do about this. Move over to the middle of the bed."

She then got on the bed and she sat in between my legs with her legs folded underneath her thighs. She smoothed one of her hands up my thighs slowly. Her touch was erotic but it still did nothing for me sexually. If this was me and Ronald he would have been hard as a steel pipe and ready for action. She didn't know that she would have to do a séance over my dick to make me hard. Women did nothing for me.

That didn't stop her from taking my dick in her hand and trying to massage it to life. She worked it and worked it feverishly. After a few minutes of that she decided to give me a blow job. She went at that for at least another five to ten minutes. I so wanted to tap her on the shoulder and tell her to give it up but I let her do what she wanted to do. I didn't know if Mateo was testing me to see if I would cheat on him with a woman or what, but this would be proof enough to him that he had nothing to worry about.

She finally decided to give up and get off of the bed. She had a disappointed look on her face.

"You're such a handsome guy. Too bad I couldn't make you happy. I guess you can pull your pants up now." I did as I was instructed once again. Then she came over to me and snuggly placed the blindfold back on.

"You can get back into the position you were in at first." So after she said that I heard the door open and then close once more.

Someone else was in the room now. They didn't speak; they just pulled me up from the bed. I was hoping that it was Mateo and it felt like him from his touch but there was no confirmation of it. I immediately felt like something was wrong. His silence was defining. I didn't know if I had won or if I had lost.

We took the same route back. I heard a door creak open and then I felt a gush of air letting me know that I was back outside. We took a few more steps and then I heard what sounded like a car door opening. I was gently ushered into the car and then whisked away. The entire ride home I was deep in thought. *Did I win? Did I lose? Was I supposed to have sex with her or was I supposed to do just what I did?* I banged my head on the back of the car seat in frustration. I didn't want to come this far and lose.

When the car came to a stop again I was helped out of the car and then the car pulled off, leaving me standing in front of my home. It was the middle of the night so I was glad that no one saw me standing in front of my house with a blindfold on and duct tape. I snatched the tape and blindfold off and then made my way into the house.

When I got in the house I showered and then walked into my bedroom and sat on the side of my bed. I felt like having a Florida Evans moment and screaming out, "Damn damn damn," but I didn't. I was just going to wait and see what happened. I was going to hope for the best.

All of what I said earlier about not having a fit and the other bullshit went out the window when I woke up in the morning and realized that I may have lost to Lewis and have to eat some crow.

I ended up being on edge the whole weekend. I stayed up late and slept little. I thought and thought about all that I could have done to change the outcome of the last challenge but only ended up back to what actually happened. Depression and hibernation were my only friends this weekend. I neglected everything, even my cat. I locked myself in my room until Sunday night when I decided to eat and feed my cat.

Monday I was back at work and back into boss mode. I threw myself back into my work and my projects. I still couldn't fathom that I lost the challenge. There was no word from Mateo. I knew why and it didn't take a genius to figure out that I had lost and it was over for me. I just couldn't stand losing and then having to look into the smug and fake face of the winner. That shit was for the birds. I walked by Lewis several times today and he was pretending as if he lost and that things were back to normal. I wanted to fire him just to get him out of my sight. But I didn't do that. I just held my ground and moved on with my life like I was supposed to do. I figured I might as well call Ronald to come back over and fuck me crazy. I was so pissed off that an orgy sounded just like it might make me forget all of this. At least that was what I hoped.

But that was short-lived. My workday had ended and I had stayed over for an additional two hours, which made it about seven at night, to get some things organized and to make sure that everyone else was already gone home. I didn't feel like seeing anyone when it was time to leave. I was finishing my last task and I was ready to head on home or go out and treat myself to some distractions. But just as I was about to leave I received a text message from Mateo that changed my whole mood. It read two simple words: You Win.

I jumped for joy and was overcome with happiness. A few tears escaped my eyes as I looked around my office.

Another text came through telling me to leave everything and meet his car at a specified location and that he would be awaiting my arrival. I drove my car to a desolate place in Baltimore County, Maryland. There was a car waiting for me there. I got out of my car and practically jumped into the back of the same type of black car I had been in before. This time Mateo was in the back seat waiting for me.

"I'm so glad to be here." I spoke with sincerity.

"I'm glad as well." He smiled. "I can't wait to show you your spot in my life so just lay back and enjoy the ride."

I did just that. I laid my head back on the seat next to Mateo, closed my eyes, and drifted off into a sound slumber. I guessed all of the drama of the last few weeks had me drained.

"We have arrived." Mateo's sweet voice and smile greeted me as my eyes fluttered open. I stretched a little as he got out and walked around to open the door for me. I got out and looked up at the mansion that I would soon be calling my home. I couldn't believe that this was all mines.

"Are you ready to spend forever with me?" he spoke as he gently turned me toward him.

"Yes, I'm ready as ever. I'm yours forever." I wanted to kiss him passionately but I didn't want to seem to rush things. But let it be known that I was going to lay it on him when we did get to the bedroom.

"Well let's go," he said as he put his hand on the small of my back and we walked toward his home.

"There is something I want to show you." We walked down a small hallway until we got to a room filled with books. He pulled on a book and a door slid open just like in a superhero's house, but this was real life and I was impressed and curious as to what he was going to show me.

The door revealed a set of steps that was surrounded with naked brick walls. As we went down the stairs the temperature changed from warm to chilly in seconds. The door behind us closed automatically with two clicks following it. Mateo was a rich guy and all that I could think about was the huge amount of money, jewels, and pricey valuables he had stored down here. He was about to show me his secret stash and I was excited. I was going to be rich. I floated down the hall with Mateo until we came to a door. He punched a few keys into keypad near the door and the door slowly slid open. We walked in as the lights fluttered on, illuminating the entire room.

What I saw before me made my heart drop.

"This is where you will be staying." Mateo spoke but my mind was focused on the things I was seeing in this room. "This is where you will be staying as a personal part of my living museum."

"Living museum?" I looked at him like he had lost his mind. This room was filled with tall glass containers with men floating in some kind of clear liquid. They were hooked up to all types of machines that looked like it was keeping them alive. Their eyes were open and it looked like they were looking right at me. It looked like one of those containers they keep the aliens alive in all of the *Alien* movies. I freaked out even more when I saw Lewis's body floating in one of the containers. My stomach began to turn and cramp up and then I threw the contents of my stomach on the ground.

"You're crazy. You have lost your mind," I said as I inched away from him and toward the door. I wasn't fast enough because he grabbed me by the arm and pulled me back toward him. This time it was not gentle and the look in his eyes was glazed, crazy looking.

"Let me show you my first lover." We walked over to the first glass container. I was crying uncontrollably. He had an engraved metal plate in front of him that read MARK HUBBARD—2004. I gasped because that meant that this guy had been down here almost seven years. I knew then that the chance of me getting out of here alive was slim to none but that didn't stop me from begging.

"Mateo, please let me go. Please just let me leave. I won't say anything to anybody. I promise. I never even met you," I pleaded.

"Mark was my first love," he said, ignoring me. "He was the prettiest, most handsome guy and as you can tell he still is. He wanted to break up with me and leave me but I couldn't let anyone else have him. I didn't want him to die so I came up with this way to keep him alive and pretty. I don't get to hold him like before but now I get to see him when I want to; just like it will be with you."

"Mateo, it doesn't have to be this way. I won't leave you. I love you." I put my hand on his chest.

"I know you do. That is why I want to put you on display to keep that love fresh and alive forever."

The door to the room opened up and two guys walked in the room.

"These guys will now help you with your transition. You will now be a permanent piece of art in my museum. Thank you for fighting so hard to win the spot. You were the best man, but I am the true winner."

I fought and fought the two guys but it was futile. They covered my mouth with a rag. I saw this in too many movies to know that this was the end for me.

Epilogue

Janice

I sat back in my living room chair and wept tears of heartache and pain. I sat here with my eyes glued to the news that was on the television station. I just couldn't believe it. I shook my head from side to side in disbelief. It was a replay of the broadcast two weeks ago that I recorded. I just couldn't get over it. I was still in complete shock.

My boss, Kardell Spencer, and Lewis Turner were reported missing about two months ago and we all were baffled at their disappearance. When I was interviewed about their disappearance I did mention their weird behavior in the weeks before but since I never asked any questions I couldn't speculate on anything. My boss was a great guy and he didn't deserve any of this. And even though Lewis and I weren't the best of friends I wouldn't wish any harm on him.

"In all of my years I haven't seen anything like this." I spoke out loud. I was in my home, alone, enjoying my retirement. I had never given up hope on finding them and I even helped with passing out fliers and information about them both with both of their families. Their families were distraught with anguish and pain. I couldn't imagine experiencing the disappearance/loss of a child as a mother. But here it was on the news and this loss made the national news circuit.

It was said that restaurateur Mateo Lopez was under secret surveillance for ties to the Hispanic mob, drug trafficking, and money laundering, but could never be caught because he was so good at not getting his hands dirty.

On a federal tip one of his homes was raided on the outskirts of Anne Arundel County, Maryland. Upon raiding the house a secret passage was discovered that was believed to be where he housed his drugs and money, but what was discovered was of epic proportion.

They said that Mateo Lopez wasn't involved in drugs at all but in something no one had any idea was going on.

Mateo Lopez was a kleptomaniac of human beings. He had a personal collection of living human beings being kept alive by some sort of physical stability machines. They had reported that there were at least a dozen men being keep alive artificially but when the door was blown open it triggered something that turned off the life support for the men being held there. Several of the men were reported missing over a seven-year period. Some men were never reported because they were gay, displaced, and excommunicated from their families. An investigator said cases like the ones for these guys were very hard to solve because of the lifestyles that the men led. I shook my head as I watched and continued to watch. It was as fresh as the first time I watched.

I received the call a few days after the television news broadcast, first by Lewis's family telling me that they had identified his body and that his funeral arrangements were being made. I attended the funeral out of respect and even spoke a few good words about him and his flair for life.

When I got the call from Kardell's family I took it harder than I thought I would. His mother and I sobbed and cried into the phone for over a half hour. His funeral service was just as beautiful as Lewis's. I broke down at the funeral as well. It was such a sad occasion but a tribute to his life. I got up and spoke words of love for a young life taken too early. He was just as much a son as he was a boss to me. The company that he started was taken over by Kardell's sister and was renamed Spencer and Lewis Advertising Group. I still stopped by to show my support and help keep the memory of the two slain guys alive. It was the least I could do for two guys who did their best at living but tragically died. I finally cut the television off, got on my hands and knees, and prayed that they were resting in peace. I even prayed for the guy who did this to them even though he put a gun to his head and took the easy way out when they raided his house.

For those of you who love happy endings keep turning the page for the alternate ending.

Chapter 40

Lewis

Blind Ambition: Rewound

When I returned home after my outing with Dennis I was just happy to be home. I surveyed my home and for the most part Kardell left everything in very decent shape. I wasn't worried about him being a slob, it was just the fact that someone else was living in my home for a week. His scent lingered on my furniture and I wasn't fond of that. I Febrezed everything I could to get it smelling the way I loved it.

I showered and primped myself for a nice slumber in my bed. I was just getting nice and cozy when my telephone chimed, letting me know I had a text message.

I rolled over to look at the message. I smiled because it was the last challenge from Mateo. It instructed me to get dressed if I wasn't and to wait outside of my apartment for someone to pick me up.

I did as I was told. I waited for about ten minutes before an all-black sedan with tinted windows pulled up. It looked just like the one that Mateo always picked me up in. The back door opened and I hopped in. I was blindfolded and duct tape covered my mouth. My heart was racing because I felt like this was it. I was going to complete this challenge and then walk off with the prize. I was going to leave all of this behind me.

Yes, I was apprehensive about where I was going and who I was with but I pushed caution to the wind and focused myself and my mind on the matter at hand. I was going to win. Besides, Mateo hadn't ever given me a reason to not trust him and I wasn't going to start now.

The ride was yet another long ride and I was getting antsy, and anticipation filled every part of me.

Then the car came to a stop. The back door opened and I was carefully helped out of the car as if I was precious cargo. I was led by the hand to an unknown location and we stopped. I heard a door being opened and I was once again led by the hand. The person leading me never said a word to me, just led me down a long hallway. All you heard was the sound of our footsteps hitting the floor as we walked. It was a warm environment wherever we were. Then we stopped once again. Another door was opened and I was led in once again. I was led to and sat down on what I assumed was a bed. Breathing only through my nose was weird for me. I couldn't speak nor could I see. They say that other senses get heightened when others are cut off. I could hear and smell. I heard only quietness and the smell was of nothing.

"Scoot back and lie still." I heard Mateo's voice speak into my ear. "This one last challenge is for you to do the unthinkable. Something you've never done before. This will prove to me if you are the best man for me. When you hear the door shut again you may remove your blindfold." That was all that he said. I wanted to reach out and touch his face but I didn't want to ruin anything by making any sudden moves. A few seconds later the door shut again.

I quickly pulled the blindfold off of my face. I blinked my eyes as I tried to focus them. When they began to focus I saw that I was in a room with low light and a very romantic setting, but what else I saw was something that blew my mind. There was a completely naked lady standing in the room. She was gorgeous. A vision of flawless beauty.

She walked over to me seductively. "Are you ready?"

I nodded my head but I didn't know what for. She then began to unbutton my pants and pulled them down to my ankles and she did the same for my underwear. Then it clicked in my mind. *He said do something I've never done before. A woman. I've never done a woman before.* Nervousness suddenly enveloped me because I was never attracted to a woman. Ever.

She put her hand on my penis and began to massage it. She was trying to make it hard, but it wasn't working. She tried and tried but nothing happened. In my mind I was trying to conjure up a fantasy with a man, any man, to get the blood flowing to my nether regions. But it wasn't working. All I could think about was the woman with her hands on my manhood trying to raise it from the dead. Then she went down on me and tried to give me a blow job. She was working feverishly but it was still to no avail. It was like working with a limp spaghetti noodle. She looked at me as I frowned in anguish. I began to thrust in her mouth to give some momentum but that too was a failed effort. *I can't believe that he would have given me this challenge.* This was not what I was prepared for. Who could prepare for this? Why would he do this knowing I would fail?

I felt heartbroken as she got up and looked at me with disappointment all over her face. I was still duct taped. I moaned for her to try again. But alas it was proven that in the fifteen minutes that she tried it wasn't happening. I was not a happy camper. I was devastated. She placed the blindfold back on and then I heard the door open and close again. Tears ran down the sides of my face and my heart sank because I knew that I had failed the challenge.

I banged my hands on the sides of the bed in a fit but ceased when I heard the door opening again. The person walked to the side of my bed. They pulled my clothes back up and then pulled me from the bed. We took the same trip that I took for me to get here. The entire ride back home I slouched in disappointment. When the car stopped, the blindfold and the duct tape were removed from over my eyes and mouth. The door open and this time I was instructed to get out. The car pulled off, leaving me standing there in front of my place of residence. I felt like a huge failure. I was sick to my stomach.

I walked the few steps to my door and went in. I wasn't feeling my best. I felt like I had lost everything. I felt cheated.

I went to bed that night confused and hurt but I was not going to work that way. I was going to fake it in hopes of another chance because that was what I texted Mateo before I went to bed that night/early morning.

I wanted another chance, another challenge, because I couldn't lose to Kardell and look him in the face every day at work. I just couldn't do it.

It was the Monday after the challenge and I was back at work dressed to impress but feeling like a wreck on the inside. I didn't do anything the whole weekend. I just lay in bed with the covers over my head. I didn't sleep much, bathed little, and I ate very little food. I didn't hear anything else from Mateo for the rest of the weekend and it almost drove me crazy. I couldn't believe that I lost the challenge. I got all the way to the end and lost. I was devastated. I didn't think that it was fair but as some people say "you win some you lose some"; but I didn't care about losing at this moment. Winning was everything and only losers said that shit. I felt so close and then to see it all slip through my fingers was just too much.

I went into the bathroom and cried at least twice today. There was still no word from Mateo. I knew why and it didn't take a genius to figure out that I had lost and it was over for me. I was now stuck at this job to look at my boss and all the rest of these boring people. *I know I am going to have to fuck a few good men to get over this one.* I just couldn't stand losing and then having to look into the smug and fake face of the winner. That shit was for the birds.

I watched my boss work today and he was pretending like he lost and that things were back to normal. I wanted run up to him and spit in his face and walk out of this muthafucka for good. But I didn't do that. I just held my ground and moved on with my life like I was supposed to do. I knew I was going dick hunting as soon as I got off. I was so pissed off that an orgy sounded just like it might make me forget all of this. At least that was what I hoped.

But that was short-lived. My work day had ended and I was headed home to get ready to go out and treat myself to some distractions. Just as I was about to leave I received a text message from Mateo that changed my whole mood. Two simple words: You Win.

I fell to my knees in sheer happiness and joy. A few tears escaped my eyes as I looked around my office.

Another text came through telling me to leave everything and meet Mateo at a specified location. I drove my car to a desolate place in Baltimore County, Maryland. There was a car waiting for me there. I got out of my car and practically jumped into the back of the same type of black car I had been in before. This time Mateo was in the back seat waiting for me.

"I'm so glad to be here." I spoke with sincerity.

"I'm glad as well." He smiled. "I can't wait to show you your spot in my life so just lay back and enjoy the ride."

I did just that. I laid my head back on the seat next to Mateo.

"We have arrived." Mateo's sweet voice said to me. I stretched a little as he got out and walked around to open the door for me. I got out and looked up at the same mansion that I had come to before. I smiled as I looked at my new home. I couldn't believe that this was all mines.

"Are you ready to spend forever with me?" he spoke as he gently turned me toward him.

"Yes, I was born ready. Here is where I belong." I wanted to kiss him passionately but didn't want to seem like the ho I used to be. But let it be known that I was going to rock his world when we did get to the bedroom.

"Well let's go," he said as he put his hand on the small of my back and we walked toward his home.

"There is something I want to show you." We walked down a small hallway until we got to a room filled with books. He pulled on a book and a door slid open just like in a superhero's house, but this was real life and I was impressed and curious as to what he was going to show me.

The door revealed a set of steps that was surrounded with naked brick walls. As we went down the stairs the temperature changed from warm to chilly in seconds. The door behind us closed automatically with two clicks following it. Mateo was a rich guy and all that I could think about was the huge amount of money, jewels, and pricey valuables he had stored down here. He was about to show me his secret stash and I was excited. I

was going to be, as Rick James said it, "I'm rich, bitch."
I floated down the hall with Mateo until we came to a
door. He punched a few keys into a keypad near the door
and the door slowly slid open. We walked in as the lights
fluttered on, illuminating the entire room.

What I saw before me made my heart drop.

"This is where you will be staying." Mateo spoke but
my mind was focused on the things I was seeing in this
room. "This is where you will be staying as a personal
part of my living museum."

"Living museum?" I looked at him like he had lost
his mind. This room was filled with tall glass containers with men floating in some kind of clear liquid. They
were hooked up to all types of machines that looked like
they were keeping them alive. Their eyes were open and
it looked like they were looking right at me. It looked like
one of those containers they keep the aliens alive in all
of the *Alien* movies. I freaked out when I saw the young
guy whose flier I had in the glove compartment of my
car. *This is what happened to him.* I now wished I paid
more attention to the flier and not getting my clutches
into Mateo. Now I was sure to be missing.

"You're crazy. You have lost your mind," I said as I
inched away from him and toward the door. I wasn't
fast enough because he grabbed me by the arm and
pulled me back toward him. This time it was not gentle
and the look in his eyes was glazed and crazy.

"Let me show you my first lover." We walked over
to the first glass container. I was crying uncontrollably. He had an engraved metal plate in front of him
that read MARK HUBBARD—2004. I gasped because that
meant that this guy has been down here almost seven
years. I knew then that the chance of me getting out
of here alive was slim to none but that didn't stop me
from begging.

"Mateo, please let me go. Please just let me leave. I won't say anything to anybody. I promise. I never even met you. I'll get selective amnesia," I pleaded.

"Mark was my first love," he said, ignoring me. "He was the prettiest, most handsome guy and as you can tell he still is. He wanted to break up with me and leave but I couldn't let anyone else have him. I didn't want him to die so I came up with this way to keep him alive and pretty. I don't get to hold him like before but now I get to see him when I want to; just like it will be with you."

"Mateo, it doesn't have to be this way. I won't leave you. I love you." I reached up and touched his face.

"I know you do. That is why I want to put you on display, to keep that love fresh and alive forever."

The door to the room opened up and two guys walked in the room. They walked toward me. I broke loose from Mateo and I tried to do a football play and zigzag past them because there was some distance between me and them. I almost made it past them until I tripped over one of my own feet and fell flat on my face. I lay there sobbing to myself and my impeding death. I didn't have the will or the hope to try to get up.

"This is what you wanted. You fought so valiantly to get here and now this is where you will be with me." Mateo spoke over me. I continued to sob and prayed to God for a way out.

The sound of a loud boom and then the resonating pounding of what sounded like stampeding feet interrupted my sobbing. Then there was a loud boom that led to dust and smoke filled the room.

"Freeze, get your hands in the air. This is a raid!" I heard what I assumed was a law enforcement officer yelling into the smoke-filled room. I silently thanked God for His intervention on my behalf.

It didn't take long before Mateo was in handcuffs along with the two men who were about take me into their custody.

One of the officers helped me off of the floor. "Are you okay?" he asked sincerely.

I was shaken up but I couldn't help but notice that this guy was a very good-looking guy, even in my current situation. He was dark complexioned with dark brown eyes to match. He was very gentle with me as he put his arm around my waist to help keep me steady.

I nodded my head as the tears flowed from my eyes. He slowly helped me out of the room, up the steps, and out to the front lawn to a barrage of police cars and various other law enforcement vehicles.

I was ushered into a nearby ambulance as a waiting attendant tended to the bruise on my head. I cried several times as I sat in there on that gurney. I played a win-or-lose game with my life and didn't even know it. It worked out in my favor but I couldn't help but think what would have happened if things didn't turn out like they did today.

Chapter 41

Kardell

Trust: Rewound

After my sister left my house tonight I was happy to do a little sprucing up and then get myself ready for a non-productive weekend. This week had been enough for me. I drew me a nice warm bath and then climbed into my bed. I had drifted off to sleep when I heard the chiming of my phone alert me to a new text message.

I rolled over to look at the message. I smiled because it was the last challenge from Mateo. It instructed me to get dressed if I wasn't and to wait outside of my house for someone to pick me up.

I did as I was told. I waited for about ten minutes before an all-black sedan with tinted windows pulled up, the back door opened, and I hopped in. I was blindfolded and duct tape covered my mouth. My heart was racing because I felt like this was it. I was going to complete this challenge and then walk off with the prize. Yes, I was apprehensive about where I was going but I knew that Mateo was behind this so I chilled out until we got to the destination. It was a ride filled with thoughts of what was next for me in my life. I figured I might as well do a little plotting about my life after I won this last challenge. The ride was long enough for me to go into great detail about packing my house and storage for the possessions that I wouldn't need once I moved in with Mateo. *I am pretty sure I won't need much. He probably has everything and adding me to his life will complete him.* I knew that was what I was thinking about him. I was so happy that my life would be complete after this last challenge. I felt sorry for Lewis though. *Since he will be the odd man out he'll probably start falling back into his hoeish pattern again and who knows where that will lead?* But that wasn't for me to think about now. He knew the risk that he took when he signed up to go head to head with me.

I was still in my thinking process when the car came to a halt. We had arrived. I sat up in the chair and waited for what was next. My heart raced in my chest again. I swallowed back the nervous lump in my throat as soon as I heard the door open. I definitely knew what Ray Charles felt like when he was being chauffeured around during his musical career. I had to wait to be helped out of the car for fear of falling flat on my face.

Pretty soon a hand reached in and grabbed my hand. It was soft and gentle. I knew Mateo's touch so this had to be his hand in mines.

"Are you ready to complete the last challenge?" Mateo's voice was in front of me. I could feel his breath; he was that close to my face. I nodded my head yes.

"This will tell me all I need to know." When he said that, it piqued my interest and made me nervous all at the same time. *What could he possibly have me do? What could be more challenging than all of the other things that he put me through?* I had watched a few episodes of that television show that made you drink horse semen or eat cow testicles or something far more unimaginable. All of that was swirling through my head. The possibilities were so innumerable in my head that they were all I could focus on as he was now ushering me by hand across some gravelly rocks until we stopped and I heard a door creak open and then we walked in. The door slammed shut, causing me to jump a little.

"No need to be afraid. You are not in any danger," Mateo reassured me. We walked down a long hallway. I counted about two dozen steps and we turned at least one corner. Then we stopped again and I heard yet another door open. We walked through that one and that door too closed behind us. Only this time this one was a lot quieter when it closed.

I was guided from behind by my shoulders a few steps and then he turned me around. "Have a seat and then pull yourself onto the bed and then lay flat with your arms at your side," he instructed me. I did as I was told. I was still a little tense as I lay there, waiting for what was next.

"When you hear the door shut again you may remove your blindfold." Mateo whispered in my ear my next instruction. I nodded my head, confirming my understanding.

It wasn't long before the door opened and closed.

I quickly pulled the blindfold off of my face. I blinked my eyes as I tried to focus them. When they began to focus I saw that I was in a room with low light and a very romantic setting, but what else I saw was something that took me by complete surprise. There was a completely naked woman standing in the room. She was a vision of flawless beauty.

"Hey, fella, is this your first time with a woman?" she asked seductively.

I nodded my head yes.

"Well, I'm going to take it nice and slow with you. Okay?" she said as she looked at me like a teacher did a student. I nodded my head again.

She walked over to the bed with her body moving fluidly with each step. At this point, or maybe before this point, a straight guy would or should have had a full erection by now. But that was not the case with me.

When she got to the side of the bed she gave me another instruction. "Unbuckle your pants and pull them down to your ankles for me." I followed the instruction and then I just lay there with my flaccid penis lying in between my thighs, lifeless.

"Somebody's not happy to see me." She frowned in disappointment. "Well, let me see what I can do about this. Move over to the middle of the bed."

She then got on the bed and she sat in between my legs with her legs folded underneath her thighs. She smoothed one of her hands up my thighs slowly. Her touch was erotic but it still did nothing for me sexually. If this was me and Ronald he would have been hard as a steel pipe and ready for action. She didn't know that she would have to do a séance over my dick to make me hard. Women did nothing for me.

That didn't stop her from taking my dick in her hand and trying to massage it to life. She worked it and worked it feverishly. After a few minutes of that she decided to give me a blow job. She went at that for at least another five to ten minutes. I so wanted to tap her on the shoulder and tell her to give it up but I let her do what she wanted to do. I didn't know if Mateo was testing me to see if I would cheat on him with a woman or what, but this would be proof enough to him that he had nothing to worry about.

She finally decided to give up and get off of the bed. She had a disappointed look on her face.

"You're such a handsome guy. Too bad I couldn't make you happy. I guess you can pull your pants up now." I did as I was instructed once again. Then she came over to me and snuggly placed the blindfold back on.

"You can get back into the position you were in at first." So after she said that I heard the door open and then close once more.

Someone else was in the room now. They didn't speak; they just pulled me up from the bed. I was hoping that it was Mateo and it felt like him from his touch but there was no confirmation of it. I immediately felt like something was wrong. His silence was defining. I didn't know if I had won or if I had lost.

We took the same route back. I heard a door creak open and then I felt a gush of air letting me know that I was back outside. We took a few more steps and then I heard what sounded like a car door opening. I was gently ushered into the car and then whisked away. The entire ride home I was deep in thought. *Did I win? Did I lose? Was I supposed to have sex with her or was I supposed to do just what I did?* I banged my head on the back of the car seat in frustration. I didn't want to come this far and lose.

When the car came to a stop again I was helped out of the car and then the car pulled off, leaving me standing in front of my home. It was the middle of the night so I was glad that no one saw me standing in front of my house with a blindfold on and duct tape. I snatched the tape and blindfold off and then made my way into the house.

When I got in the house I showered and then walked into my bedroom and sat on the side of my bed. I felt like having a Florida Evans moment and screaming out, "Damn damn damn," but I didn't. I was just going to wait and see what happened. I was going to hope for the best.

All of what I said earlier about not having a fit and the other bullshit went out the window when I woke up in the morning and realized that I may have lost to Lewis and have to eat some crow.

I ended up being on edge the whole weekend. I stayed up late and slept little. I thought and thought about all that I could have done to change the outcome of the last challenge but only ended up back to what actually happened. Depression and hibernation were my only friends this weekend. I neglected everything, even my cat. I locked myself in my room until Sunday night when I decided to eat and feed my cat.

Monday I was back at work and back into boss mode. I threw myself back into my work and my projects. I still couldn't fathom that I lost the challenge. There was no word from Mateo. I knew why and it didn't take a genius to figure out that I had lost and it was over for me. I just couldn't stand losing and then having to look into the smug and fake face of the winner. That shit was for the birds. I walked by Lewis several times today and he was pretending as if he lost and that things were back to normal. I wanted to fire him just to get him out of my sight. But I didn't do that. I just held my ground and moved on with my life like I was supposed to do. I figured I might as well call Ronald to come back over and fuck me crazy. I was so pissed off that an orgy sounded just like it might make me forget all of this. At least that was what I hoped.

But that was short-lived. My workday had ended and I had stayed over for an additional two hours, which made it about seven at night, to get some things organized and to make sure that everyone else was already gone home. I didn't feel like seeing anyone when it was time to leave. I was finishing my last task and I was ready to head on home or go out and treat myself to some distractions. But just as I was about to leave I received a text message from Mateo that changed my whole mood. It read two simple words: You Win.

I jumped for joy and was overcome with happiness. A few tears escaped my eyes as I looked around my office.

Another text came through telling me to leave everything and meet his car at a specified location and that he would be awaiting my arrival. I drove my car to a desolate place in Baltimore County, Maryland. There was a car waiting for me there. I got out of my car and practically jumped into the back of the same type of black car I had been in before.

The whole ride over, I was all smiles. I thought about my new life with him and what it was going to be like in a steady relationship. Who wouldn't be happy to find the one they knew would be in their corner no matter what? It didn't hurt that he was wealthy as well. I had my own money but he had much more. The ride was quite relaxing as I listened to the soft music that the driver was playing in car. When the car finally stopped, I sat there in anticipation of the next moments that I was sure were going to change my life. When the door opened, to my surprise, Mateo wasn't on the other end. I was completely confused.

"Sir, can you please step away from the car?" a Caucasian guy with a badge on his belt asked me. As soon as I stepped from the car the scene that was before me caused my mouth to gap open in awe. There were police cars and FBI covering Mateo's estate.

"Wh . . . what is going on?" I asked in confusion.

"Can you come over here with me for a second? I have a few questions for you," he said.

I followed him away from the car I arrived in. There were a few questions I wanted to ask as well. There was so much going on around us, people being handcuffed and foreign women crying and sobbing.

"How do you know Mateo Lopez?"

I knew I was supposed to have a lawyer present and all of that before I answered any question, but that wasn't what happened. I was too shook up to care and I knew that I wasn't guilty of anything. "He was . . . He was . . ." I looked at the cop trying to figure out who Mateo really was. "Damn, what was he?" I looked at him in confusion.

"Well, we thought he was a drug kingpin, but come to find out he was something on a whole different level. It's like something I have never seen before in my twenty-year career." He looked like he was just as shocked as I was right now.

"What was he?" Extreme curiosity caused me to ask.

"He was a human kleptomaniac."

"A what?" I asked, confused.

"In layman's terms, he collected people and that guy over there was about to become the next one in his collection."

I looked over in the direction he was pointing and saw Lewis in the back of an ambulance with someone attending to a wound to his head.

"Oh my goodness." I covered my mouth in shock.

"Yes, that is what I said as I got a look at the sight in this sick bastard's house."

All I could think about was what could have happened if the police hadn't gotten here in time or waited until another day. The thought caused my legs to crumble beneath me.

"Sir." He rushed to catch me but didn't make it in time. "Are you all right?"

"I . . . I will be," I said as he helped me back up to my feet.

It didn't take long before Lewis and I were in the back of an unmarked police car. Neither one of us had any words to say to each other. I only could assume that he too was letting all of the things that happened today and the last few weeks sink into his mind. We made complete fools of ourselves for the attention of a guy; and even more importantly, a guy who we didn't know at all. *But how do you know if the person you are dating or pursuing is crazy?* What if there were no signs? I felt like a real fool right now. But I was extremely glad that I was a living fool instead of a dead one.

We were escorted down to the nearest FBI office for further questioning and then released.

Kardell's Epilogue

Honey, I'm Home

"Hey, babe, I'm home." That was the sweet sound of my reformed man coming through the door and greeting me. He walked into the kitchen with flowers in his hand and in his fresh officer-in-training uniform. Yep, Ronald and I were a couple and he was in the final steps of being a police officer. I knew I said it was over and even though he did cheat on me once I forgave him and put him on probation. It had been two years since the whole Mateo fiasco and my life couldn't have been any happier. I never thought that I would have given Ronald another chance, but since I got another chance I thought that he deserved one too. Yes, it was rocky at first, but over time he had become quite the mate for me.

"You happy to see me?" he asked as he wrapped his arms around my waist and kissed me in between my neck and shoulder. It sent shivers down my spine like it always does.

"Yes, I'm glad you are home. How was your day?" I continued to shuffle around in the kitchen, preparing our meal of veal parmesan, scallops, and pilaf rice. He took out a chair from under the kitchen table and sat down.

"It was tough but good," he said.

I turned around and saw a smile on his face. I had been really tough on him about being stable and my need for a stable man in my life. But I also had to give him room to grow and mess up, because I expected the same treatment from other people when it came to me. He was doing a great job at it but there were a few times when he wavered and almost made me regret my choice to give him another chance.

"Don't worry, Ronald. It will all be worth it when you start bringing home the big bucks," I said and then walked over and behind him. I slid my hands down the front of his shirt to get a feel of his hard, tight body through his uniform.

"Do I need to make a citizen's arrest in here?" he said jokingly.

"Do what you have to do. I won't go down easy." I whispered seductively in his ear as I eased my hands down to his crotch. Just like normal he was already aroused. I thought he was born with a hard on or maybe it was me.

"I'm always up for a physical confrontation, the rougher the better." He put his hands over my hands on his crotch and ground into them roughly.

"You are going to mess around and have me burn this food for a quickie," I said as I pulled away and went back to finishing up our meal.

"So you are going to leave me horny over here." He whimpered a little. I had to admit he was spoiled and so was I.

"Don't worry, baby. I'm going to take care of you right and proper later on. I need to give you the food for the fuel you are going to need in the bedroom later on." I turned and looked over my shoulder. The look in his eyes was that of excitement. Don't get it twisted now. We didn't fuck anymore. Well, sometimes. But now he took his time with me and treated me with care.

Ronald and I now had conversations. We related a lot more when I pushed some of my high-ass standards off of the table and let him open up my world to him and vice versa. You'd be surprised how well you get along with someone when you're not trying to make them make you happy and just live with them flaws and all. No one is perfect and we all are struggling in this world to find happiness and companionship. Most of the time we get in our own way with standards that we don't even live up to. I had to sit myself down and tell myself to get off of my high horse and stop being so controlling and stuffy. Well, I learned some of that from Lewis and him being just him.

Anyway, Ronald and I were getting closer because I was home a little more to have fun and do things that he likes and that I had grown to love. I still had my company and it was still doing great. I just let my workers work and not try to do it all myself. I even gave Lewis more responsibility.

Lewis and I had a newfound bond and an understanding of each other. We both realized that we weren't that different, but we went about things differently. He was actually a very great guy when you sat down and talked to him. I'm not saying we were best friends or that he had completely calmed down. I'm saying that I was enjoying the person he was even if I didn't like all the things that he did or said.

Now I was able to enjoy my life with Ronald, my sister, my mother, and father. We were doing more family-oriented things and we were actually having open discussions about our lives. No, we were not a drama-free family, because my sister still had a slip of the tongue every now and then and my father slipped off to the racetrack from time to time as well. I am happy to say that my mother loved Ronald and they even had their own special bond. So in the end I can truly say that the best man won; the new me. Life was good. Plus, Mateo got life in prison without the possibility of parole for kidnapping and murder because two of the guys he had in stasis passed away. I still couldn't believe that there was a person in the world who collected people and kept them alive for their pleasure. It was the craziest thing that I ever heard of or had ever been a part of.

Lewis's Epilogue

Arrested By Love

It'd been two years since Mateo almost made me a part of his living museum. I relived that scene in my head every so often and it still rocked my world that he was that type of person. Who would have known?

Well, I can say that one good thing had come from all of that. And that was my new man, Justice. Yes, his name was Justice and he was all mines. He was the same guy who helped me out of Mateo's house that scary night. He was all that I was looking for in a mate and a friend. I am so happy to say that he was one of the best things that had ever happened to me. I mean he made me so happy and he had even calmed me down a little. Who would have thought a man would be enough for me to calm me down?

Justice was so patient, hardworking, and cultured. He was a few years older than me but that was a good thing to me because with age comes wisdom. He was teaching me all kinds of new things. I was going fishing, playing pool, and even going out to jazz clubs from time to time. He was opening up my life to new and exciting things.

I would have never thought that almost losing my life would open up a new path in life for me. Not only was my love life fresh but even work was better. My boss had found love and would take random days off and leave me in charge. He actually said I did an okay job when we switched places for that week of the challenge. I was shocked when he said it to me in front of the whole staff. I even got emotional and let a tear slide down my face. I wasn't the outwardly vulnerable type, but I was changing and being vulnerable was a part of life, especially when you start a new relationship. I always thought that I was wild and fancy free but I was just as uptight with my emotions and feelings as Kardell was with his life. I just didn't want to see it or I thought I was better than him just like I secretly accused him of being that way with me. I guess we were mirrors at different angles, as they say.

Kardell and I were friends now and not just boss and employee like we were in the past. We actually took time to relate and share. And since both of our mates were in law enforcement we had a lot we could discuss and even laugh about. We'd had dinner together as couples and all. And guess what, it was him who made the suggestion. Life was good for me now and even if tomorrow was crazy I still got a flashback of what could have been and I secretly say to myself, "I won." That did the trick for me every time because I did win a chance at newness and each day I woke up feeling like I won the lottery of life. Yep, I felt like the best man I could be, in the making, and I definitely felt like I was a winner.

THE END

Book Club
Discussion Questions

1. Which character could you relate to the most? And why?

2. Would you have gone through the great lengths that these two characters went through to get a mate?

3. Do you have rules that you set for yourself when pursuing a mate?

4. Have you ever broken your rules in a relationship?

5. Would you compete with someone for a mate?

6. What would you never do to get a mate?

7. Is it possible to know everything about a person you have been dating, even over a long period of time?

8. What is the worst date you have ever been on?

9. Have you ever had an attraction for a person who was all wrong for you?

10. Is there a perfect mate?

ORDER FORM
URBAN BOOKS, LLC
97 N18th Street
Wyandanch, NY 11798

Name (please print):_____

Address: _____

City/State: _____

Zip: _____

QTY	TITLES	PRICE
	16 On The Block	$14.95
	A Girl From Flint	$14.95
	A Pimp's Life	$14.95
	Baltimore Chronicles	$14.95
	Baltimore Chronicles 2	$14.95
	Betrayal	$14.95
	Black Diamond	$14.95
	Black Diamond 2	$14.95
	Black Friday	$14.95
	Both Sides Of The Fence	$14.95
	Both Sides Of The Fence 2	$14.95
	California Connection	$14.95

Shipping and handling-add $3.50 for 1st book, then $1.75 for each additional book.
Please send a check payable to:
Urban Books, LLC
Please allow 4-6 weeks for delivery

ORDER FORM
URBAN BOOKS, LLC
97 N18th Street
Wyandanch, NY 11798

Name (please print):_____

Address: _____

City/State: _____

Zip: _____

QTY	TITLES	PRICE
	California Connection 2	$14.95
	Cheesecake And Teardrops	$14.95
	Congratulations	$14.95
	Crazy In Love	$14.95
	Cyber Case	$14.95
	Denim Diaries	$14.95
	Diary Of A Mad First Lady	$14.95
	Diary Of A Stalker	$14.95
	Diary Of A Street Diva	$14.95
	Diary Of A Young Girl	$14.95
	Dirty Money	$14.95
	Dirty To The Grave	$14.95

Shipping and handling-add $3.50 for 1st book, then $1.75 for each additional book.
Please send a check payable to:
Urban Books, LLC
Please allow 4-6 weeks for delivery

ORDER FORM
URBAN BOOKS, LLC
97 N18th Street
Wyandanch, NY 11798

Name (please print):_____

Address: _____

City/State: _____

Zip: _____

QTY	TITLES	PRICE
	Gunz And Roses	$14.95
	Happily Ever Now	$14.95
	Hell Has No Fury	$14.95
	Hush	$14.95
	If It Isn't love	$14.95
	Kiss Kiss Bang Bang	$14.95
	Last Breath	$14.95
	Little Black Girl Lost	$14.95
	Little Black Girl Lost 2	$14.95
	Little Black Girl Lost 3	$14.95
	Little Black Girl Lost 4	$14.95
	Little Black Girl Lost 5	$14.95

Shipping and handling-add $3.50 for 1st book, then $1.75 for each additional book.

Please send a check payable to:

Urban Books, LLC

Please allow 4-6 weeks for delivery

ORDER FORM
URBAN BOOKS, LLC
97 N18th Street
Wyandanch, NY 11798

Name (please print):_____

Address: _____

City/State: _____

Zip: _____

QTY	TITLES	PRICE
	Loving Dasia	$14.95
	Material Girl	$14.95
	Moth To A Flame	$14.95
	Mr. High Maintenance	$14.95
	My Little Secret	$14.95
	Naughty	$14.95
	Naughty 2	$14.95
	Naughty 3	$14.95
	Queen Bee	$14.95
	Say It Ain't So	$14.95
	Snapped	$14.95
	Snow White	$14.95

Shipping and handling-add $3.50 for 1st book, then $1.75 for each additional book.
Please send a check payable to:
   Urban Books, LLC
Please allow 4-6 weeks for delivery

ORDER FORM
URBAN BOOKS, LLC
97 N18th Street
Wyandanch, NY 11798

Name (please print):_____

Address: _____

City/State: _____

Zip: _____

QTY	TITLES	PRICE
	Spoil Rotten	$14.95
	Supreme Clientele	$14.95
	The Cartel	$14.95
	The Cartel 2	$14.95
	The Cartel 3	$14.95
	The Dopefiend	$14.95
	The Dopeman Wife	$14.95
	The Prada Plan	$14.95
	The Prada Plan 2	$14.95
	Where There Is Smoke	$14.95
	Where There Is Smoke 2	$14.95

Shipping and handling-add $3.50 for 1st book, then $1.75 for each additional book.

Please send a check payable to:

Urban Books, LLC

Please allow 4-6 weeks for delivery